SAVING FERRIS

a novel by
A R KENNEDY

Dedication

To all my pups through the years—C, L, H & h—
for teaching me Kelly was not "just a dog"

CHAPTER 1

CECILIA WOKE UP. She'd never get used to the darkness of country nights. She rolled over to return to sleep and heard the noise that must have been the cause of the early wake-up call. A small yip from the window. She mumbled her displeasure and slapped her husband's side of the bed.

"Joey, wake up." No response. "Joey." She reached for him again and found nothing but his cold pillow. A small yip again. "Dumb dog," she mumbled. She was fully awake now, remembering why her husband's side of the bed was empty. Why it would forever be empty.

Cecilia sat up at the edge of the bed and hung her head. She no longer wanted to be in the empty bed. A low growl emanated from the dog. "Okay, Ferris. I'm coming."

She snapped on a nightlight and shielded her eyes from the small, yet bright, light. In the city, she could have seen the bedroom without such an aid. Some people called it light pollution. Cecilia called it the life of the city.

She could make out the profile of Ferris, staring out the window onto their backyard. He stood tall enough that his head rested on the windowsill. She often found the golden retriever looking out any window of the house like this. Waiting for Joey to return, she assumed. She had done it for weeks too.

But tonight, he stood at alert.

"Do you want to go out or what? Remember, I'm not the one who likes you, so hurry up."

He turned his head briefly and looked at her, then returned his attention to the backyard. "I am not taking you out in the middle of the night to chase a squirrel." The backyard's motion sensor light was on and she cursed the squirrel that must have triggered it.

She started to lie back down and return to her dreamless sleep. The dreams, in reality and in sleep, had disappeared with Joey. The call of nature diverted her and she headed to the bathroom instead.

With the door to the hallway open and the rest of the house now available, Ferris took off and ran down the stairs. "I'll take that as I got to go now too, woman."

Putting Ferris's bathroom needs before her own, she followed him downstairs to the kitchen's sliding glass door, his exit to the spacious backyard. It was far more likely he'd have an accident than she and she didn't want to spend the rest of the night cleaning up his mess.

She snapped on the kitchen light. Now that she was fully awake, the light no longer caused discomfort. She doubted she'd return to sleep again tonight anyway.

"Calm down," Cecilia told the dog as she struggled to put on his leash. "I know Joey lets you run around but I'm not chasing you at two in the morning." It was no surprise that Ferris continued to move. Listening was not his forte. It was how he got homed here.

Cecilia finally got the camouflage leash on Ferris's collar and opened the sliding glass door. Ferris squeezed through before she had it fully open, pulling her through as well. An alarm beeped and she reached for the doorframe to stop her momentum. "Ferris, come on!"

Ferris had a lot of flaws but pulling her on their walks was not one of them. Holding the leash in one hand and firmly placing her foot over the doorframe, she quickly punched in the alarm code. The incrementally louder and faster beeping stopped. She stepped onto the patio and Ferris pulled her onto the backyard's grass. "You really are a pain in the tush tonight."

The motion light flicked on as Ferris pulled her into the middle of the yard. He stopped and surveyed what Cecilia figured he imagined as his kingdom. Again, he was in high alert.

She looked around the yard but could only see as far as the backyard's light illuminated. She couldn't see the fence that ran around the acre of land. She couldn't see her closest neighbor's home. She couldn't see anything but Ferris. And her breath in the cool night air.

"What's wrong with you?" She patted him on his back. Usually when she petted him on his back, he squirmed in glee. Tonight, she didn't think he even noticed the touch.

With the damp grass soaking through her socks, Cecilia wished she had put on shoes. The chill ran up her body and she regretted not putting on a jacket as well. Joey's T-shirt and boxers did little to keep her warm. Hoping to generate a little warmth, she told Ferris, "Come on, one lap and we're back in." Several pulls on his leash yielded no movement. With no motion, the yard's light flipped off. Suddenly engulfed in darkness, Cecilia let out a short scream.

Ferris twirled around, yanking Cecilia with him. As the light flipped back on, Cecilia screamed again.

CHAPTER 2

T HE BACKYARD WENT from complete darkness to light in a second. She registered what she was seeing as she hit the ground. Her head slammed against the grass. She screamed out for help, "Joey!"

Ferris pulled on his leash again and this time she didn't have the strength to hold him.

She started to scream for help once more but the intruder punched her in the face before covering her mouth. He was shorter than her but heavier. He was able to keep her pinned to the ground. Ferris barked continuously but she had no view of him.

With the intruder's full weight on top of her, she was unable to move. Her struggles only produced micro-movements that did little to free her. He leaned in to her and his hot breath stung her ear. She tried to pull away but his hand over her mouth kept her still. "Just stop. It'll be over in a minute." He held a knife to her throat. The cold steel blade against her skin froze her. "Be quiet. Am I making myself clear?" he asked.

He had made himself clear. Very clear. Cecilia didn't know what he wanted but he could take anything he wanted from the house. She tried to speak but his hand smothered any attempt. She tried to nod her head, slowly to avoid being nicked by the knife, but his hand kept her firmly in place. With her head pushed against the cold, wet grass, she looked at him out of the corner of her eyes. Cecilia hoped eye contact would signal she understood and would remain quiet.

"I didn't hear you." He laughed. Ferris's barking had stopped and the night had returned to the country quiet she had always hated. The laugh echoed through the cool night air. She hated that laugh more.

With the hand that remained over her mouth, he pushed her head harder into the grass. His other hand, the one with the knife, moved down her torso. She felt the cold blade through Joey's worn T-shirt. As the knife slid down her body, his eyes tracking its movement, Cecilia realized what he wanted—her. And that she wouldn't give.

She resumed her fight with all she could muster as she heard him start to unbuckle his belt. He slammed her head against the ground. "Quiet!"

The backyard light flipped off again. Startled, he lessened his grip slightly. She kneed him in the crotch and pushed him off.

She struggled to her hands and knees and then to standing. Ferris was now at her side, nuzzled against her leg. "Ferris! Get in the house!" she yelled. They ran for the still partially open sliding glass door. She took one backward glance to see the intruder still on the ground, writhing in pain. Ferris now leading the race back to safety, Cecilia crashed into him at the door. She pushed him in and fell in behind him. She landed hard on her back, hitting her head again.

She blinked several times trying to clear her vision. The flashing alarm system's box caught her eye. It reminded her of what Joey called "My Backup."

Using the kitchen island, she tried to pull herself up. But her hand was smeared with blood and she slipped back to the floor. Using both hands, she hauled herself up.

With tunnel vision, she headed to the safe, not noticing the still-open sliding door or the trail of blood she'd left on the floors and counter.

Her wet socks slid on the hardwood floor as she entered Joey's office. She held onto the doorframe for support. She swayed and tried to focus on her goal. Her vision was clouded by the trail of blood from her head wound. She wiped it away and refocused on her destination. She stumbled again and held onto the desk for support. Two more steps, using the desk to steady herself, and she stood in front of the safe. Her fingers shook as she pressed his code. Zero–six–two–five. Her finger trembled as she tried to hit the five, hitting eight instead. A series of beeps signaled the incorrect code. She tried again and quickly failed. Her shaking finger hit the eight instead of the zero. She glanced over her shoulder, fearing she'd see the intruder behind her. She saw no one, not even Ferris.

Cecilia cleared out her second failed attempt by hitting the eight three more times. The safe beeped again, signaling the incorrect code. She took a deep breath before her third and final attempt. One more failed entry and only a locksmith could open it.

Zero–six–two–five.

There was a soft click signaling entry. She pulled open the door and grabbed what she needed.

Cecilia ran back to the kitchen but stopped short at the counter when she saw them.

"Oh no," she mumbled. "Please not Ferris. Oh, please God, don't hurt Ferris." Cecilia's body shook. Her voice quaked as she asked, "Please let him go."

The intruder stood on the patio, holding a knife to Ferris's throat. One hand was on the scruff of his neck to keep control as Ferris struggled. The knife remained gingerly at his throat.

"Just let him go. I haven't seen your face. Just let him go. I can't tell the police anything."

The balaclava masked his identity. She had seen little that the police would find helpful. Dark jeans. Dark hoodie. Dark shoes. Dark eyes. Slightly shorter than her. Heavier than her.

Now, all she could see were his brown eyes and his knife. He pressed the knife firmer into Ferris's golden coat. The dog whimpered. She continued to beg. "Please just let him go."

"And if I don't?" he asked.

Cecilia slowly raised the gun.

He laughed again. That slow, resonating cackle that would haunt anyone's dreams.

The gun shook in her hands. Ferris continued his

light whimpering and the intruder remained in place. The sides of his mask moved, as if raised in a grin by the muscles underneath.

She saw a drop of blood on Ferris's coat.

And she shot.

CHAPTER 3

Then

"CECE, I'M HOME," Joey yelled as he entered the front door. "And I have a surprise."

"If it's anything like your last surprise, I don't want it," Cecilia called from the kitchen.

His laughter filled the entryway. "No, this one's alive."

"I think that's worse," she called back. She stirred the homemade chicken noodle soup, Joey's favorite, one more time before putting the cover back on the pot.

Two weeks ago, he'd come home with a dead deer strapped in the bed of his truck. He honked until Cecilia came running out of the house. She had screamed in horror as he pointed excitedly at the carcass. "First day of the season and I got this!" He was like a child on Christmas morning.

"What is that?" she asked.

"Dinner," he answered.

She ran to the bathroom to vomit as he described, in detail, how it would go from the truck to their dinner table.

With trepidation, Cecilia met Joey in the foyer after he assured her it wasn't another deer.

"You know I love you," he told her.

"Uh oh," she responded.

He kissed her on the neck and whispered into her ear, "Not the answer I expected."

"I love you too," she said before kissing him on the lips.

He put his arm around her waist and escorted her outside into their front yard.

"What's that?" she asked.

"I know you are a city girl. But you've seen a dog before!"

Cecilia looked at her husband out of the corner of her eye. The yellow-furred dog was running around the front yard. An orange butterfly fluttered about. The dog seemed to be chasing it. Every few steps, he'd jump in the air after it. She wasn't sure if he was trying to eat it or play with it. Was it dinner? Or a new friend?

"What's it doing here?" she asked, trying to keep her tone even.

"He needs a home."

"What's he doing here?" she asked again, less successfully keeping an even tone. The dog jumped again and landed against the fence. It looked at the fence, as if considering how it got there, then returned its attention to the butterfly.

"Come here, Ferris," Joey yelled.

At the sound of his name, the dog's attention

turned to Joey and he sprinted toward the couple. Joey held his arms out for him. The dog jumped and landed a foot away from Joey, onto Cecilia.

They fell hard to the ground. The dog jumped up, placing all paws onto Cecilia's body. She groaned at the strain of his weight. He stood over her to inspect her. Appearing to be pleased, he licked her face. Then he scampered off for his other playmate, the butterfly.

Joey put a hand out and helped Cecilia up.

"What is that doing here?" she asked again.

"He failed out of service school. He needs a home." Joey's eyes never left Ferris. The smile never left his face.

Cecilia's glare remained fixed on Joey.

"A dog failed school?" she asked.

"He was training to be a service dog," he explained.

"And he failed?" She touched his arm to get his attention. It took two more times before he turned from watching Ferris to her.

"Yes," he answered. A smile still lit his face. He turned back to watch Ferris. Cecilia did as well. The dog ran from one edge of the front yard to the other. She would have thought he was chasing something but there was nothing there. More than once he bumped into the fence when he turned around.

"And you brought him here?"

"Yes." He nodded.

"To live."

"Yes."

"Ferris?" she asked.

At the sound of his name, the dog came running over again. Cecilia stepped to the side before the dog could tackle her once more. He jumped toward her, missed, and landed hard on the grass. He sprung back to his feet and shook his body. Spotting something new, he ran toward the far corner of the yard, where a squirrel had appeared.

"Ferris like Ferris Bueller?" she asked.

Joey laughed. "That'd be funny. A dog struggling to get a day off of school, feigning illness, and then spending the day with his friends."

Cecilia had always loved Joey's laugh. It was the first thing she had noticed about him. Could you fall in love with someone at first listen? If so, she had.

She kissed Joey on the cheek, knowing she wouldn't be able to convince him to find the dog another home. She doubted a dog, especially one who had failed out of training, had a return policy. As much as she didn't want it living in her home. Shedding in her home. Doing whatever else dogs did in a home.

But she knew when Joey loved someone, that was it. She counted herself lucky to be in his loved category and now Ferris was too. She hoped the bumbling dog understood how lucky he was.

"So he's not named after Ferris Bueller?" Cecilia asked.

"Nope, he's named after a ferris wheel." They watched as Ferris began running tight circles, chasing his tail. "Because he likes to run around in circles."

CHAPTER 4

CECILIA WOKE UP on the kitchen floor. Ferris sat next to her, licking her face. She heard male voices shouting. Suddenly, one stood over her.

"Ma'am?" he asked. "Ma'am, are you alright?"

She looked around. There was a lot of red. Blood, she thought. It must be blood. Ferris licked her on the face again. She turned to face him. "Oh, thank God."

"Ma'am, please don't move," the officer told her. "The paramedics are coming. Just stay where you are."

She ignored him and pulled herself up and leaned against the kitchen's island. Ferris stepped next to her and sat at her side. Cecilia pulled him in closer and whispered in his ear, "Thank God you're alright." She petted his head, leaving a trail of red on his golden fur.

"Ma'am, are you alright?" Officer Vincent Pugliese asked again.

Bright red blood trickled down Ferris's neck. She knew it was not transferred from her and she gently pulled his hair away trying to find the source. "Ferris...I think he's hurt."

"But you, ma'am, are you alright?"

She inventoried herself. She couldn't feel any pain.

Truth was she couldn't really feel anything. She looked around her kitchen and saw red all over their white kitchen floors, cabinets, and appliances. Then she saw a lot of blue as more officers ran in.

Officer Pugliese stood to attention. "He's outside, Chief," he said as an older man walked in. He pointed toward the backyard. "It's the Gabbert kid." Chief Holden Owens nodded his head, scanned Cecilia and Ferris, then walked outside.

Officer Pugliese used the radio clipped to his shoulder. "ETA on ambulance?"

The radio chirped, "Pulling up now."

Cecilia's head began pounding. She rubbed her temples and felt a wetness. She was still bleeding. Holding her hands in front of her, she marveled at the redness. Her blood.

Paramedics came running in. The officer directed one to Cecilia. "Where's the other one?" the female paramedic asked. "First call said two at the scene."

"Gone," Pugliese answered.

Gone, thought Cecilia. She doubted the police would ever find him. She only hoped he never came back.

"Ferris. I think Ferris needs stitches." Cecilia tried to pull herself up using the counter.

"Stay where you are, ma'am," the paramedic directed her. He firmly placed his hand on her shoulder and she returned to sitting on the floor.

"He's bleeding." She pointed to the dog. "Can you help him?"

The paramedic looked to the officer for help. "I can help her. I don't know what to do with a dog." He turned back to Cecilia, peering at her forehead. He placed his bag on the floor and opened it. Cecilia watched as he put gloves on before attempting to place gauze on her forehead.

Cecilia swatted him away. "Please just help Ferris. I'm fine."

"You don't look fine, ma'am," he told her. He reapplied the gauze. She tried to move her head away but a wave of dizziness made her stop.

When it passed, she reached in his bag for gauze. "Ma'am, please stay still."

"I just want to help Ferris." She placed the gauze on Ferris's neck. He squirmed for a moment but then allowed the gauze on the cut.

Pugliese could see Cecilia's increasing anxiety and the paramedic's increasing frustration with her. Only one thing could stop both.

"The vet, Dr. Kinney, lives a few blocks over. The house with the big white columns, black BMW in the drive. Go get him for the dog," Pugliese ordered a younger officer.

The other officer hesitated. "It's three in the morning."

"Just go get him. Trust me, the whole neighborhood is up."

The female paramedic returned. Her partner looked up. "Yep, gone."

Cecilia looked back and forth between them before

returning her attention to Ferris. The female paramedic placed her bag on the floor and opened it. She pulled out a cuff and started to take her blood pressure.

Ferris placed his head on Cecilia's shoulder and gently moaned. She took the gauze off and judged that the cut was clotting.

"Ma'am, you're bleeding. You have multiple wounds. We need to take you to the hospital," the male paramedic told her.

The female paramedic left and returned with a stretcher.

"No, I can't leave Ferris. He'll get upset," she told him.

"What?"

"The dog, Ferris. He has anxiety. He's been hurt. I can't leave him. Joey wouldn't want that."

"Who's Joey?" Officer Pugliese asked.

"My husband."

"Where is he?" Pugliese asked.

She paused. Her head throbbed. Her kitchen was full of strangers. She struggled briefly for the answer. For the second time that night, she had to remind herself where her husband was.

"Dead," Cecilia answered.

CHAPTER 5

A T SEVEN IN the morning, Cecilia returned from the hospital. She was stitched, bruised, and exhausted.

She walked down the driveway to enter through the side gate, like she always did. Realizing she had no keys, she headed to the back of the house. The yard was now lit by the early morning sun. She tried to put out thoughts of the night's attack.

Despite her pleadings not to be taken to the hospital, they had taken her. A doctor stitched her head wound and ordered an MRI. She was diagnosed with a mild concussion and sent on her way with several papers on post-release care.

She was thankful she didn't have to argue with the doctor about being released. Her head throbbed and her body ached. She knew an argument with the doctor would only exacerbate both. She barely had enough energy to call for a cab to take her home, never mind an argument.

The sliding glass door was now closed but not locked and she slipped into her house. She barely took notice of the mess that her kitchen was in. Blood, footprints, dirt, more blood, and footprints. She was only looking for one thing.

"Ferris," she called out. Usually, when she called out his name, she could instantly hear him. His paws would smack the flooring as he ran to find his caller. Any hesitation usually meant he had gotten into something he shouldn't have. "Ferris," she called again. Still nothing. Her calls became more urgent as she recalled the last time she had seen him. He was bleeding and moaning as the paramedics dragged her away.

She opened the front door to call out and found a note taped to the door from Dr. Kinney. Ferris was at his clinic.

She ran to her car before she realized she had no keys or purse or shoes.

Everything was where she always put it. Her purse hung on the hook and the keys were in the dish by the side door. Her run-around town shoes, gray boat shoes, were on the floor.

Before leaving, she double-checked that she'd locked the sliding glass door in the back and the front door.

As she locked the side door, she glanced down at her clothes. The blue scrubs they'd given her at the hospital were ill fitting. But it was better than the blood-soaked and ripped nightclothes with which she had arrived in the emergency room. The scrubs hung two inches too short and she had to cinch them in tightly at her waist. They were not made for her tall, slender frame. But the scrubs were all they could find for her.

Cecilia plopped in the driver's seat of her purple Ford Escort. Her clothes might be clean but her hair certainly wasn't. Matted with blood and dirt, it hung in every direction. It explained the odd look the cab driver at the hospital had given her when she got in. She didn't have time to shower. Ferris had already been at the vet's for hours and was probably at new levels of anxiety.

She hand-combed her hair as best she could, pulling the brown strands back off her face into a ponytail. Grabbing a hair band from the gearshift, she wrapped it around to keep the hairs in place. She leaned in closer to the rearview mirror. Bruises were already developing on her face and neck.

Cecilia backed out of the driveway. She drove to the corner, stopped at the stop sign, and realized she didn't know where she was going. She had never been to the veterinarian's office. She put Dr. Kinney's name and Folley into her phone's search engine and only one option popped up. She put the address into her phone's directional app and waited to be told which direction to drive in. A car behind her beeped. She waved her hand in apology. In the city, she would have waved only one finger but Joey had taught her you didn't do that here. Everyone knew everyone else in this town and everyone knew her purple Escort. She turned left as the app's voice told her.

Five minutes later, she was at the town's only veterinary clinic. "I'm here for Ferris," she told the secretary. The secretary didn't move or answer, just stared at Cecilia. "Ferris Chandler," she clarified.

Cecilia looked around the office. The large waiting room was empty. She had expected a smaller office. Being the only vet in town must be good business, Cecilia thought.

Taking Ferris to the vet had been Joey's job.

Now every job was hers.

The secretary still made no move to get Ferris.

"The golden retriever," Cecilia added. "The emergency from last night. Dr. Kinney brought him in last night."

"Ooh, you're Mrs. Chandler?" she asked.

Cecilia nodded yes.

"Okay, let me get the doctor."

She didn't say she was getting Ferris and Cecilia became alarmed. "Is he alright? Is Ferris alright?" She tried, but failed, to keep the stress from her voice.

The secretary hesitated but answered, "Ferris is fine. Dr. Kinney thought he'd be with us for a while."

She continued to stare at Cecilia as if something were wrong. Cecilia reminded herself there was plenty to stare at—developing bruises, a split lip, stitches on her forehead, ill-fitting scrubs.

"Go into exam room one." She pointed to the room to the right. "I'll get Dr. Kinney."

Cecilia did as she was told. Waiting rooms always felt like a time stretcher. The minutes felt like hours. Finally, the door opened and the veterinarian entered with Ferris walking in slowly behind him. He slinked over and sat at Cecilia's feet. He slowly slid to the floor. His head lay across her shoes, while his front legs splayed out on either side.

She got on the floor with him. "Is he alright?" Cecilia asked. She petted him gently and he moaned slightly.

"I thought he'd be here all day so I gave him a sedative," Dr. Kinney told her.

Cecilia nodded, never taking her eyes off Ferris.

"A few stitches," he continued. "He'll have to wear an e-collar so he doesn't scratch at them. The stitches are dissolvable. Bring him back in a week for a checkup."

Cecilia nodded again.

"You sure you don't want him to stay with us for a bit?" Dr. Kinney asked.

"No, why can't he come home with me? He's never not been home with us—I mean me."

Dr. Kinney hesitated and tried to avoid eye contact. "Ferris shouldn't be alone and I figured you'd be busy today."

"Busy?" Cecilia asked. Her only plans were to lie down and try not to move. The pain was starting to set in at all her joints and her head ached intensely.

He shrugged. "Make sure he doesn't touch those stitches. One of the techs will help you with him."

A technician came in to put a cone on Ferris. Ferris's only movement was his ribcage slowly rising and falling while the tech put the cone on him. The tech left as quickly as he came in and said nothing to

Cecilia. She didn't mind. She was used to Folley residents having little to say to her. At least he didn't stare at her injuries.

She gently coaxed Ferris to standing, using his favorite kibble. A small bag of it was always in her purse now. She lured him out of the exam room and toward the exit. Every few steps, she'd give him one little piece. He'd munch on it slowly and she'd lead him a few more steps. Cecilia took no notice of the staff who stood watching her and her slow progression to the door with Ferris.

She breathed a sigh of relief as she got to the door. She could see the finish line, her car, on the other side of the door.

But she was stopped by the secretary. "Mrs. Chandler, the bill."

CHAPTER 6

Then

"A THOUSAND DOLLARS!" Cecilia screamed. "A thousand dollars!"

"Calm down, CeCe." Joey sat across from her on a stool at the kitchen's island. He took a sip of his kale juice. Cecilia paced back and forth. "Please sit down. Have a glass of wine." She knew it had been bad when he had come in with the bottle of chardonnay.

"You were all over me when I spent a hundred dollars on shoes."

"They were two hundred dollars, CeCe." She turned sharply and glared at him. "And I was not 'all over you' about them. I fixed them, didn't I?"

Ferris had chewed off one heel of her favorite cobalt blue, three-inch shoes, the ones that matched the floral wrap dress she loved. She had sat on the front stoop an hour that day waiting for Joey to come home. When he arrived home, he was met with an angry wife, waving the broken blue-heeled shoe, while cursing his dog.

Fortunately, Joey had been able to repair the heel.

"You're always going on about saving for a family

and you spent a thousand dollars on the dog!"

"It was nine hundred and fifty-two dollars, CeCe."

"It's a thousand dollars on the dog!" She slammed the bill down on the counter.

"He's part of the family, CeCe. Our family." He reached for her hand. She started to pull it away but didn't. He pulled her around the island onto his lap. "I'll plump up someone's bill at the job."

"You would never do that." She took his arms and wrapped them tighter around her waist.

"The rich ones would never notice." She knew they wouldn't.

"But you would never do that," she reminded him.

"We'll be fine. The business is doing well. We're getting more jobs."

Cecilia knew how hard Joey was working to expand what was once his father's business. He inherited the construction company when Mr. Chandler died last year. Initially, he struggled for the town to accept him again. The prodigal son did not receive the loving welcome he had hoped. They viewed him with suspicion, fearing the years in the city had turned him into the city folk most of them despised.

Cecilia sighed as Ferris came over and rubbed his head against her leg. He sat down and looked up at her, waiting for a pet. "I'll take the job Kenny floated last week," she told him.

"You said you'd never work with them again," Joey reminded her.

Kenny was difficult but he paid well and on time.

"What are you gonna do?" She shrugged and relented—to working for Kenny again and to petting Ferris.

Content, Ferris plodded over to his bowl, hitting his water bowl with his left paw when he got there, spilling water on the clean floor. He slopped up water loudly. He came back over to the couple and rubbed his wet mouth against their legs. Cecilia squealed and Joey laughed. He petted him on his back before Ferris returned to his bed in the living room.

"What could I have done? I love him. I took him in, promised to take care of him. He was sick."

"I know." She turned to face him and planted a kiss on his lips. "You love me too, took me in too. Promised to take care of me too. If I got sick, you'd do what you had to take care of me too."

Joey pulled away from her and tried to act repulsed. He suppressed his smile poorly. "What? Spend a thousand dollars on you? No way!" He laughed and pulled her in for a long kiss.

CHAPTER 7

CECILIA STRUGGLED TO get the doped-up Ferris into the car. She regretted not taking Joey's F-150 truck. He had a ramp Ferris could have walked up. Maybe.

But that was Joey's truck. And it hadn't been driven, or even touched, since its return to their garage after his death. She could barely look at it.

Exhausted, Cecilia rested her head against the headrest. She glanced at the full page receipt the clinic had given her. Emergency home visit, emergency transportation, waste removal, stitches, X-rays. The itemized list was large, as was the bill.

She glanced back at Ferris before she started the car. He was sleeping on the sedan's back seat. He remained sleeping as she carefully drove home, trying to avoid any bumps or sharp stops. She snuck peeks at Ferris when she could. He never seemed to move.

There was a police car sitting out front when she pulled in her driveway. The two officers got out of their patrol car, put their hats on, and met Cecilia as she got out of her car.

She opened the car's back door and looked at Ferris, who was still sound asleep. She gently shook him

27

to wake him. No response. He was breathing regularly so she didn't become alarmed. Dr. Kinney had said he'd probably sleep the rest of the day.

"Good morning, Mrs. Chandler," Chief Holden Owens said. The other man, Officer Vincent Pugliese, stood two steps back. He nodded a greeting.

She tried to smile but never took her eyes off the dog. It was late summer and the day wasn't predicted to get hot. She might have to leave him in the car until he woke up. She headed to the garage to get a chair so she could sit by him.

"Mrs. Chandler, how are you?" Holden asked again.

She turned to face him. "Fine."

"And the dog?"

"He'll be fine. I just picked him up from the vet's. He has some stitches." Holden looked at the dog and thought there was more wrong with him than a cut that required stitches. "They gave him some medication. I'm afraid to move him."

Her whole body hurt already from the attack. She feared the pain moving the seventy-pound dog would elicit.

Chief Owens nodded understanding and leaned into the car to take a closer look at Ferris. He reached for the dog and Cecilia grabbed his arm to stop him. "What are you doing? He's hurt. Don't touch him."

Pugliese stepped toward Cecilia. "Get your hands off the Chief, ma'am," he ordered.

She looked up at him, surprised. "Stand down,

Pugliese," Owens commanded. He returned his attention to the dog. Holden stroked Ferris's golden fur and Ferris didn't move. He turned to Cecilia. "Don't worry, I wouldn't hurt him." The gentle smile assured Cecilia that he was telling the truth.

He gently picked Ferris up and cradled him against his chest.

"Get the door, will you, Pugliese?"

Vinnie did as instructed, closing the car door but never taking his eyes off of Cecilia. Her full attention on Ferris, she didn't notice and walked up to the side door to open it.

"Where should I put him?" Holden asked.

"Um..." Cecilia said, as she tried to decide.

Ferris usually slept in his bed in the master bedroom. Unless she was working, then he slept at her feet.

When Joey was alive she didn't allow him on the bed but on more than one occasion she had found him stretched out on the bed when he didn't hear her come home. Or she found the evidence—his hair. But things had changed since Joey died. A lot of things.

Cecilia pointed to a dog bed in the living room and Holden gently placed him down. Ferris groaned a bit as Holden pulled his arms from under him.

They stood over him for a moment until they were sure he was comfortable.

"We need to ask you some questions, Mrs. Chandler," Owens told Cecilia.

She turned to face the Chief. "I'm sorry, what?"

she asked.

"We need to ask you some questions, Mrs. Chandler," he repeated. Pugliese stood behind him, in front of the front door, arms crossed.

"Can we do this later?" she asked.

"No, we have to do this now," Pugliese ordered. Owens shot him a look.

She slowly nodded understanding. "Um...okay." She pointed to the couch for them to sit.

Holden sat while Pugliese remained in his ready stance. "Thank you, Mrs. Chandler."

"Cecilia. Or CeCe, please." She figured the polite thing to do was to offer something to drink. "Do you want something to drink?"

He shook his head no. "You probably don't want to go in there right now," Holden told her.

The brief look she had earlier flashed in her mind. The cleaning would have to wait. The short nod she gave to agree intensified her headache. She grabbed her head, trying to ease the pain. Holden jumped up, putting his arm around her shoulders. "Are you alright?" he asked.

"It's been a long night and my head hurts."

He tried to guide her to the couch with him but she refused and chose the chair next to Ferris's bed. She watched him breathe several steady breaths and she did the same.

Pugliese cleared his throat to get her attention and was successful.

"Did you catch him?" Cecilia asked. "Or do you

need me to give a description? I really didn't get a look at him. He had that ski mask thing on." She mimed that the intruder had something over his head. "It covered his whole face."

The two officers exchanged a glance.

"Mrs. Chandler...Cecilia, the intruder...he's dead." Holden cleared his throat in order to continue. "You killed him."

CHAPTER 8

DANIEL BRISCOE HAD been locked in his office all morning. Folley's prosecutor leaned back in his chair and looked at the man sitting across from him and, for the third time that day, he questioned himself regarding his hire.

Of course, Alex Sanders was the only campaign manager who had agreed to come to Folley. None of the others wanted anything to do with the small town lawyer's pursuit for the state senate.

Briscoe had wasted time on the phone with each prospective manager, helping them find Folley on the map. He described it how most residents did: quaint. Briscoe usually called it old and small. He'd long outgrown the town and wanted out.

The town's website boasted "small town charm." It had been part of Mayor Townsend's failed attempt to increase tourism to the town. The only attraction was a lake and plenty of other towns had better lakes. And with only one hotel in town, few tourists arrived.

Briscoe had watched Mayor Townsend's career drive slowly evaporate. The mayor had big aspirations when he was first elected. He'd thought Folley would be a stepping-stone to the capital as well. Briscoe didn't want that to happen to him.

A firm knock on the door disturbed Briscoe from his thoughts. He yelled, "What?"

His assistant, Marcy Thompson, walked into the room. He glared at her. He could not think of one reason she should break his "Do not disturb" order. He also could not think of one time she ever had. "Yes, Marcy?"

She nodded to the middle-aged Sanders, who ignored her and pulled out his phone.

"I think you need to call the Chief." She hesitated and Briscoe held his tongue. He did not want to snap at his assistant in front of Sanders. He'd worked all morning on portraying himself as a calm man, for Sanders. A man he could sell to the constituents to work at the capital for them. If Sanders dropped him, he didn't know what he'd do. He doubted he could run a successful campaign himself. He wanted out of Folley and he saw this as his only chance. Time was slipping away.

Briscoe stared at Marcy, jaw clenched, waiting for explanation. "There's been a murder," she told him.

Briscoe sat up. "A what?" He could not have heard her correctly. A murder in quaint Folley? The biggest case he'd ever had was an armed robbery.

"A murder," she repeated.

Sanders perked up as well. "A murder? Does that mean a murder trial?" He turned to Briscoe. "Has there ever been a murder trial in this town?"

Briscoe shook his head. "Not since I've been here."

He looked to a lifelong resident of Folley. "Marcy?"

"Not that I can remember," Marcy answered. "I can call my mother—"

"No," Briscoe interrupted her.

"This will help your campaign immensely," Sanders told him. It was the first time he had seemed interested in Briscoe since his arrival. He smiled and Briscoe returned the smile. A big trial was exactly what Briscoe needed to bolster his career. Sanders made a few notes on his phone. "Will the mayor support you?" he asked.

Out of character, Marcy answered for him. "The mayor will definitely support you after this case."

CHAPTER 9

" AREN'T WE GOING to arrest her?" Vinnie asked as they left the Chandler home.

Holden hesitated. He certainly didn't want to. She was a recent widow struggling with enough and he didn't want to add this to her plate.

"She killed him," Vinnie said. As if Holden needed to be reminded. But he knew several people, with higher ranks and bigger egos, would be reminding him when he returned to the office who she killed.

"It was self-defense. He attacked her. On her property," Holden responded. "You heard her."

They had listened to her brief account of the night. He appreciated her succinctness. The recollection was devoid of emotion. Holden didn't know if it was shock or just Cecilia's way.

He'd heard in town she was some kind of computer wiz. Something he knew very little about but something many in the town, whose computer knowledge did not extend past how to turn one on and off, felt the need to comment on. He'd heard more than once how surprised they were that she still lived here after Joe Chandler's death. They all gossiped how she belonged in the city, not here. They'd said that when she'd arrived a couple years ago too.

"Did you know the husband?" Vinnie asked when he got in the driver's seat.

"Joe? Sure. Grew up here. Couple years younger than me. Real shame." Holden was thankful he hadn't had to give the death notice to Cecilia. He didn't like having to tell a wife her husband was never coming home again. Especially the young wives. It always made him think of his mother.

Holden recalled arriving on the scene last December.

An ambulance had been pulling away as he parked his car. Another ambulance remained on the scene.

The sheriff was waiting, talking on his cell phone. He waved him over. The construction site was outside city limits but the business, Chandler Construction, was in city limits.

"The owner's dead," Sheriff Walter Winkins announced after they shook hands. "Joseph Chandler." Wally lit a cigarette. He offered one to Holden, who passed. "You know the wife? Want to come with me?"

"No," Holden answered. "No, I don't know her," he clarified. And no, he did not want to go with him to tell her. "I've seen her around town but not to talk to."

Mrs. Chandler was tall and slender, always meticulously dressed. She stood out in the rural town. He'd seen her more than once in the local grocery store. She smiled politely as people passed but she was clearly uncomfortable. He'd never seen her stop to talk to anyone. Or them stop to talk to her.

He knew how uneasy he'd felt when he moved here ten years ago. He hadn't moved from a metropolis like she had but it was a bigger town than this one. He had found it a big transition. It must have been a monumental transition for Mrs. Chandler.

His marriage hadn't survived such a move. Annabelle had left after seven months.

Maybe Mrs. Chandler loved her husband more than Annabelle had loved him. Maybe the Chandlers were simply a better match.

They watched as the coroner's van pulled in.

"What happened?" Holden asked.

The sheriff pointed to the construction site. "Right over there. The heating and cooling unit broke free from the crane." He took a drag of his cigarette. "No hard hat going to protect you from that."

"Everything up to code?" Holden asked. He'd never heard anything negative about Chandler Construction, before or after Joe had taken over from his father. And this town talked. If there was a problem, he was sure he'd know about it.

"Yep. All the permits are up to date. Preliminary findings, the equipment is in good shape. All inspections up to date. All the workers legal. Appears to be an accident."

They walked toward their cars as the coroner's van pulled away with Joseph Chandler inside.

Sheriff Winkins finished his cigarette and flicked it

away. "So you want to come with me or what?"

"No, you don't need me with you to watch a pretty woman cry."

Holden looked at the Chandler home and was glad he hadn't made Cecilia cry, today or last year.

Vinnie was talking again. "She killed him outside her home. After she had already gotten away from him. And was safely in her house."

"But he was still there. He was still threatening her."

"Outside her home. She could have just closed that glass door and called 911."

"But he had the dog. He was going to kill Ferris."

"The law says—" Owens stopped him before Pugliese could recite the statute.

"I know the law, Pug." But Chief Holden Owens never had a case like this. He didn't know how the law applied.

"The Castle Doctrine says you can use deadly force to protect you and your family, not your property."

Owens didn't want to argue with Pugliese any longer. He knew he'd be facing a bigger fight when they got back to the station. He hoped he could win the fight so he could save Cecilia from more stress.

"Just drive, Pugliese."

As they pulled away, they didn't notice the first news truck pull up.

CHAPTER 10

Then

"WHY ARE WE here?" Cecilia asked when they pulled into the dirt parking lot. There was a white trailer at the end of the parking lot.

"For a little education," Joey responded as he parked his Ford F-150 among many other similar trucks.

"It's a Saturday. Can't I have a day off from the learning about country life?" Cecilia sighed and rested her head against the headrest. Dressed in wide-leg floral patterned pants, a pink silk tank top, and a white blazer, she felt overdressed for a dirt parking lot and the trailer. Cecilia had hoped they were going out for a nice meal. But she had left nice meals in the city.

Her clue that they weren't going anywhere nice should have been when Ferris jumped in the truck. He rested his head on Cecilia's shoulder and she gently pushed him off. She cringed when she saw the dirt his muzzle had left on the white blazer. The dirt wiped away easily.

"Learned? CeCe, I don't think you've learned anything about country life." He laughed and the laugh filled the truck. "You just need to be glad we don't have the farm anymore. I would pay any amount to see you getting up with the roosters and milking the cows...oh and feeding the chickens..." The thought of each new chore made him laugh harder and he had more difficulty speaking it. "Oh and the pigs. You walking among the pigs!"

Cecilia lightly slapped him on the shoulder. "Why are we here?" she asked again.

"Today you're going to learn how to protect yourself."

Excited to be somewhere new, Ferris ran from one window to the other, smacking Cecilia with his tail each time he turned. "I think Ferris here is the one who needs protection."

"Let's go, boy," Joey instructed him as he helped Ferris out of the car. Then he came around to the passenger side and helped Cecilia out. She slid down his body and asked, "Is there something else we could do today? Go somewhere a little more romantic than this?"

"Maybe later," he answered.

Joey held her hand to steady her as they walked on the graveled parking lot. Her fuchsia high heels were not made for this terrain.

The popping sound she heard when she got out of the truck got louder as they walked closer to the trailer. "Hey, Boomer. How you doing today?" Joey said to the man inside.

Boomer gave Cecilia a thorough once-over, as if

he'd never seen a woman before. Cecilia looked around and took in the trailer. Boomer sat behind a glass case that held guns for sale. Pictures of guns hung on the walls behind him. She slowly turned to take the place in. Pictures of people holding guns, people shooting guns, pictures of guns hung on every wall. Boxes of bullets were displayed for sale on a rack by the door. It slowly dawned on her what her date night was.

A shooting range was not what Cecilia had planned for their Saturday night out.

Boomer grunted hello when Joey introduced them.

"The usual, Boomer," Joey told him as he got cash out of his wallet.

"I'll put you in the end," Boomer said after inspecting Cecilia again.

"Yeah, probably best," Joey agreed. "You get my order?"

Boomer nodded and handed Joey a bag, along with a gun and two sets of headphones.

Joey handed Cecilia the bag. "I got you a little something."

Normally, she would smile when presented with a gift. But she doubted something at a gun range would ever appear on her wish list. Joey took her hand and led her out the back exit of the trailer.

Two lanes of the eight shooting lanes were occupied. Once finished shooting, the two men, at the far right, reeled in their targets. They removed their headphones and pulled down their targets. They glanced up at the open door to check out the new arrivals. "Hey, Joey," one called over. Then he did a double-take when they noticed his wife.

Joey returned their greeting and Cecilia gave a little wave. Each looked at Cecilia before returning to their conversation about who shot their targets better.

Joey escorted Cecilia over to the leftmost shooting lane. Cecilia opened the bag to find pink headphones.

"Pink headphones?" She held them out and wondered how she would wear them without messing her hair.

Joey nodded. "Nice, right? Knew you'd love them."

She pulled her hair back and to the side, placing the headphones around her neck.

"Look, they even match," Joey said, pointing to her pink tank top. He put one pair that he was carrying around his neck and placed the other pair on Ferris. "You and me boy, we get black ones." Ferris sat patiently between them. Cecilia struggled daily to put a leash on Ferris but he let Joey put earphones on him without a wiggle.

"So this is going to be a usual Saturday night date?" she asked.

"No," he answered, helping Cecilia put her headphones on, with no regard for her hair. The headphones rested askew on one ear so she could still hear him. She sighed relief.

"We can come any night," he added. Joey put a target up and pointed to the center. "This is what you're aiming for."

"I don't like this, Joey," she said as he placed the gun in his hands.

"You need to learn how to shoot a gun."

"I've lived twenty-seven years without even holding a gun. I've done just fine."

"But we live here now. It'll take over twenty minutes for police to get to us if there's a break-in. You need to know how to use a gun." Using the clothesline apparatus, he placed the target ten feet away.

The target wasn't simply expanding rings but a picture of a man, with rings transposed on top of him. She could clearly make out his eyes. "I can't shoot something that close."

Joey laughed. "Well, I doubt you'll be able to shoot anything farther."

He turned her to face the target and placed the gun in her hand. She recoiled. "Really, Joey, I don't like this."

"CeCe, living here, you need to learn." He held his hands firmly over hers and kept her facing the target.

"What kind of neighborhood have you moved us into?" she asked, turning her head to meet his eyes.

He took the gun and placed it on the shelf in front of them. "The neighborhood is fine. It's just isolated."

Removing the headphones, Cecilia turned to face him. She smiled and hoped she could flirt herself out of the gun range without ever having to shoot a bullet. It was bad enough she had held the gun. Joey, six inches taller than her, looked down at her and into her eyes. He returned the smile. "Can't we get an alarm?" she asked.

Joey placed his hands on her upper arms and gently squeezed. "We already have an alarm. You never set it."

"How about a guard dog?" she asked.

"We have Ferris." They both laughed. Joey pulled her in to hug her and she placed her head over his heart as he squeezed her tight. She watched Ferris, who sat a foot behind them, headphones still in place. His tail tapped urgently, wanting to get in on the hug. "Really, CeCe, I need you to do this. For me. I worry when I get stuck at work and you're home alone."

She nodded but said nothing. His guilt for working late was not enough to sway her.

"I'm serious, CeCe. What happens if someone broke in? You need to be able to protect yourself. Our children." He knew a hypothetical, like an unborn child, would not sway her. She would need a concrete example. "How about me? Would you use it to protect me?"

"Of course, I would." Cecilia loved him more than anything and couldn't picture her life without him. He was her best friend since the moment they met five years ago. "But goodness, Joey. I don't think I could shoot someone."

CHAPTER 11

C ECILIA WAS DOZING on the couch when something
woke her. She immediately looked for Ferris,
who remained sleeping in his bed. The doorbell rang
again.

Since the funeral, she couldn't remember ever hearing the doorbell. It rang fairly constantly in the days
after his death, before his funeral. Joey's friends
coming to pay respects. Neighbors dropping off
casseroles. As if she had any appetite. Floral deliveries
from friends and family from out of state.

Today, like then, she had no desire to answer it. If
she ignored it, they would go away. A third time, the
doorbell rang. A low moan emanated from Ferris.
Fearing that another ring would wake him up, she
answered the door.

Cecilia didn't recognize the woman standing at the
door. She couldn't make out the man behind her
either, whose face was blocked by a large video
camera. The camera had a local news station's logo on
the side.

The reporter thrust a mic toward Cecilia and,
without introducing herself, she asked, "Tell us why
you killed the local teenager, Robert Gabbert."

Cecilia stood shocked. She hadn't been out of the house in hours. In front of her house, there were now two media trucks. Cecilia looked up and down the block and couldn't see any neighbors. The houses were separated by at least a quarter of a mile on the block. It was nothing like their old home, where you could shout from your window to the neighbors and they could make out every word you said.

Despite the spread-out neighborhood, she often saw neighbors walking their dogs or pushing baby carriages up and down the quiet street. Especially on a cool late summer day like this, she expected to see neighbors. She wouldn't know their names but she'd recognize their faces and wave politely as they passed. And they would return the wave.

The reporter asked the question again.

Cecilia had thought she'd been attacked by a man. Not a boy. He was strong. He had held her down. That was no child. What he had wanted to do to her was certainly not motivated by a child's yearnings. Something had to be wrong. Her head hurt too bad to process what the reporter was saying. She still couldn't process what Chief Owens had told her. How was it possible that she had killed the intruder?

The reporter asked the question a third time. This time with more urgency. "*Ma'am*, why did you kill local teenager Robert Gabbert?"

Cecilia finally mustered the ability to speak, but not the ability to answer that question. "Please stop ringing the bell. The dog is resting."

She closed the door.

On her side of it, Cecilia slid down it and held her aching head.

DANIEL BRISCOE MARCHED into the station. His entourage, being only his assistant Marcy Thompson, trailed a step behind him. Marcy's legal pad was held close to her chest, ready to take notes whenever he barked them at her.

Briscoe and Owens had a good working relationship. They usually communicated via email or through Marcy. They rarely interacted with each other face-to-face. They both liked it that way. They had only ever argued over one subject, Robert Gabbert, and they were headed for another round.

Briscoe stormed into the Chief's office and shouted, "Give me one good reason that Chandler woman isn't in your holding cell."

Marcy scribbled on her pad. Owens wasn't sure if she had been ordered to keep a transcript of his every word or was trying to make herself look busy.

"Good afternoon, Dan. Please come in," Owens answered. He plastered a fake smile on his face. He wanted to avoid escalating the argument and ignored the fact that Briscoe had barged into his office. "Marcy, always a pleasure."

"I asked you a question," Briscoe spat.

Briscoe's entourage had grown as he had stomped

through the station. Now, everyone in the station stood outside Owens's office and waited for an answer.

"Close the door, Dan."

The prosecutor made no move for the door. Owens slowly stood and leaned on his desk. Even leaning over, he was an intimidating figure and Briscoe buckled. He signaled for Marcy to close the door. She scurried over and shut it. With a wave of Owens's hand, the group outside scattered.

He sat down again before answering. "It was self-defense, Dan."

Briscoe remained standing, his arms crossed over his chest. "She shot him. He was defenseless."

"Defenseless?" Owens shook his head. "He had a knife."

"A knife versus her gun? He had no chance." Marcy stood behind Briscoe scribbling down every word uttered.

"He had every chance, Dan. She told him to leave." Owens looked at Marcy and added, "Repeatedly." He stared at her, ensuring she wrote that down. He watched as she underlined it.

Briscoe harrumphed. "A grown woman versus a boy."

Owens shook his head. "He was *not* a boy. He was an adult."

"A teenager!" Briscoe shot back. Marcy flinched at the shout, but she kept transcribing the conversation.

"An eighteen-year-old man who you know was

trouble."

"Trouble? He was spirited is all." Briscoe smirked and sat down in one of the two available chairs. Marcy didn't leave her post, standing behind him.

"Spirited? Bull."

It was the worst-kept secret in the town. The mayor's nephew, Robert Gabbert, had been arrested several times. And every time he was, he was given a second chance. Owens had known it was only a matter of time before he escalated. He had told Briscoe this, repeatedly.

"He was trouble. You of all people should be glad he's dead. How many more times could you sweep his crimes under the rug?" Owens asked.

"Indiscretions," Briscoe corrected him.

"Indiscretions? Bull!" Owens slammed his fist onto his desk.

Startled, Marcy recoiled and her writing hand flew off the page. She furiously erased the stray mark.

"He was escalating and you know it." Owens lowered his voice. "You're lucky he didn't rape the Chandler woman. There's no way she'd let that be pleaded out to community service."

"Well, he didn't, did he?" he asked, with a smirk on his face.

Owens used all his strength not to slap that smirk off his face. He knew assaulting the prosecutor wouldn't be viewed as an "indiscretion." Not with the whole station watching. "He didn't even serve his community service since his last 'indiscretion', did he?"

"Irrelevant." Briscoe leaned forward and tapped his finger on Owens's desk. "She shot him." He tapped the desk again, a little harder this time. "She killed him." With more force, he tapped the desk a final time. "You will arrest her for it."

"Oh come on! What am I charging her with?"

"Second-degree murder."

CECILIA WAS RESTING on the bed, not sleeping but not awake either. Ferris was lying next to her. A luxury he had never been afforded before. The stresses of the night forgotten, he snored lightly. Cecilia's cell phone rang, disturbing her from her attempts at sleep. It did not disturb Ferris.

She answered it without checking the caller ID. She quickly regretted it when she heard her sister's voice. "Did you kill a child?" her sister asked.

"What?" Cecilia asked.

"I got a Google Alert for your town. Nothing ever happens there. But today for the first time ever I got a Google Alert."

Cecilia got up and walked to the front of the house to look outside. There were now three media trucks.

"They said there was a murder. And they showed Joe's house." She sounded excited at the hint of a scandal. "Your house," she clarified. "I saw you on the news. What were you wearing?"

Cecilia looked down at herself. She had changed out of the scrubs, having thrown them out after scrubbing the kitchen clean. She now wore her usual life-after-Joey attire—one of his shirts and whatever she could find for pants. Today was a Van Halen T-shirt and black leggings.

Cecilia plopped in the chair next to the window. She continued to peer out at the street, hoping not to be seen.

"I gotta go, Janna."

"Cecilia? What's going on?" Janna pleaded for information.

Cecilia didn't miss that she didn't ask if she was alright. She only wanted gossip. It reminded Cecilia how different she and her sister was.

Cecilia would not have called at all.

She watched as activity sprang from the three vans. Cecilia leaned forward to see what the cause was. She knew they thought it was good. For them. She doubted it be good for her.

The newscasters, with their camerapersons at their heels, smoothed out their hair and their outfits. Those behind the cameras readied themselves for the shot as well, placing their cameras on their shoulders and fiddling with controls.

The front of the house was blocked by the news trucks, so the police car pulled into her driveway.

"I have to go, Janna," she said again.

"What? You have to tell me what's going on!"

"I don't know," Cecilia answered, after she ended

the call.

There was only one other time Cecilia could remember seeing a police car in her driveway.

That one had brought bad news as well.

CHAPTER 12

Then

CECILIA SAT AT her desk in Joey's office. Hers was the smaller of the two desks in the office. The large antique mahogany one had been her father-in-law's. They both held it in such reverence that even Joey avoided using it, even though it was rightly his now.

Cecilia was completing her last job of the day. The last item on her to-do list before she could shut down the computer for the weekend. She checked her watch. Joey should be home in under two hours. She'd have enough time to shower, pack, and be ready when he got home. He promised this weekend they'd go back to the city for a relaxing weekend. She hadn't been there in over six months. And that had only been for an afternoon for a funeral.

Ferris was at her feet. He would be remaining in the country for the weekend, stowed away at the local veterinarian's for boarding.

The doorbell rang.

Ferris remained at her feet, undisturbed.

"Aren't you supposed to bark? Aren't you supposed to hear someone approaching before they ring the bell? Isn't that what dogs do?" she asked.

He looked up at her but his body remained at her feet.

The doorbell rang again and this prompted Ferris to move. She checked her watch again. She never had visitors this time of day. She never had visitors any time of day. The only people who regularly came to the house were the mailman and the UPS driver. The mailman never rang the bell. The UPS driver would ring once, before depositing her package at the front door.

The doorbell rang again. Both Cecilia and Ferris left the office to check out who was the cause of their midday disturbance.

Cecilia walked from the back of the house, through the kitchen, to the front door. Ferris followed her. She opened the door without asking who was there. She would never have done that when she lived in the city. She wondered when she had started doing that.

"Mrs. Chandler?" he asked. He was dressed in a brown uniform and a cowboy hat. "May I come in?"

She nodded yes to both questions.

He removed his hat as he crossed the threshold and sat in the living room. "I'm Sheriff Winkins."

Cecilia nodded understanding.

"I'm here about your husband."

"Joey?" she asked. She could not think of a reason why a sheriff would be at her house about her husband. She doubted the police made home visits if he'd been arrested. But Joey would never get arrested.

She stood at the doorway into the living room. Ferris stood behind her. His head cowered down by her knees, trying to sneak a peek at the stranger.

"Yes, Joseph Chandler. Ma'am, could you sit down, please?"

She and Ferris remained frozen at the doorway. "Joey's at work, sir. I can give you his phone number, the address. He's at the office."

"Ma'am, can you please sit down?"

A pit began to form in her stomach. She looked down at Ferris and wondered if he felt that same dread. The low moan coming from Ferris indicated his mutual distress.

She pulled her cell phone from her pocket. "I'll call him."

He motioned for her to stop and tried to get her attention. "Ma'am."

She ignored the sheriff. She didn't like being called "ma'am." She didn't like this stranger in her house. She didn't like the growing fear in her heart. She didn't like the dog rubbing himself against her leg, leaving his golden hairs all over her pants.

Cecilia pulled up her call history and tapped the last call, Joey cell. The phone rang before going to voicemail. "I spoke to him a couple hours ago. He was going out into the countryside to check some site."

She had laughed when he'd said it. She retorted that they were already in the country. Joey assured her they were not.

Cecilia dialed his number again. Four rings, then voicemail. She struggled to find her voice and the voicemail disconnected before she could leave a message.

"Sometimes the cell doesn't work at the sites. Or maybe he left it in his car. He does that." She tapped her phone again, calling the office number. It rang several times and then went to voicemail. She checked the time and stared at her phone. "The secretary should be there. Unless Joey let her go early. He does that." She stared at the phone, willing it to ring. To see Joey's face pop up on the screen. Him calling her back. "We're going home this weekend...into the city...soon. Once Joey gets home."

The sheriff put his hand over hers. Ferris growled softly. She hadn't even noticed that the sheriff had gotten up. "Please, ma'am, have a seat."

Keeping her hand, he escorted her to the couch. Ferris jumped onto the couch.

She started to tell him to get off because he didn't belong on the couch. But she knew it didn't matter. She feared nothing would matter ever again. Ferris placed his head on her lap. He returned to his light moaning. Cecilia placed her hand on his head and gently stroked his fur.

"Ma'am," she heard the sheriff say.

"No, please, no."

"I'm sorry, Mrs. Chandler to tell you—"

"No, just one minute. Please, let me have one more minute." She took a deep breath. "Just give me one more minute to be his wife."

CHAPTER 13

HOLDEN OWENS SAT in the passenger seat, looking at the Chandler house. He did not want to be here. He didn't want to go in that house. Worse, he didn't want to come out of that house with Cecilia in handcuffs.

Pugliese got out of the car. Arresting a woman who had been assaulted only a few hours ago did not weigh as heavily on his mind. He had been first on the scene and saw this as a career opportunity. He straightened his hat and readied himself for the cameras.

Owens heard the shouts of the reporters, coming up the drive. "Tell them to stay back," he ordered Pugliese.

"Keep off the property," Vinnie told them in his most commanding voice.

Holden slowly got out of the car. Pugliese was answering reporters' questions. "Let's go, Pugliese," Holden commanded. "I told you to keep them back, not talk to them."

"Well—"

Holden stopped Vinnie before he could voice an insolent reply. "Yes, you needed to talk to them to tell them to stay back. No, you did not need to say anything else."

Pugliese nodded understanding and started to walk to the front door.

"No, get back to the car. Call for backup. I want those vipers held back when I come out with her." Holden watched Pugliese's smile vanish from his face. He was looking forward to arresting Cecilia far too much. He remained standing in front of Owens.

"I gave you an order, Pugliese. I expect this one to be followed. Are we clear?"

"Yes, sir."

Chief Holden Owens rarely pulled rank. He rarely felt the need to. He feared this was just the beginning. He could read a room. The station had no qualms about arresting Cecilia. The woman from the city had killed one of them. They all knew Gabbert was a bad one of them. But he was still one of them.

He passed secretaries crying for "Bobby" as he and Vinnie had headed out of the station. These same women who had shaken their heads at Gabbert the last time he had been arrested. Owens couldn't even remember what that arrest had been for. There had been so many.

Those women weren't crying for the woman he attacked and had planned to rape. Nope, it was always us versus them in a town like Folley. He knew that too well.

For a time, it had been them against him. When he had first moved to Folley. But at some point, he had become one of them. Usually, he thought that was a good thing. Now, he wasn't so sure.

Most had probably forgotten he had been born outside of Folley. Most, but not all. His resistance to arrest Cecilia had reminded them.

Owens glanced back, confirming Pugliese had done as he was told. He stood, arms crossed, leaning against the trunk of the car. The frown on his face suited him to his first assigned task. The media remained at their post, off Cecilia's property. Owens resumed his walk to the front door. He took a deep breath before ringing the front doorbell.

Cecilia was headed down the stairs before the bell rang. Ferris plodded down the stairs behind her, seemingly still feeling the effects of the drugs.

She opened the door, knowing who it was but not knowing what he could want. She had answered all their questions hours ago. What else could the Chief want?

He stood large in the doorway, blocking her from the reporters' cameras. She was eager to let him in, not wanting to be seen on the news again. But she paused and looked at him closely. She hadn't recognized him earlier in the day.

"We've been here before, haven't we?" she asked.

And he nodded yes.

HOLDEN PULLED UP in front of the Chandler home the

day of Joe's funeral. He'd overheard a pair of ladies talking about how lovely the Chandler house was in the coffee shop this morning. They were discussing how much they'd love to call it their own. One had already called her real estate broker to let her know when Mrs. Chandler listed it for sale. The other feigned shock. Holden guessed she had also called. If she hadn't, she soon would be.

"Only a matter of time," the blond one had said. "Lady like that isn't going to stay in this town. She has no reason to. Not with the husband gone."

The other blond one added, "Bless her heart," to assuage her guilt for coveting a recent widow's house.

The husband wasn't even buried yet and they were redecorating his home.

As he got out of the car, he agreed it was a nice-looking home. It was a two-story residence with off-white siding and a large porch. He guessed there was a large backyard as well.

Holden was surprised his car was the only one here. Joe Chandler was a town son. Born and raised in Folley. He'd returned when the family business needed him. He couldn't believe no one had come to the Chandler home to pay respects.

Mrs. Chandler wasn't a town favorite but he didn't think she was disliked. She was just ignored.

His hands felt noticeably light as he walked up the walkway. He regretted not bringing something. But what does one bring? Food? Who could eat when your spouse recently died tragically? Flowers? That would be unwise. The divorced police chief showing up at the pretty new widow's home with flowers. Tongues would wag.

His ex-wife, Annabelle, would have known what to bring. She knew all the manners and customs of country life. This was the first time in years he wished he could talk to her.

Holden walked up the two steps onto the porch, surprised the home was so quiet. He rang the bell, disturbing the silence.

A dog let out a dull bark and Holden waited.

Mrs. Chandler opened the door. She was wearing jeans and an oversized T-shirt. It wasn't her usual stylish outfits that showed off her figure. It certainly wasn't the mourning clothes he had expected.

She smiled at him. It was the fakest, saddest smile he'd ever seen.

"How can I help you, Officer?" she asked.

"I came to pay my respects for your husband."

"Okay, thank you," she answered.

They stood in the doorway. Neither knowing what to do. Remembering her manners, she asked, "Would you like to come in?"

Not wanting to but feeling obligated to, he agreed and stepped into the entryway. Again, neither knew what to do. They stood there in an awkward silence. The house was empty save the three of them. Ferris sat by Cecilia's feet and watched Holden.

"I'm sorry. Am I early?" Holden asked.

"For what?" she asked.

"The funeral."

He watched tears well in her eyes. She swallowed hard before she could answer. "It was yesterday."

Holden mumbled profanities and then looked up at Cecilia, ashamed that he had cussed in front of her. "I'm so sorry, Mrs. Chandler. I...I thought it was today. I wanted to pay my respects. Joe was a nice man."

She smiled at the mention of his name. "He..." She paused and struggled to say, "was." Cecilia walked toward the kitchen, turning away from Holden so she wouldn't cry in front of him. Mother had taught her crying was a private activity. "No one needs to see your bodily fluids, dear," she'd told her at her grandmother's funeral when she was a child.

"Would you like a cup of coffee?" she asked.

"Okay," he answered. He watched as she stood in front of the empty coffeemaker. It was as if she didn't know how to use it. Not wanting to put her out any more than he had already, he said, "You know, something cold would be nicer."

She turned to the refrigerator and, again, it looked like she had no idea how to use it.

"Why don't you have a seat?" he asked, pointing to one of the kitchen stools. "I'll get it myself."

She plopped on a stool and Ferris plopped next to her. Holden opened the refrigerator and asked, "Can I take this?" holding out a can of Mountain Dew.

"You can take anything you want," she answered.

Ferris barked. "I wasn't talking about you. No

one's taking you from me." She patted him on his head and smiled. It was the first time he had ever seen her smile genuinely and it was beautiful.

Cecilia looked up and caught him staring at her. She pointed to the full countertops. Every inch was food—casseroles, pies, cakes. He'd been right. The neighbors had done their neighborly duty and supported the widow. Many had probably visited with thoughts of how their furniture would look in the Chandler home.

"Lots of food. Everybody brings food." She shook her head. "Like I can even think about eating." She turned from the food to Holden. "Thank you for not bringing any food."

"You're welcome," he responded, feeling awkward again that he had arrived empty-handed.

"And look at all those flowers." She pointed to the dining room. The room was full of arrangements. Lilies, roses, carnations. Mostly white. "They'll be dead in a few days. That'll only remind me that everything dies. That he's dead too." She cleared her throat. "Thank you for not bringing flowers."

Holden hesitated, then responded, "You're welcome." The uneasy quiet returned until Holden opened the soda can. Fearing the house would reverberate with every sip he took, he asked, "Where is everybody?"

"Who's everybody?"

"Your family. Joe's family."

"I asked them to leave." She bit her lip. "Told

them, actually. They were just so...annoying. I heard them talking about the lamest of things—the weather, the football season, how I need to take down the Christmas lights. Joey just put them up. He loves them. How can I take them down?"

Holden started to offer that he'd take them down but that is not what she meant. It wasn't that she couldn't take them down physically. It was that it was mid-December and Joe would want them up for the holidays.

The silence returned. Holden sipped his soda and Cecilia stroked Ferris's back.

"You a big Beastie Boys fan?" Holden asked. He instantly regretted it. Cecilia would probably deem this question annoying and kick him out too.

"What?" she asked.

"Your shirt." He pointed to the black tour shirt, which hung on her thin frame.

She looked down and smiled. "No, Joey's the fan. He dragged me to more than one of their concerts. This was his favorite shirt." She grabbed the collar and brought it to her nose. Inhaling deeply, she could still smell Joey. "He loved to walk around the house singing their lyrics."

"Was he good?"

"Of course not!" she answered, with a smile on her face. The smile quickly faded and tears formed in her eyes.

He selfishly wondered if a woman would ever mourn him like Cecilia was mourning Joe.

He doubted it. Holden had once been hurt in the line of duty. When he woke up, he found Annabelle holding court outside his hospital room with dried tears on her face. Crocodile tears, as his grandmother would say.

"I...I don't want to be rude. But I'm going to cry soon and I'd rather do that alone." Ferris nuzzled against her leg as she stood.

Holden scurried around, trying to find the garbage receptacle for the soda can. He decided to take it with him as he hurried after Cecilia to the door. She held it open and he walked out. He turned to say goodbye but she'd already closed the door.

Holden stood staring at the front door, wishing there were something he could do to help her.

Cecilia leaned against the door, using it for support. She wished she could hear Joey quoting the Beastie Boys one more time.

CHAPTER 14

"YOU KNOW LAST time you were here, you never told me your name. I realized after you left. All I knew was that you were a police officer."

"Chief Owens," he answered. "Holden Owens."

"I'd say it's nice to meet you but not really under these circumstances, right?" He nodded. "Or last time either," she added. He nodded a second time.

She started toward the kitchen. Again, she was trying to hide tears from him. He followed her into the kitchen again. As did Ferris, who hit her leg three times with his cone. She went to the refrigerator, got out two cans of Mountain Dew, and slid one to him.

Cecilia eased herself down, fearing the pain every movement caused. She sat on the same barstool and Ferris sat in his same spot as last time. She was again dressed in a band T-shirt that had been Joey's. Motley Crue today.

Holden sat down at the barstool across from her. He marveled that the kitchen had been returned to the clean state he had seen during his visit last year. A significant change from this morning, when it was covered in blood.

"How's he feeling?" Holden asked. He tried calling Ferris over but he had no interest in leaving his Cecilia.

"Fine," she answered.

"How are you feeling?" he asked. The bruises on her face were beginning to show. Her movements were slow and controlled. She was clearly in pain and it wasn't even twenty-four hours. It was going to get worse before it got better.

"Fine," she answered. When Holden's last girl-friend would answer "fine," he knew an argument was brewing. He knew Cecilia was lying to him too but he didn't fear a row. Until he went to arrest her. Then things could get ugly.

They both sipped their sodas and placed them on the counter. She turned the can around in her hands.

"You took down the Christmas lights, didn't you?" she asked.

She caught him off guard. He had forgotten.

"Did the neighbors complain?" she asked. "Is that why? It was only the first week of January."

"No...I...I just wanted to help."

She took another sip and he did as well. "Thank you," she told him. Before he could reply, she spoke again. "I'm guessing this isn't a social call."

"No," he answered while staring at his soda can.

"Do you have more questions for me?" she asked.

His head still down, he shook his head and answered, "No."

"I don't want to be rude. Even though everyone in this town thinks I am. I feel we should get to the point." They both looked up from their half empty sodas and looked at each other. "Why are you here?"

"I'm here to arrest you."

Cecilia took the news better than he expected. Better than he would have. She took the news better than he did when Briscoe had ordered him to arrest her.

She finished her Mountain Dew. "Last drink as a free woman. I really wish I had chosen something a little stronger."

She threw the can in the recycling bin and held her hand out for his can. Holden marveled at her calmness. It was probably shock.

"Should I be doing something? I'm not really sure what someone does when they're arrested. Although I am guessing most have not just shared a drink with the arresting officer in their home."

Holden laughed, then realized how absurd that was. "I'm sorry," he said. "You probably should call a lawyer to meet you at the station."

She nodded. "True. Lawyer. I need a lawyer." She considered it for a moment. "I'm guessing the business attorney wouldn't be the right choice."

"He's probably the only choice you have to meet you at the station soon. You can hire a criminal attorney later."

"Criminal attorney," she mimicked back. "Never really thought I'd need a criminal attorney." She pulled out her cell phone and placed a call to her lawyer. She cut off each of his questions politely. She hung up when he agreed to meet her at the station. She looked at the phone and mumbled, "How could he be dead? I've held a gun two times in my life. I've shot a gun two times in my life. How could he dead?" She looked up at Holden and asked, "Now what?"

"There's a lot of media out there. I'm going to have to do this by the book." He asked her to turn around and put her hands behind her back. She did as she was told.

"You're not going to read me my rights?" she asked.

"I'm not questioning you right now so I don't have to," he answered as he placed the handcuffs on her, as gently as he could, trying as best he could not to cause any more pain. Ferris growled.

"Don't worry, Ferris," she told him. Cecilia looked over her shoulder, cringing when she did so. "What about Ferris?"

"I'm hoping you'll be home tonight."

Holden had let go of her and she turned to face him. "I hope so too."

They stood looking at each other until a knock at the sliding glass door disturbed them. Office Pugliese was standing there and yelled, "What's taking so long? I thought maybe she shot you too."

"That's not funny," Owens told him as he approached the door. "Bring the car to the garage. We'll take her out the back."

"They'll still see her," he shouted back.

Owens opened the sliding glass door. "I know

that, Pugliese. But they won't see her face."

Pugliese looked at Cecilia. He grimaced. "No one's gonna want to see that face."

"Pugliese!" Owens rebuked.

"I'm talking about the bruises and the swelling. She looks terrible." Owens pointed to the door and Pugliese left via the side door.

"I haven't looked in a mirror since this morning. Is it that bad?" Cecilia asked. "Because it feels that bad."

Holden had learned any woman who asked a question about how she looked did not necessarily want the truth. But Cecilia didn't seem like any woman. "Well, it's not good," Holden answered. He pointed her to the side door.

Cecilia nodded and did as instructed. She avoided her reflection in the mirror by the door.

Vinnie pulled the patrol car to the back and Holden hurried Cecilia out. There was a commotion in the front of the house. But the extra officers held the media back and no one got a clear shot of Cecilia.

Holden helped her in the car, placing his hand over her head. "Just get down and stay down."

"Okay but—" she started.

"I'll lock up the house," he assured her.

Cecilia stayed put, and silent, in the back of the police car until Holden returned. "Drive," Holden instructed Pugliese, as he hopped in. "And don't hit one of those reporters! I have enough problems today without Briscoe having me arrest you for vehicular manslaughter."

CECILIA STARED AT her fingers. They weren't stained with black ink as she figured they would be when they took her fingerprints. The officer had taken her hand and placed it on a scan. Then, by the elbow, she took her to stand by a wall, with height measurements behind it for her mug shots.

And then she waited.

She sat alone in the holding cell until Chandler Construction's attorney, Clayton Hindel, arrived.

"Are you alright, Cecilia?"

She didn't bother to answer. "What do we do now?" she asked.

"I don't know." He looked over his shoulder. "They don't know either. We haven't had a murder in this town in decades."

"It wasn't a murder, Clayton. It was self-defense."

"Okay," he said, motioning for her to lower her voice.

They turned their attention to the approaching chief of police.

"Chief Owens, how are you?" Clayton asked.

Holden ignored him. "I found a judge for a bail hearing. I don't know what bail he'll set, but between the house and the business you should be fine."

"Good, good," Clayton said. "What are they charging her with?"

"Second-degree murder."

"Second-degree murder!" Cecilia and Clayton shouted in unison.

"Have you lost your mind?" she asked.

"Cecilia!" Clayton rebuked.

"Not me. Briscoe. He's the one pushing for this," Holden explained.

"Good God," Clayton mumbled.

"Briscoe? Who's Briscoe?" Cecilia asked.

Someone called for Holden from the other side of the station before he could answer her. Holden acknowledged him and turned back to Cecilia.

"Okay, they're ready. We'll take you to the courthouse. Same as before. Okay, Cecilia? Keep your head down and stay down in the car."

Owens placed the handcuffs on her again and escorted her to the patrol car. She moaned as she laid down on her side on the back seat. "I'm sorry," Holden said, fearing he had caused her the pain.

"Not your fault," she told him. "I'm bruised all over from last night."

He looked her up and down and nodded understanding. "We need to get photos of that."

She stared at him, hoping she'd heard him wrong. "I'm sorry?" she asked. She struggled to find a comfortable spot but there was none. Her beaten body would not find a good position scrunched in the back of the police cruiser.

"Evidence of the attack," he explained.

She abandoned her attempt to get comfortable and

tried to joke. "And not nudie pics for the station?" She laughed but quickly regretted it. Her body gripped in pain.

Owens winced at the sight of her in extreme pain and tried to assure her. "No, definitely not. I'll talk to Clayton when we get to the courthouse." In her house, he had smiled at her, but this was Chief Owens and not Holden having a soda. Chief Owens was all professional.

"We need to get photos of Ferris as well," he added before closing the car door.

Pugliese slid into the driver's seat and Owens into the passenger seat. "Take Fifth," Owens instructed him.

"Main is quicker."

"I know that. But it has a big pothole and a couple of speed bumps. We need the smoother ride on Fifth," he told him, before glancing back at Cecilia.

Pugliese shrugged and did as he was told. For the ten-minute drive, he drove like his grandmother, in an attempt to keep Cecilia comfortable and the Chief calm.

Clayton was waiting in the courthouse lobby when they arrived. "What took so long?" he asked.

"Had to drive like Granny Pugliese. I have no idea why I couldn't have put on the lights and flown over here."

"Because she's hurt and in pain. Need I remind you she was viciously attacked last night?" Owens spat.

"Yes, I know. Before she murdered Gabbert," he mumbled. But not low enough.

They glared at each other until the bailiff called them into the courtroom.

Daniel Briscoe was waiting at the prosecutor desk, Marcy seated to his right. Cecilia followed Clayton to the desk on the left. Owens and Pugliese remained on the other side of the railing until the back door opened.

Everyone stood when the judge entered. No one missed Cecilia's struggle to stand, with her arms still handcuffed behind her. From behind, Holden gently helped her up.

Briscoe spoke when Judge Arthur Lowe looked to him. "We are charging Cecilia Chandler with second-degree murder of Robert Gabbert, Your Honor."

"How do you plead Ms. Chandler?" the judge asked.

"Not guilty," she answered, "Your Honor."

The judge returned his attention to Briscoe. "We are asking for Ms. Chandler to be held without bail," Briscoe told him.

"Without bail?" Clayton asked.

"Yes, *without bail*," Briscoe repeated with emphasis.

"Your Honor, Mrs. Chandler is not a flight risk. She has been a solid citizen of this town for years with no criminal record." Clayton leaned toward Cecilia, "Do you have a criminal record?"

"No," she whispered back.

With the pause, Briscoe spoke, "She has no ties to the community and is being charged with second-degree murder."

"And she's innocent until proven guilty," Clayton reminded him.

"The body in her backyard says otherwise," Briscoe retorted.

"Briscoe!" Judge Lowe rebuked. "Are you a flight risk, Mrs. Chandler?"

"No, sir," Cecilia answered.

"Will you surrender your passport?" the judge asked.

She nodded and answered, "Yes, sir."

"And wear an ankle monitor?" he asked.

"Yes, sir."

"Good enough for me. Bail five hundred thousand," Judge Lowe announced before slapping his gavel. The judge vanished through the back door.

Briscoe dropped his briefcase on the desk and threw his papers inside, muttering "Five hundred thousand. Absurd." He looked up to find Cecilia glaring at him.

"What is she still doing here?" he asked, pointing at her. "Get her back to jail, Owens."

Briscoe stomped out of the courtroom, Marcy at his heel.

Owens came around to the defense table. "Let's go. And we need to take those pictures," he reminded her.

"Pictures?" Clayton asked.

"Of my injuries," she answered.

Clayton looked from Cecilia to Holden. "They didn't do that at the hospital?"

She shook her head no. "Can you handle the bail, Clayton?"

"Yes," he assured her. The three headed out of the courtroom. "But we need to find you a criminal attorney."

She sighed. She was exhausted. She wanted to go home, check on Ferris, and go to sleep, until all this was over. "Do we need to do that right now? Can we do it tomorrow?"

"Of course," Clayton answered. "I need to make some phone calls."

"The bail. You'll take care of bail first, right?" she asked. She started to panic. "I...I can't stay a night in jail. Ferris can't spend another night at the vet's."

Clayton put his hand lightly on her shoulder. She winced from the light pressure. "Yes, bail first. Then, find you a criminal attorney." He scribbled on his pad. "I'll stop by tomorrow first thing with options."

Cecilia nodded and mumbled thanks. She watched Clayton walk down the hallway to exit the courthouse before turning to Holden. "Okay, picture time, I guess," she told him. He escorted her to an empty room in the courthouse and posted Pugliese at the door.

"I'll go get one of the female officers to take the pictures," he said before walking away.

"Wait," she called out. He turned and she waved

him closer to her. She bit her lip. "Look, could you just do it? I don't know them. It'll be less embarrassing if you just do it." She saw how uncomfortable he got at the request. "I've got a sports bra on and boy shorts. You'd see more of me if we were at the beach."

His face blushed.

"Please," she pleaded.

He hesitated.

"It's been a long day," she added. "I really want to get this over as quick as we can and I'm sure you'd do it fast."

He nodded agreement.

"Thank you," she said.

She slowly stripped. Not to be seductive but to avoid as much pain as she could. As the day wore on, the pain was worsening.

Holden tried to look everywhere but at her slender frame. But he couldn't. Her body was covered in bruises. Deepening purple bruises marked her back and stomach. A deep cut ran along her side.

"Did you show this to the hospital?" he asked, pointing to the wound.

"No, they were worried about my head. There was so much blood from the head laceration, they didn't see it. I didn't notice it until I got home."

"Doesn't it hurt?" he asked.

"It all hurts."

In silence, Holden took several pictures of Cecilia's bruised and beaten body.

CHAPTER 15

"NEWS TRAVELS FAST," Clayton announced as he slid in the side door.

"I'm sure the media is to thank for that." The four media trucks remained outside. She'd closed all the blinds upon their arrival yesterday. This morning, she snuck a peek out the bedroom window, expecting them to be gone. She was disappointed to see they were still there. With the arraignment completed and the trial date not set yet, she wondered why they remained. It must be a slow news week.

"Wyatt Sewell," Clayton announced.

"Who?" she asked. She poured Clayton a cup of coffee and topped off her own. She heard Ferris's protective cone hit the kitchen island three times before she felt him at her side. Ferris tapped her leg with his paw and she gave him a treat. He walked over to his bed, hitting his e-collar on the kitchen island two times, which was an improvement.

"He wants your case," Clayton told her.

"*Wants* my case?"

"This is a big case in the criminal world. A lot of exposure, free publicity. I didn't even have to make any phone calls to find you a lawyer. They all called me!"

Cecilia had never seen Clayton so excited. He was gleeful at the prospect of this Sewell lawyer representing her.

"And we're choosing Mr. Sewell why?"

"Wyatt Sewell. You can't be serious. You don't know him?"

She shook her head no.

"The Collin Franks case? The Pro Bowler accused of rape? The Ginger Simms case? The actress accused of drug trafficking?"

She continued to shake her head no.

"I can't believe you haven't heard of these cases," he said.

She'd never been a news junkie and had never watched entertainment news. She had only one concern. "Did he win?"

"Of course he won. He always wins."

That's all Cecilia needed to hear.

CLAYTON LEFT AFTER finishing his coffee, promising to return with Wyatt Sewell in the afternoon. He was picking him up at the local airport. "He's flying in on a private jet!" Clayton announced before leaving.

Cecilia wanted to rest. The less she moved, the less she hurt. The emergency room had given her a prescription for pain medication but she had no way to get it. Going to the pharmacy was not an option.

She envisioned a caravan of her Escort and four media trucks to the local pharmacy and then being swarmed by the reporters as she tried to get in the store.

As she walked to the stairs, the weight on her ankle reminded her of her ankle monitor and home imprisonment. A trip to the pharmacy would lead to a trip to jail.

She'd suffer with the pain instead.

Cecilia walked to the stairs to go back to bed. Ferris plodded behind her. His cone hit the wall twice. She stood at the foot of the stairs and sighed. She found the full flight too daunting and headed to the couch. Ferris agreed and lay down next to the couch. She put a throw next to him and he scratched at it briefly to get it the way he wanted.

She dozed briefly. Every time she closed her eyes, she relived the attack. It reminded her of the injuries she sustained, which intensified the pain. She resolved to remain on the couch, lying still, staring at the ceiling.

Horns honking outside disturbed Ferris from his sleep. He tried to stand on his back legs to look at the window but the e-collar hit the closed shades. Too tired, from either the pain or the pain medication, he sat back down on the throw. He sighed and looked to Cecilia to check it out. She didn't care enough until the disturbance got louder. She slowly got up, wincing in pain, and hobbled over to the door. She hoped she could peek out the peephole and ascertain what was going on.

Cecilia looked out to see a crowd on her porch. Several people stood on the porch, with their backs to the front door. The media stood facing them, microphones thrust out, shouting questions at them. She recognized Clayton from the brown suit he'd been wearing this morning and assumed the others were Mr. Sewell and his staff.

The tallest man, dressed in a navy blue suit, stood in the center, with a man and a woman to his side. Clayton stood slightly off to the left.

Mr. Sewell held up his hands to quiet the crowd. "Please. No questions now. I'm here to meet with Mrs. Chandler and discuss her case. A woman already victimized once, *in her own home*, is now being victimized by the state."

He shook his head in disbelief. He promptly turned, and the others followed suit. It felt choreographed. The media, the lawyers, the "impromptu" press conference.

Clayton rang the bell and Cecilia opened the door. She hid herself from the cameras, staying behind the door.

"Oh, you look terrible!" Mr. Sewell said upon seeing Cecilia. Her beaten face was bruised and swollen. She had avoided mirrors after a cursory glance while brushing her teeth this morning. He smiled when he said it, reminding her of the Cheshire cat.

He turned to the woman. "Abigail, need some photos of this." She tapped on her cell phone and nodded understanding. "Make sure to take photos of everything."

Cecilia was wearing a white T-shirt, and a gray-and-red flannel long-sleeved shirt, both Joey's, and sweat pants. The clothing was a bit heavy for late summer but it hid all the bruising.

Clayton escorted them to the living room and made introductions. "Thank you for coming, Mr. Sewell," Cecilia said. She nodded thanks to his assistants, Abigail Hodson and Michael Bloomington, also.

"Mr. Hindel here filled me on the details. The ones the media conveniently left out. I'll be rectifying that soon." He pointed to Abigail, who made another note in her phone. Cecilia had yet to hear either of the assistants speak.

Wyatt Sewell made himself comfortable on the living room couch. He patted the spot next to him for Cecilia to sit and she did. The assistants stood in the background, observing.

"Before I take a case, I like to talk to the defend-ant."

"To see if they are innocent?" she asked.

They all laughed except Cecilia, who didn't get the joke. "No, to see if I can win."

He pointed to Abigail. "You are twenty-nine years old, work from home, computer work, independent contractor, setting up websites, etcetera, college graduate, bachelor's in computer science, recent widow, spouse of Joseph Chandler, now owns

Chandler Construction, no children, parents dead, one sister, Janna, who lives a few hours away, one dog, Ferris, golden retriever, a rescue." Ferris barked softly at the mention of his name.

"And no criminal record," she added.

"Anything else I need to know?" Sewell asked.

She was astonished and a little horrified by the thoroughness. And there was one fact that was news to her. "No, seems like you know everything about me already."

He leaned in and glared at her. "No hidden secrets that will hurt us at trial?" he asked.

She shook her head no. Killing an intruder was as bad as it got in Cecilia's world.

CECILIA COULDN'T REMEMBER the last time there were so many people in her house. Not including the night of the attack. She had no idea how many police officers had traipsed through her home that night. But they weren't invited in. The three defense team members and Clayton, she had invited them in. She needed them here.

Ferris and Cecilia watched them and wondered what to do. She felt like an outsider in her own home. It only took a few minutes to realize they didn't need them. Cecilia went into Joey's office and laid down on the leather couch. Ferris stretched out next to her, on the floor. They both moaned as they tried to find a comfortable spot for their beaten bodies. "They'll call us when they need us," she told him.

Cecilia was lightly dozing on the couch when Clayton stepped into the office to say goodbye. "They told me they don't need me. So I'm going to go."

"Thank you for your help, Clayton," she told him.

He mumbled, "You're welcome," as he plodded out, shoulders slumped.

She glanced down at Ferris, who was sleeping soundly. Cecilia's phone rang. She muted it quickly, trying to avoid waking Ferris. She glanced at the caller ID. Her sister, Janna, again. She couldn't remember the last time her sister called her three times in one week, never mind three times in one day.

But she could remember the last time Janna had called. For money as usual.

CHAPTER 16

Then

"WHAT DO YOU want, Janna?" Cecilia asked when her cell phone rang.

Her sister as well did not provide a greeting and got to the point. "I need money."

Cecilia should have been clearer when she answered the phone. She should have answered, "What do you want money for?" Or "How much do you need?"

Since Cecilia had married Joey, this was the only reason Janna called.

"I need money to search for Dad."

Joey had been patient with Janna and her money requests. He'd often convinced Cecilia to give in to her. But Joey was gone and so was her patience.

"No," she answered.

Ferris trotted over and rubbed himself against Cecilia's leg before heading to his bed. She wiped off his stray hairs from her trousers. She looked at Ferris, realizing she treated him better than her father had treated her.

When the person she loved died, she didn't abandon Ferris. She might not love him. She might not be as affectionate with him as he was used to. But she stayed and took care of him.

"Why not?" Janna asked.

"Because he left," she answered.

"He was grieving." Janna was always quick to excuse their father's behavior.

"We all were," Cecilia reminded her.

"It was harder for him." It had been hard for all of them to watch their mother die of cancer. Cecilia started to argue that it was toughest on her. She was the one who cared for their dying mother while raising Janna and attending online college classes.

But it wasn't a competition. No one wins with grief.

"Well, he sure found comfort in the drugs," Cecilia said. She tried not to think about the other comforts he had found—in other women—so soon after her mother's death. She had tracked him down, more than once, to drug dens, and found him in compromising positions. It was no place a twenty-year-old should have to go.

Cecilia had given him a second chance at Joey's urging when they got engaged. It was short-lived. He had taken the money she had given him to get a tuxedo for the wedding and used it on drugs. He never arrived at the church to walk her down the aisle.

Cecilia looked at the photo of Joey's dad. He hadn't walked away when his wife died. He stayed. He raised his children. He loved his family. And he loved the woman his son married.

She was thankful he had stepped in on their wedding day.

"Time to go, CeCe," he announced when he found her in the church's entryway. She'd been watching the street for her father's arrival. Part of her praying for his absence, to avoid the pain of seeing him high. Part of her praying for his arrival, to avoid the embarrassment of walking down the aisle alone.

As the last bridesmaid walked down the aisle, the ushers closed the doors, to allow for the bride's big entrance.

"You don't have to call me Dad like Jeremiah does," he had said. She smiled, knowing how much he disliked his son-in-law. "You can call me whatever you want." He paused for a moment, before adding, "How about JJ? I'll be your JJ to your CeCe, okay?"

Cecilia nodded and kissed Mr. Joseph James Chandler, now JJ to her, on the cheek.

It was the last time she had wished to have her father in her life.

CHAPTER 17

PUGLIESE CAME STROLLING into the Chief's office. "Have you watched the news?"

"Little busy here today," Owens said, pointing to his piles of paperwork. "You should be busy too. Out on patrols, right?"

"Patrol what? Everyone is in their houses watching the news on Folley and the Gabbert murder." Vinnie sat down in one of the office's green cushioned chairs. Holden didn't hide his annoyance. "And now we add celebrity attorney, Sewell, to the mix."

Holden put his pen down. "Who?"

"Wyatt Sewell," Vinnie answered, pronouncing the name slowly for emphasis.

"He took the case?" Owens knew that Clayton wouldn't keep the case but he was shocked a high-profile attorney had been hired. And so fast.

"Yes! She must be scared!"

"Scared?" Owens asked. "Briscoe is the one who should be scared." He could only hope Briscoe would come to his senses and drop the charges. At worst, work out a plea deal. He couldn't picture Cecilia surviving in jail.

Vinnie shrugged. "Briscoe's going to love this.

Even more publicity," he said.

Holden hated to agree that Vinnie was right. Which meant Briscoe wouldn't be able to back down, he thought. Like a cornered animal, Briscoe would feel forced to attack. He had hoped once things settled down, Briscoe and Cecilia could agree on a plea deal. A calm and rational defense lawyer could convince Briscoe she hadn't intended to kill Gabbert. Her only intention was to get him to leave, get off her property without causing her or Ferris any more harm. How could a city girl be such a good shot anyway?

He hoped hiring Sewell wasn't a mistake. From all media accounts, Sewell wasn't a lawyer who made deals. He made splashes. But he did always win.

"She is guilty," Vinnie told Holden.

There was no point having this discussion with Vinnie again and Holden returned to his paperwork. He pointed for Vinnie to get out of his office. "She's guilty of protecting herself."

"The dog," Vinnie corrected him as he got up and left. "She was protecting *the dog*."

OWENS LEFT THE station, needing a break from the buzz of the office. He pulled into the park's parking lot, glad to see only a few cars. And none that he recognized. He wanted to go for a run and clear his mind. Jogging always helped clear Holden's mind.

He stretched at his car before taking off on the

trail around the lake. He pushed thoughts of Cecilia from his mind. He passed a fellow jogger, running with her chocolate Labrador retriever, and nodded hello. The dog reminded him of his dog.

Roles reversed, if Baxter were still alive, would he have acted differently? Holden couldn't say he would. But he doubted Briscoe would have prosecuted the chief of police.

After a mile, Holden settled into a good pace. Thoughts of Cecilia, Ferris, and Gabbert were far from his mind. Until he saw Briscoe, jogging toward him, and it all flooded back.

Media coverage was increasing in Folley and the case. They'd both chosen this trail in hopes of avoiding people who would recognize them. Briscoe, like Holden, wanted to get in a workout without intrusion. While Holden wanted to keep the case out of his head, it was all Briscoe wanted to focus on.

Holden hoped he could nod a greeting and keep going. Those hopes were quickly dashed when Briscoe turned around and started running in Holden's direction.

"Did you pick up the autopsy results yet?" he asked.

"Not ready." Holden couldn't understand the urgency. No one needed an autopsy to know Gabbert was killed by a gunshot to the head.

Holden noticed Briscoe stepping up the pace. He was always competitive. Holden easily kept up. He was tempted to up the ante but didn't give in to the temptation. Holden watched as, more than once, Briscoe would give a wider berth to those joggers with dogs.

"Did you...send over all...the files?" Briscoe asked.

Holden hid his smile as Briscoe struggled to keep up the brisk pace. "Of course, whatever was ready was sent," Holden answered, easily.

Instead of answering, Briscoe nodded and focused on running. Holden was grateful for the quiet but would be more grateful for solitude. Knowing his run was almost done, the car park about half a mile away, Owens increased his pace. Out of stubbornness, Briscoe kept pace.

They were both thankful when they got to the car park. Owens stopped and did his post-run stretching while Briscoe leaned over, hands on knees, struggling to catch his breath.

A walker, with a dog, approached. The friendly dog pulled the owner over to Holden, who patted him on the head. The dog lost interest in Owens and approached Briscoe. He scowled at the dog and stepped back, out of reach of the dog. The owner pulled the dog back and they went to the trail.

Owens finished his stretching and waved goodbye to Briscoe.

"You make sure I have everything I need ASAP," Briscoe told him.

"It's like any other case, Briscoe. You'll get everything." Another dog, and his owner, got onto the trail.

Briscoe stepped several feet away from them. "Are you doing this just because you don't like dogs?"

"Just get me what I need. I'm prosecuting a murderer."

CHAPTER 18

WHEN THE PHONE rang again, Cecilia answered it. If she didn't, her sister would just keep calling. Plus, Cecilia had some fact-checking to do.

"Wyatt Sewell!" she screamed. "Your lawyer is Wyatt Sewell!"

Janna began peppering her with questions but never paused long enough for Cecilia to answer. "Is he as handsome as he is on television?" Cecilia had no idea.

"Did he talk about Ginger Simms?" Cecilia had no idea who that was.

"Is he single?" Cecilia had no idea.

Cecilia spoke the moment Janna took a breath. "I'm fine, Janna. Thank you for calling."

Remembering the manners their mother had taught them, she asked, "Oh, yeah, how are you?"

"Is our father dead?" Cecilia asked. It was odd that she had learned of this from a brief biography from her defense team, during Abigail's recital of facts. It should be odder that she had no reaction when they told her.

"Yes, a couple months ago," Janna answered.

Cecilia wasn't shocked. Their father had looked

terrible the last time she'd seen him. He was so strung out on drugs she'd known it was only a matter of time. "And you didn't think to tell me?" Cecilia asked.

"I didn't?" she responded. "Are you sure?"

Cecilia didn't bother to answer her. Of course, she was sure Janna hadn't told her. That was not something one would forget being told.

"Well, I posted it on Facebook," Janna said.

"I don't check your Facebook feed for obituaries, Janna." Cecilia sighed and shook her head. She didn't bother to remind her sister that she wasn't on Facebook.

"Well, I didn't think you'd care," Janna explained.

Cecilia would have preferred to make the decision on how she would have reacted. Would she have gone to the funeral? Other questions floated through her mind. Was he buried with their mother? Who arranged the funeral? She couldn't imagine Janna capable of such a task.

Before she could decide what to ask, Janna started again. "You need to tell me everything about Wyatt Sewell!"

"Check my Facebook feed," Cecilia answered.

"But you don't have a Face—" she heard her sister start, as Cecilia clicked the end button.

Ferris plodded over to her, hitting his e-collar on the coffee table. He made the most curious expression, having no idea what the collar was. He'd been wearing it for days, yet still seemed surprised by it. "I wonder if you have any brothers or sisters." She patted him on the head. "Not that I'd want them here. I used to not want you." He lay his head on her lap. "Couldn't make it without you, though."

Of course, she wouldn't be in this mess if not for Ferris. She tried to push the thought from her head. It was really Joey's fault. He had forced her to promise to protect their family with a gun. He had made Ferris a part of their family. He died and left her alone to protect themselves.

Nothing like putting the blame on a dead man.

She lay down on the couch, hoping to sleep. She hadn't slept more than an hour since the shooting. She stared at the ceiling. Ferris tried to get his head comfortable on her stomach. He moved right and left, trying to flatten out the e-collar, while Cecilia tried not to scream in pain as it dug into her bruised skin. He sighed gently once he got settled, with her help.

She closed her eyes but could only see the flashes from earlier, when Abigail took pictures of her beaten body.

It was like a bizarre photo shoot. Instead of trying to get the most beautiful shot of a model, they were trying to get the most hideous shot of her.

Mr. Sewell sat in the living room, working on his phone, while Abigail and Michael directed her right and left to shoot every side of her. For fifteen minutes, they photographed every inch of her, starting with wide shots, then proceeding to close-ups. She wished Chief Owens were the one taking the pictures again. He hadn't looked at the camera's viewfinder and pointed and whispered, like Abigail and Michael had. She was forced to stand half naked in her dining room and wonder if they were marveling at the shades of purple her damaged back had become or at the cellulite on her thighs.

In five minutes, Owens took the same shots Abigail and Michael had taken in fifteen, but with Cecilia feeling less violated.

They showed the results to Mr. Sewell, who appeared pleased. She declined to look at the results when Abigail offered. If she had wanted to see, she could look in a mirror. She'd avoided mirrors and covered her skin with pants and long-sleeved shirts. Cecilia wanted to forget about the attack. But the pain reminded her.

Before Abigail put the camera away, Cecilia asked her to take photos of Ferris.

"Why?" she asked.

"Chief Owens said we should. Since he was attacked too."

The two assistants exchanged a look.

"The chief of police told you take pictures of the dog? To strengthen your case?" Michael asked.

"Yes," she answered.

"Okay," Abigail agreed.

Cecilia struggled to get the protective collar off of Ferris. With pain medication in his system, he was much calmer than usual. Cecilia gently held his head up and Abigail crouched down to get the shot. Michael held a ruler up as a reference for the photo.

Ferris's photo shoot was much quicker and less embarrassing than Cecilia's. Exhausted, Cecilia stayed on the floor next to Ferris until the defense team left for the day.

As Cecilia tried to sleep, her imagination wouldn't let her rest. Snapshots flashed in her mind of what she looked like in the photographs. She tried not to think about how the photos would be used. Large printouts at trial? The whole lot printed out and passed around for the jury to inspect? A few grizzly photographs provided to the media?

"Oh God," she mumbled. The defense team would be back in the morning, for a full briefing of the night's events. She could ask what their plans were with the photos but she knew she wouldn't.

Joey's voice echoed in her head. "They are the professionals, CeCe. Let them do their job. They're my best guys. Don't interfere." He'd said it more than once to her as they renovated the master bath. And more than once, she had ignored him. In the end, he was right.

She was too tired to fight now with anyone. She'd been struggling every day to make it through life without Joey, and the intruder had beaten the last bit of energy out of her. She had to trust that Mr. Sewell knew what he was doing. Even if she was at full "CeCe force," as Joey would say, Mr. Sewell appeared to be a formidable opponent.

Cecilia just hoped the prosecutor agreed.

CHAPTER 19

THE SEWELL DEFENSE team arrived at precisely nine. Mr. Sewell again held a brief meeting with the media on her porch, promising a press conference in the upcoming days. The media seemed appeased and they returned to their trucks.

Michael carried enough coffee and donuts to feed a team twice their number. Cecilia wondered for a moment if they were going to ask the media in. She closed the front door before they could.

As if they'd been there a hundred times, they proceeded to the dining room. Cecilia and Ferris stood at the dining room's doorway and watched as they sipped their coffees, pulled out notepads, laptops, and pens from their bags and arranged their papers. Ferris approached Michael when he picked up a donut. He sat up at his feet, in hopes of a dropped crumb.

"Ready?" Mr. Sewell asked. Abigail and Michael nodded yes after setting up their devices and sitting down. Michael placed his phone in the center of the table to record the proceedings. Abigail propped her tablet up to video it.

Mr. Sewell pointed to a chair at the dining room table, across from them. "Cecilia, are you ready?"

She nodded and sat down. She felt as if she were on a job interview. A job she didn't want.

"Tell me what happened," Mr. Sewell instructed her. "Do not leave out a single detail."

Cecilia nodded and tried to collect her thoughts. For days, she had flashbacks of the night, the attack, the aftermath. But now she struggled to put it into words. She opened her mouth, but nothing came out. She cleared her throat and tried again. She didn't know where to begin. Ferris walked over to her. The donut was gone and so was his interest in Michael. He sat down next to her. He nuzzled into her hand, forcing her to pet him. She did and then found her voice.

"Usual night. I took Ferris out into the backyard. He did what he needed to. I checked all the doors were locked and the alarm was set and we went to bed." That summed up her last night before she was arrested.

She started to recount the night, but made the mistake of using the word "out." Ferris heard the word and started running around, hitting his collar on furniture several times. They paused the recordings as she got up to let him into the backyard.

Cecilia returned five minutes later and resumed the tale from where Ferris had interrupted her. She told them about Ferris waking her up and continued until she fired the shot. She took a deep breath and they allowed her to collect herself before she continued. They paused the recordings and she went out to get a drink of water. Ferris followed and did the same.

When she returned to the dining room, they were huddled talking to each other. Mr. Sewell was speaking. "I thought they arrested her because of the good shot. I thought it was a sexist case. If a man had made a shot like that, they'd state the Castle Doctrine and that's it. But a woman, an outsider, with one shot, a kill shot, they arrested her."

Cecilia sat down and Mr. Sewell looked up at her. "You killed the intruder to save the dog?" he asked.

She looked at Ferris and nodded her head. She looked back to Mr. Sewell and answered, "Yes."

"Why?" he asked.

All three stared at her as she considered the question. "Why did I save Ferris?" she asked.

"Yes. Why did you shoot to save the dog?" Sewell asked.

"He's Joey's...He's *my* dog." She looked down at Ferris again. His big brown eyes looked up at her. Joey used to say those looks were Ferris "hugging you with his eyes." She'd laugh at him and tell him he was out of his mind. But now she thought he was right.

It was the first time she had considered Ferris hers. She'd always regarded him as Joey's. Even after Joey had died, she'd referred to Ferris as Joey's. But he wasn't. Ferris had been their dog. And now he was hers. Cecilia looked at Sewell before adding. "This is his house. His home. Our home." Ferris poked her in the thigh with his e-collar and she rubbed his head. She looked down at him before admitting, "I love him."

Mr. Sewell grinned from ear to ear. Michael and Abigail were typing on their computers furiously.

"Oh, this is good. This is real good," Mr. Sewell said. "Better even. We do love our pets, don't we?"

OFFICER VINNIE PUGLIESE sat in the station's break room and considered asking the Chief the question that had been bothering him for days. He knew he should let it go. He thought Mrs. Chandler was guilty and should be convicted. But it nagged at him.

As a child, he had inundated his parents with questions starting with why. That often left his father asking aloud, "Why did we have you?" Vinnie would ignore him then and he was ignoring his better judgment now. He had to know.

He'd walked past the Chief's office a few times but he didn't want to disturb him. The door was closed during each pass. That was unusual and a clear sign of concern. Owens had been inundated with phone calls and paperwork. This small town police chief was unaccustomed to the scrutiny of a murder. Pugliese was born and raised in Folley and had never heard of one committed in the town.

The small town had small town crimes. The residents tended to police themselves. Except Bobby Gabbert. He was a frequent flyer in the station. Every officer knew him by sight. Anyone other than the mayor's nephew would have been shipped to a juvenile detention center, or more likely the state penitentiary, by the time his rap sheet reached the second page.

Pugliese was contemplating his options, staring at his mug. He could ask the Chief, he could forget about it, or he could look into it himself.

"What is wrong with you?" Owens asked. Pugliese jumped, spilling his cold coffee. "Never knew you to not finish your cup." Owens refilled his own coffee mug.

Pugliese got up and cleaned up the mess. Owens had enough problems on his plate and considered not asking. He had an open door policy with his staff—all the staff, police officers, and supplemental personnel—which he had ignored today. His door had been closed all day dealing with the Gabbert murder. "Something wrong, Pugliese?"

"I was just thinking..."

The hesitation signaled to Owens that he wouldn't like what Pugliese was thinking about. He rarely hesitated when speaking, when he probably should always hesitate before speaking. Owens didn't prompt Pugliese but waited for him to continue.

Pugliese finally uttered aloud the question he'd been mulling over for days. "Why would Bobby pick Cecilia?"

"What?" Owens asked. He was in the middle of pouring his coffee and lucky he didn't spill it.

With more conviction this time, he asked, "Why

did Bobby Gabbert choose to attack Cecilia Chandler?"

"I know *who* you're talking about Pugliese." There were no other people this town was talking about. "I'm asking *what* you're talking about. What does it matter why?"

"I guess it doesn't. But it bothers me." The why—the why always bothered Vinnie.

"Bothers you? A woman is arrested after being attacked on her property and this is what bothers you!" He slammed the coffeepot back onto the burner.

"I was just wondering—"

"I got enough to deal with without your ruminations. Get back to work." Owens finished stirring the sugar into his coffee and threw the stirrer into the trash. The same question had floated through his mind the first night. If he thought it could help Cecilia, he'd look into it in a heartbeat. But why Gabbert attacked her didn't matter.

"I'm off duty," Pugliese explained.

Owens headed out of the break room. "Then get out of the station."

"Well, I was wondering, could I look into it?" he asked.

"Look into it? Do we not have enough to do!" Owens stomped away, murmuring under his breath.

"Well, I didn't hear a no," Pugliese mumbled when the Chief was out of earshot.

WITH A FEW quick taps on her phone and a brief phone call, Abigail ordered lunch.

Cecilia didn't know any restaurants in town that delivered. Maybe for her, they wouldn't have. For the famous Wyatt Sewell, rules were different.

Cecilia wasn't hungry. Having been forced to sit all morning, recounting the attack, the pain in her back was severe. She lay down on the couch, Ferris at her side, until Michael called her back in.

The remnants of their lunch were gone and they were ready to get back to work. Michael and Abigail set up their devices for round two. Mr. Sewell didn't speak until they both nodded, signaling they were ready.

"Thank you for your thorough recollection of the attack. I'm sure that was difficult for you," Mr. Sewell told her. Cecilia nodded. "Now I have some additional questions."

He pulled out a transcript of the morning's proceedings. It was typed, with areas highlighted in yellow. She could see neat handwritten notes on the margins.

Cecilia looked around her dining room. It no longer resembled the dining room where she had held romantic dinners with Joey. Or where holiday dinners were hosted, before JJ died. It was now an office. In the lunch break, besides eating, they had set up a printer, two laptops, and a router.

"When the Chief came to speak to you, did he read you your rights?" Mr. Sewell began.

She paused and furrowed her eyebrows. "You mean, 'You have the right to remain silent'?"

"Yes, did one of them read you your Miranda rights?"

She thought for a moment before answering. "No, he and the other officer just came in to talk to me." Cecilia had never felt she was in danger of being arrested. When they had started, she hadn't even known the intruder was dead. Regardless, she thought she was protected by the law Joey had once told her about. She had protected herself and her family on her property. If they had read her the Miranda rights, she would have known she was in trouble.

She didn't miss the smiles the three exchanged. "Love a small town, right?" Michael whispered. Abigail nodded agreement.

"Did you feel your life was at risk during the attack by the intruder?" Mr. Sewell asked.

"Of course I did." Had they not listened to her recounting of the night? "He had a knife. He had me pinned to the ground. He was beating me. He was going to rape me. He would have killed me if he didn't get what he wanted."

"At the moment you shot," he clarified, "did you feel your life was in immediate danger?"

"Of course, I was still in danger. Well, not my life exactly...but Ferris. His life was in immediate danger.

He had a knife to his throat."

Again, they exchanged glances. This time they weren't as pleased.

"It was either he raped me or he killed Ferris," Cecilia said. "That was my choice."

"At any point was the intruder in your home?" he asked.

"I don't know." She glanced over her shoulder toward the kitchen. She could see the mess the kitchen had been, covered in her blood. "I...I never saw him in the house."

"Could he have been in the house?" Mr. Sewell asked.

"You mean that night? Or at any time?"

"That night," Sewell clarified.

"I...I don't know. I left the door open when I ran in for the gun. I should have closed the door, I should have locked the door. I should have—"

Noticing the oncoming emotions, Sewell interrupted her and asked, "How did the intruder get Ferris?"

"I...I don't know." The intruder could have come in and taken him out or Ferris could have run out after him. Cecilia didn't know.

It had been bad enough recounting the attack. But this was worse, questions she didn't have answers for. Realizing her errors. What she should have done. She looked at her watch. They'd only been back from lunch fifteen minutes.

Sewell whispered to Abigail, "Check the crime scene photos." She nodded and made a note. Abigail's list of things to do must be enormous.

Abigail's phone rang and she looked to Sewell. He nodded for her to take it. "Okay, let's take ten," he told them. Abigail left the room to take the phone call.

"Anyone thirsty?" Michael asked as he headed to the kitchen. Ferris followed him.

"No," Sewell answered. He remained in his chair and flipped through a file in front of him. Cecilia remained glued to her chair. She didn't think her legs could support her if she tried to stand.

"Something on your mind, Cecilia?" Sewell asked.

That was a loaded question. There was a lot on her mind, not least of which was the possibility of spending the rest of her life in prison.

"Why was I arrested, Mr. Sewell? I thought it was a justified shooting."

He motioned for her to sit in the chair next to him. She slowly got up, glad her legs could support her. Using the table for support, she walked around to his side of the table. He turned the chairs so they were looking at each other. "First, call me Wyatt."

She nodded. "Joey told me that if I ever shot someone in our home it would be alright. Some Castle law, defending a man's castle. Something like that."

"There's some interpretation within the law." He took a moment to collect his thoughts so he could explain this to a layman as best he could. "Every state is a bit different and we've been familiarizing ourselves with this state's laws. Self-defense laws vary by state. Some states have stand your ground laws, meaning you don't have to retreat if you're threatened, even if you're not on your property. Some have the Castle

Doctrine, where you don't have to retreat if you're on your property. And some have a duty to retreat, where if threatened you have to retreat. You can only use deadly force as a last resort."

Cecilia couldn't imagine a situation in which one wouldn't use deadly force unless it was a last resort. She also couldn't see how she had violated the law, regardless of which law her state had. "And this state?" she asked.

"Yes, this is a Castle Doctrine state."

"Yep, that's what Joey said. So I was on my property, threatened and I, inadvertently really, used deadly force. I was just trying to scare him away. I...I never thought I'd kill him. What am I missing?"

"One, when claiming self-defense, you have to prove it. It's really your word versus a dead man's." He leaned in. "Some people lie, you know."

She mocked shock. "You don't say."

He returned to his upright posture and resumed his lecture. "Self-defense laws mean you can protect yourself and your family."

She nodded. She understood that. Before and after the shooting. "That's what I did."

He tried to clarify. "It means you can protect yourself and your family but not your property."

"*Yes*, that's what I did." Cecilia knew she wasn't a lawyer but how could Wyatt, and the prosecutor Briscoe, not see she hadn't violated the law. "I protected my family."

"You protected your dog," he corrected.

"Yes, Ferris." Having heard his name, Ferris returned to the dining room, his entrance signaled by his e-collar hitting the doorway. He sat next to her and she rubbed Ferris's back. She hadn't violated the law. She had protected their family, their Ferris. Wyatt looked from Cecilia to Ferris and back again. He had a sad smile on his face while he waited for Cecilia to understand. "Are you saying Ferris isn't family?"

Cecilia had often heard there were dog people and not dog people. She had never thought about it herself until Ferris's arrival. She had always felt neutral regarding animals. She didn't know if she was a dog person but she was a Ferris person.

"No, *I'm* not saying Ferris isn't family. I've got two dogs at home, Klondike and Snickers. I love them. I love them like they're part of my family." She expected him to pull up photos of them on his phone. He didn't. "I agree with you. They're family."

"But…" She waited.

"But the law doesn't agree."

"Well, if he's not family, in the eyes of the law, what is he?"

"Property."

HOLDEN WAS SUMMONED to Dan Briscoe's office at the courthouse.

"That Sewell held a news conference." Briscoe pointed to the television. "Did you see it? The slimy bastard."

Holden found that ironic coming from Briscoe.

Using air quotes, Briscoe said, "Mrs. Chandler is too distraught to attend this press conference." He turned on the television. "He showed her picture. Her wedding picture!" CNN was replaying the impromptu news conference, held on Mrs. Chandler's front porch. Flanked by his assistants, Mr. Sewell began talking about Mrs. Chandler. He held up an eight-by-ten photograph of her on her wedding day. Radiant was the only word Holden could think of to describe her.

Holden couldn't remember his own bride being that beautiful on their wedding day. But too many arguments had tarnished all the good memories of his ex-wife.

"Trying to sway the media to their side," Briscoe mumbled.

"Isn't that what you were trying to do at your news conference?" Holden asked.

Briscoe shot him a look. "I don't need to sway the media. I've got the law on my side."

Not justice, Holden thought.

Briscoe paused the television. "Marcy," he yelled. She scurried in, pad and pen in hand. "Get me everything you can on Robert Gabbert." She paused. This was going to take her some time. The files on Gabbert was immense. "All the good stuff. There has to be good stuff." She scurried out.

Holden couldn't take his eyes off the frozen image of Mrs. Chandler's bridal picture from the television.

CHAPTER 20

CECILIA WAS SITTING in the living room, scrolling through work emails when she heard a light tapping. She looked at Ferris, who had also heard the noise.

Both of them perked up when they heard the noise again. Tap, tap, tap. Ferris led the way toward the noise, which when it happened a third time, they garnered was coming from the kitchen. Ferris only hit his protective collar once in his route to the kitchen.

Ferris ran to the sliding glass door, jumped up, and licked the glass. When he returned to all fours, Cecilia let out a short scream. Chief Owens was standing outside the door, but not in his police uniform. He was dressed all in black, with a headlamp, light on, across his forehead. He gave an awkward wave. Cecilia put in the alarm code and opened the door.

He slid in and promptly closed and locked the door. She stood at the door and marveled at the dark backyard. He looked around the first floor, ensuring all the shades were closed. Ferris followed him.

"How'd you get through the yard without setting off the motion light?" Cecilia asked.

"Stealth," he answered, pointing to his headlamp.

She turned to the front of the house. There was no commotion coming from the street. "How'd you get past the media trucks without them seeing you?"

"I told you, stealth." He smiled and winked.

Cecilia tried to suppress a grin. "What are you doing here, Chief?" The last time Chief Owens was here he arrested her. The time before that, according to Mr. Sewell, Owens violated her rights by questioning her without reading her the Miranda warning.

"Please, it's Holden." He sat down on the same stool he had occupied during previous visits.

"Well, you do have half-naked pictures of me, Holden. Which I pray you have not shared with the other men at the station." She stated it lightheartedly but stared at him with concern. Holden shook his head no. "Then, you can call me CeCe." She waited for him to answer. He didn't. "You're not here to arrest me again, are you?"

He bristled when she mentioned the photos and then the arrest. He hated being reminded that he was the arresting officer. "Of course not," he assured her.

Cecilia stood against the refrigerator and watched Ferris walk around the kitchen island. He was recovering much faster from his injuries than she was. Each day the bruises on her legs seemed to expand and get darker. She didn't want to see what her back and face looked like. The pain and stiffness remained debilitating.

Each lap, Ferris got a bit faster. Soon he'd be running if she didn't distract him. "Can you give him a treat?" she asked Holden, pointing to Ferris's biscuit jar.

"Sure," Holden answered, quickly getting up. He was glad to have a distraction from the mental images of her standing in front of him, only in her underwear. He had no trouble picturing that body free of bruises.

Trying to complete another lap, Ferris ran into Holden. Seeing the treat, he sat and waited. "Good boy, Ferris," Holden said and handed him the treat.

Cecilia never took her eyes off Holden. He sat back down and she asked again. "Why are you here, Holden?"

"I realize this is a little risky but I wanted to check on you."

"And you couldn't have just called?" she asked.

"I didn't want that appearing on your phone bill."

"Why?" she asked, as she got out two Mountain Dews from the refrigerator.

"Briscoe will be running your life through a fine-tooth comb. Bank accounts, phone bills. You name it, he's checking it now."

She walked over to him and handed him the soda. The stiffness in her joints made the five-foot journey feel like a mile. She sat on the barstool across from Holden, slowly easing herself down, stifling a moan as she did.

"I guess it is risky for you professionally to check on the alleged murderer." She looked at the windows, glad the shades were drawn. The media wouldn't be able to report on her late-night visitor.

"No, I meant it's risky because you have a gun."

Her eyes bulged at the insinuation that she was dangerous. He suppressed a grin. She reminded him, "But you took that gun."

"True," he responded, nodding his head. He swiveled his head around. "But you might have more."

"Oh no." She shook her head vehemently. "One is enough. Too many actually."

They both knew she didn't have another gun. A complete search of the home had been completed after the shooting. For a few minutes, they drank their sodas in silence.

Holden tried to hide his surveillance of her but she could feel his eyes on her. He noticed every time she shifted her weight to try to find a comfortable spot on the stool and when she cringed as Ferris's collar bumped into her leg. It should have been off-putting. But there was something about him that put her at ease and that was a rarity. She tried to remember the last person she met, other than Joey, who made her feel that way.

"How are the injuries?" Holden asked.

"How do they look?" She pointed to her face. "I'm avoiding mirrors to avoid scaring myself."

Holden didn't want to lie to her but he certainly couldn't tell her the truth. The left side of her face was one big bruise. Big and purple and larger than when he had last seen her. Her split lip was puffier. He understood why she winced every time she took a sip of the Mountain Dew.

Cecilia interpreted the silence. "That bad, huh?" she asked.

"It'll clear. In a week, or maybe two, it'll be all gone. You'll be back to your"—he started to say beautiful but didn't—"back to your usual self."

"But I'll still be under house arrest."

He wished he could comfort her but knew he couldn't. Briscoe was out for blood. This was going to trial, whether they liked it or not.

Holden finished his drink and stood up. "I better be going."

Cecilia stood up, slowly, as he walked by. He didn't miss her grimace, despite her attempt to hide it. Holden put his headlamp back on his head and turned it on. A red light glared out. "Night vision," he explained. "Stealth."

Cecilia thought he looked like an alien with a third eye.

She didn't notice the pain when she smiled. "You know you look ridiculous, right?" she told him as he slid out the back door into the darkness.

CHAPTER 21

Then

"YOU KNOW YOU look ridiculous, right?" Janna said as Cecilia came out of the bathroom.

"You know I could have met you at the church."

Janna scowled at her and took another drink from the minibar. A childish retort from her immature sister, Cecilia thought. She was quickly regretting asking Janna to be her "plus one" at Debbie's wedding. Cecilia had wavered on the request. She knew Janna would jump at attending the posh wedding and reception. Cecilia had decided attending with her sister was better than the recent widow attending alone.

Not attending her sorority sister's wedding had not been an option.

She was desperate for some normalcy. To get dressed like a normal woman, not wearing her dead husband's clothes. To be around people. It had only been Ferris and her in that big house for weeks.

Cecilia looked at the full-length mirror. She thought she looked nice. She was pale, thinner than usual, but not ridiculous. The champagne-colored Grecian gown was not her style but was flattering to her figure. She'd seen worse bridesmaid gowns.

It would be the first time she'd see Debbie and the other sorority sisters since Joey's funeral.

She was surprised she hadn't heard from any of them yet. She was shocked she hadn't been asked to do everyone's makeup. That was her usual job at a sorority sister's wedding. Her expert hand had been used to deftly apply makeup. It gave her a purpose at these events. And today she needed a purpose more than ever before.

"Make sure you're at the church by five," Cecilia reminded Janna, as she reapplied her lipstick.

Janna nodded, more interested in the free booze. Cecilia grabbed her matching champagne clutch and made to leave the hotel room.

"CeCe," Janna called out.

Cecilia turned to find Janna holding her hand out. "Cab fare?"

Cecilia didn't bother to argue or point out that the church was two blocks away. She grabbed a twenty from her purse and handed it to her sister.

Cecilia watched her and wondered, not for the first time, how they could be sisters. "Aren't you going to ask how I am? You've been here two hours and never asked."

Janna rolled her eyes. "I don't need to ask. You look terrible. I don't need to hear an old widow moan on. I got that enough when you used to stick me with Gran."

"When our mother was dying? Yes, Gran was the

only one who could watch you while I took care of Mom and everything else."

Janna raised her hand. "Oh, stop, CeCe."

Cecilia agreed. They didn't need to rehash their mother's death and their father's incompetence. They saw the past very differently.

"Why don't you focus on the living?" Janna asked.

Wasn't that what I was trying to do? Cecilia thought. Coming here to a wedding. Inviting her sister for support. She would have much preferred to avoid such a public spectacle of love and happiness while she mourned the loss of her husband. A wedding was the last place a recent widow wanted to be.

Cecilia's phone beeped. The alarm signaling it was time to meet the bridal party for photos downstairs. She left without reminding Janna again to be at the church on time.

She no longer cared.

Cecilia was relieved when the elevator arrived, empty. She'd have a few moments to compose herself before plastering on a smile for the rest of the day. Nine floors later, the doors opened onto the main floor. She got out and didn't know which way to go. She hadn't gotten any emails on the event's itinerary since the shower months ago.

But how hard could it be to find a bride in a large white dress and seven bridesmaids hovering around her?

Cecilia roamed the hotel's main floor trying to ignore the onlookers. She didn't know if they could tell she was moments from tears or if they just thought she was overdressed for a mid-February day. She was relieved when she saw Debbie's mother.

Cecilia smiled at the mother of the bride but the smile was not returned. "What are you doing here, dear?"

Cecilia checked her watch. "In the email, the maid of honor said we were meeting the photographer now."

"Well, we thought you weren't coming."

Cecilia started to ask why when the commotion from the elevators signaled the bridal party's arrival. The giggles of happiness reminded her of her own wedding, and Cecilia fought back tears.

Debbie stopped short when she saw her. More than one bridesmaid bumped into another at the abrupt halt. Debbie glanced at her mother before speaking. "CeCe, how...how nice to see you."

The rest of their sorority sisters said nothing. They held the deer in headlights look each of them had given her at the funeral. They didn't know what to do with her.

"You look beautiful," Cecilia told her. "I told you that was the right dress."

Cecilia approached her and made to kiss her. Debbie stepped back. "Oh no...you'll mess my makeup." It was as if widowhood was contagious and Cecilia the carrier.

No one would look at Cecilia, embarrassed by the situation. Or maybe believing tragedy was spread by eye contact, as well as by touch.

"Oh, there's the photographer. Let's go," Debbie announced. The bridal party scurried off, leaving Cecilia behind.

Cecilia wondered what to do, but Debbie's mother made it clear what they wanted her to do. "You don't look well, dear." She went into her purse and took out a tissue. "Why don't you go home?"

Home. Cecilia's first thought was Ferris. She realized she'd rather be in Folley with Ferris than here with her former friends.

Debbie's mother walked away and joined the posing bridal party. All of them had pushed thoughts of Cecilia out of their heads.

No one wants a young widow at a wedding. It only reminded the bride of all that could go wrong.

CHAPTER 22

B RISCOE HEARD THE deliveryman come in and watched as Marcy signed for an envelope. She didn't immediately get up, so he dismissed it as unimportant and returned to his work on the Chandler case. Unimportant was anything not related to the Chandler case or his upcoming campaign.

Five minutes later, Marcy slowly walked into Briscoe's office. Briscoe knew it must be bad. She was scared of him on a good day. Today, she looked terrified.

He knew she must have defied his order of bringing anything Chandler-related to him immediately. She must have peeked at the brief and held onto it, waiting for him to leave for lunch. Most days, he'd be headed to CB's Diner for lunch by now. But everything was different now with the impending murder trial.

She placed the envelope on his desk and slowly turned to exit. "What's this?" he asked.

Marcy answered without turning toward him. "I don't know," she answered. She resumed her escape of the office.

"Wait," he ordered. He knew she was lying.

She resigned to her fate and returned to his desk.

She held her breath while he opened the envelope and read the documents from the courthouse. His face began to redden within seconds.

"Son of a...ah! That Sewell!" He threw the papers across the desk. "Throw out the confession!" he yelled. "That's ridiculous!" He slammed his fists on the desk. "Get me Owens!" Marcy remained standing at his desk, frozen in fear. "Get me Owens now!" he ordered again.

She didn't bother running to her desk and used Briscoe's phone. He was too mad at Owens and Sewell to be annoyed. She told the officer who answered, "Chief Owens needs to see Mr. Briscoe immediately."

For twenty tense minutes, they sat in his office in silence. He hadn't dismissed her so she stayed.

"You summoned," Chief Owens announced when he arrived.

"Get in here, Owens!" Briscoe barked.

He smiled at Marcy as he walked in, "Afternoon, Marcy." He'd learned early on that if he was nice to Marcy, life was easier between the two men. She was a great buffer for them. Briscoe's last assistant had not been as nice, or easy to work with.

Briscoe yelled, "Close the door, Owens!" He threw the paperwork at Owens as he sat down. He looked at it briefly and threw it back.

"Legalese not my thing, Dan." He looked to Marcy, "What is this?" he asked. He knew she'd answer succinctly and devoid of Briscoe's arrogance.

"It's a—" she started.

"Shut up," he yelled at her. "It's proof of your incompetence, I fear."

Owens held his temper and through a clenched jaw asked, "What's wrong?"

"Did you or did you not read Ms. Chandler her rights when you spoke to her?"

"We do everything by the book, Dan. You know that. When are you talking about?"

"When you spoke to her at her house after the shooting."

"I didn't speak to her when I arrived. Paramedics were working on her."

Briscoe's face was red when Owens arrived. It was quickly becoming alarmingly red. "When you spoke to her later, that day, *in her house,* did you read her her rights?"

"When me and Vinnie went over? After she got back from the hospital?"

Briscoe's head made a slight nod of yes. All his facial and neck muscles were so tense Owens was surprised they could make the movement.

"Um…no. Why would I?"

"*Because you were questioning her about murdering someone?*"

"I thought we were getting a statement on a home invasion and sexual assault that led to a self-defense murder. How could I have foreseen you losing your mind and charging her with murder?"

"I don't know. Because you're the chief of police and it was a murder!"

"If his body was positioned a few feet differently, if he'd been in the house, we wouldn't even be having this conversation."

"But it wasn't. You knew it wasn't. You saw where the body was."

"So what do you want me to do?"

"Nothing. I'll fight this with Judge Lowe and hope he doesn't throw out the confession. If not, you've made my job a bit harder." Owens got up while Briscoe continued his tirade. "I'll still win this case even though you're an imbecile!"

Owens knew this was his cue to leave. Otherwise, he might throttle the prosecutor. "You're the imbecile for bringing this thing to trial!"

CHAPTER 23

D AN BRISCOE AND Wyatt Sewell sat outside Judge Lowe's office waiting for their turn. Their assistants sat across the hall from them. Abigail and Michael were furiously working on their phones. Marcy fiddled with her pen.

The judge opened his door and signaled the two lawyers in. Everyone stood. "Just you two. I don't need everyone crammed in here." Abigail handed Wyatt a few papers. The assistants sat back down and the lawyers went in.

Once Judge Lowe sat, Briscoe started. "Miranda warning was not necessary, Your Honor."

"Your Honor, in this scenario it was," Sewell retorted. He sat in one of the two chairs on the other side of the judge's desk.

"Miranda warning is required when a person is being questioned for a suspected crime *and* is in custody." Briscoe glanced at Sewell sitting at ease. His comfort grated him. "In this scenario, Ms. Chandler was not in police custody."

"Custody does not need to be at the police station. Custody depends on the suspect's perception of whether he or she felt like they were in custody. Mrs.

Chandler did not feel free to leave."

"They were having a pleasant conversation in her living room, Your Honor." Briscoe sat in the other chair and leaned back. "She was free to leave any time."

"Pleasant conversation? Talking about the brutal attack by a sexual predator—"

"Your Honor," Briscoe interrupted. The judge signaled him to be quiet.

"The brutal attack she withstood in her own home. She was concussed, in severe pain from the beating. Two officers came into her home and started questioning her. She asked if it could be done later and was told no. One stood in front of the door, blocking her exit." Sewell handed the judge a close-up of Cecilia's beaten face. "She was in her own home. Where was she going to go?"

Briscoe started to speak but the judge held up his hand to stop him.

"I tend to agree with Mr. Sewell. They should have read her rights."

Mr. Briscoe clenched his jaw but knew better than to talk back to the judge. He changed his tactic. "Spontaneous utterance, Your Honor."

"What?" Sewell asked.

"Spontaneous utterance of the crime does not need a Miranda warning." Lowe and Sewell looked at Briscoe to clarify. "When the police arrived immediately after the shooting."

"Do you have any officer statements of this?" the

judge asked.

"No, but I'll get it," Briscoe told him.

"I'm sure you will," Sewell muttered.

Judge Lowe ignored him but Briscoe didn't. He glared at his opponent, furious that he would question his ethics. Especially in front of the judge.

"I've read all the police documents. There was no spontaneous utterance at the scene, Briscoe," the judge told him. "Confession's out."

Sewell smiled as they left. Their respective assistants knew instantly who won. Abigail and Michael headed out of the courthouse, victorious. Marcy remained sitting, waiting for instruction and fearing Briscoe's wrath.

"I've still got plenty to convict her with," Briscoe yelled after them.

Sewell yelled back, "Not by the time I'm done with you, Briscoe."

CECILIA WAS SITTING at the kitchen barstool, staring out onto the dark backyard. Wyatt's law session the day before was sobering. She could see the trouble she was in.

Wyatt had tried to assuage her fears but she could see he was worried. "Briscoe has overshot with a charge of second-degree murder. I think we can fight that easily. He would have been better off charging you with voluntary manslaughter. Imperfect self-defense."

"That's what I did? Imperfect self-defense?" she asked.

He shrugged. "It's all up to interpretation. It'd be more difficult to fight. You honestly believed that lethal force was justified under the circumstances but that belief wasn't reasonable."

"Should we make a plea deal? Voluntary manslaughter, what kind of punishment comes with that?"

"Depends on a lot of things. If convicted of that, the judge takes in mitigating factors. For you, the mitigating factors are you have no criminal record, you're taking responsibility for the crime, your attachment to Ferris since the death of your husband."

"So a plea deal then? Should you ask for that?"

Wyatt shook his head. "Briscoe's not going to deal. We've asked around. He wants this publicity to propel him in his career. Senator, state attorney, I don't know. But he thinks this is the case that gets him out of Folley. He wouldn't plead this out. He wants to win."

"This isn't a game, Wyatt! It's my life. Ferris's life! What are we going to do?"

"I'm going to win, Cecilia. *We're* going to win, Cecilia."

He reached for her hand and held it gently. "We have more research to do but I think most juries in this state would side with you. The women would have acted the same way. The men have taught their daughters to protect themselves. They are not going to convict you if they would have, or their daughters would have, done the same thing."

Michael and Abigail arrived shortly after that and Cecilia was banished from the dining room. They had worked throughout the day on her case.

Staring out into the black backyard, the scene of the crime, she tried to remind herself that if Wyatt said he'd win, they'd win.

Cecilia screamed when a man dressed all in black appeared at the sliding glass door.

She got up to open the door when she recognized him as Holden.

"How did you do that? I was looking out there and had no idea you were approaching!" She looked to Ferris. "How did you not know?" He tilted his head from side to side, the protective collar swinging with each tilt.

"It's my stealth," Holden explained.

"What is wrong with you?" she asked.

"Sorry, I didn't mean to scare you." He walked in and placed his headlamp and backpack on the kitchen island. He pulled out a couple sandwiches from his backpack. "Thought you might be hungry." She opened the fridge and displayed the mountain of sandwiches and salads that the defense team had delivered earlier. "Oh...didn't expect that." Trying to change the subject, and avoid an awkward exit, he blurted the first thing he thought of. "Your face...your face looks better. Less purple."

"Thank you?" She assumed one's face being less

purple was a compliment.

He handed her a sandwich and she declined. "Not hungry."

"You need to eat. Keep up your strength. You need to be strong for the fight."

"Men. It's like it's some kind of game to you. You realize this trial, it is for my life, don't you? And what about Ferris? If I go to jail, what happens to him?"

"We'll find some place for Ferris," Holden assured her. Ferris walked over to Holden, his e-collar hitting everything in his path. Holden liked the golden retriever and patted him on his head. "He can come live with me."

Horrified, she yelled, "You can't take Joey's dog!"

Again, Holden was struggling. He'd forgotten the dizzying effects of an argument with a woman. Ferris looked up at him. He looked as bewildered as Holden felt. "I think we can take the collar off for a bit."

"Really? Are you sure?" she asked.

"We'll watch him. If he scratches the wound, I'll put it back on."

She nodded approval and Holden removed the collar. Ferris swung his head around. Noting the freedom, he ran around the house several times before stopping to collect one of his toys. He trotted to his bed and chewed on his favorite toy, one Joey had given him a week before he died, a stuffed duck.

"What do you think of him?" she asked.

"I think he looks fine without the collar, as long as you're watching him. Put it back on before you go to sleep."

"No...I mean...do you think he's family or proper-ty?"

"Oh..."

"Yep. I got a law lesson from Wyatt."

Holden debated his answer. They both knew he shouldn't be here. They both knew the lawyers on the case would erupt if they learned they were talking to each other. If called to the stand, he would answer honestly on the charges. So Holden answered her honestly.

"If I thought you were guilty, I would have arrest-ed you when I first arrived on the scene. Or I would have taken you to the station for questioning after they cleared you at the hospital."

"Do most of the officers feel like you do? Is it only Briscoe who wanted the arrest?"

This question was harder. He again chose the truth, knowing it would hurt. "Most in town think an outsider killed a town son. No matter what they might have thought of Gabbert, he was one of them."

"You think if Joey were here things would be dif-ferent?" she asked.

Holden shrugged. They both knew if Joey were alive life would be much different.

"Have you noticed the mayor hasn't spoken on the subject?" Holden asked.

She shook her head no. "No, I haven't watched any news coverage. I really never watched the news before. Figured now would be a bad time to start."

"That's a good move." Gabbert's mother had been at Briscoe's news conference. But no sign of her brother. The mayor couldn't win either way. If he supported Briscoe, it would be nepotism. If he opposed him, he would alienate his family. Neutrality was Mayor Townsend's best political move. "I'm sure your lawyer will use the fact that Mayor Townsend wants nothing to do with this case."

Cecilia nodded, hoping the mayor wouldn't change his mind. She didn't need another opponent.

CHAPTER 24

Pugliese went through the files of Gabbert's previous complaints and arrests.

Using Google and Facebook, he pulled up photos of the victims and printed them. He scanned them and he was still plagued with the question. "Why Cecilia?"

Armed with data, Pugliese marched into the Chief's office and closed the door. "I told you I was wondering about Gabbert."

Owens looked up from his computer and tried to hide his annoyance.

Pugliese spread out the photos and pointed to each one of them. Owens recognized the pretty young women from the town.

"Each one of them had a run-in with Gabbert." Owens nodded. "Again, I'll ask, why Cecilia?"

Run-in was a loose term. None had been physically assaulted by Gabbert. But each incident inched closer to one.

"Pug, I have no idea why this matters."

Pugliese knew he had limited time to plead his case. The Chief was already annoyed. "She just doesn't fit in." Holden couldn't argue with that. She had never fit into Folley.

"Are you saying Cecilia's not pretty?" Holden did not want to argue about Cecilia's attractiveness with Pugliese and fortunately didn't have to.

Pugliese was bothered by the chief's use of her first name. They always referred to suspects and arrestees by their last name. Referring to them by their first name was too personal.

"Oh no, Mrs. Chandler is striking, but Gabbert clearly has a type." Holden looked at each photo again and could see their similarities. "And none of them had a dog. They were the most obvious women to attack. No dog. No alarm. Isolated home. Chandler's home had that dog. It has a pretty sophisticated alarm."

Holden looked up from the photos. "What are you saying?"

"A lot of people knew about Gabbert and his troubles. It was a secret." Owens nodded. Briscoe and the mayor did what they could to keep it quiet. Pugliese leaned in. "But a well-known one." Owens didn't argue with that either. Mayor Townsend had succeeded in keeping it out of the local paper. But a small town talks.

"And..." Owens prompted him.

Cecilia wasn't his usual victim and Pugliese suspected Gabbert didn't have his usual motive. "I think he chose Cecilia for another reason."

"And what reason would that be?" Owens asked.

Pugliese had been pondering the 'Why did Gabbert chose Cecilia?' question for days and he uttered the only plausible reason he had come up with. "Money."

Owens contemplated that. The Chandlers lived in a nice home. Robbery wasn't on Gabbert's list of crimes but he could have been branching out. He shrugged. It was a stretch. "I don't know, Pugliese."

He explained further. "I think someone hired him to scare Cecilia."

"What?" Now Owens knew Pugliese had stretched too far. "Ridiculous."

"I want to check into his financials," he told him.

"Financials?" Owens asked. Pugliese had lost him and any support he had toyed with. "He's an eighteen-year-old delinquent. There are no financials."

"Well..." Pugliese had expected the Chief's support and struggled to find another way to support his claim. "Let me go through his phone. Go through his room. Talk to the mother."

"We'd need warrants for the phone, the room. And harassing a grieving mother? No way. Can you imagine what the media would do with that?"

"Why are you so worried about the media?" Pugliese snapped back.

Owens glared at him. "I'm only worried about this town." And all of its residents, he didn't add. If this could help Cecilia, he'd let Pugliese do whatever he wanted but he couldn't see how it would. He picked up the photos and handed them back to Pugliese. "I hope you did this on your own time. And not wasting city time." Pugliese took the photos and put it back in the file he had compiled. "This whole thing is ridiculous. I know people didn't take to her but want her gone. No way. I cannot think of one person who would hire someone to scare Cecilia."

But Pugliese could.

CECILIA WAITED FOR Clayton Hindel to arrive for their monthly meeting on the status of Chandler Construction. It was the one time each month, since Joey's death, she would get dressed up and leave the house. Today, with the meeting being held in her home, she didn't bother. She answered the door in jeans and Joey's college sweatshirt.

"Thank you for coming here, Clayton," Cecilia said when she answered the door.

"Don't have much choice, do we?" Hearing himself, he apologized. He should have stopped at Glinton's for his twenty-four-ounce cup coffee, which he always needed to start his day. "I didn't mean it like that. Sorry."

"Need coffee?"

He nodded and she poured him a cup. He longingly looked at the carafe, and she half expected him to grab the carafe and drink from it for his caffeine fix. With the small cup in his hand, Clayton followed her into the office. Ferris followed them and sat by Cecilia's chair. She stopped at her desk, the small one in the corner. Clayton proceeded to the large one, JJ's desk, and sat in the waiting chair. Cecilia hesitated but knew it was the obvious choice. As she sat behind their desk, she felt uncomfortable.

"I haven't been in here since Mr. Chandler died," Clayton commented as he pulled out a binder. "Joey's dad, I mean."

The office was as Joey had left it. And he had left it as his father had. Cecilia looked at the two framed wedding photos on the desk. Joey's older sister and her husband. Joey and Cecilia.

Cecilia and Clayton ran the meeting as usual, reviewing payroll, current projects, and upcoming bids. Everything was running smoothly and profitably.

"Anything else?" Clayton asked.

"Have you heard from them?" Cecilia asked, pointing to Brittany and Jeremiah's wedding photograph. If they wanted to strike again, this would be the time. She'd struggle to fight two court battles simultaneously.

"No," Clayton answered.

"That's odd isn't it?" she asked.

CHAPTER 25

Then

FERRIS WAS WAITING at the foot of the stairs when Cecilia returned from the funeral. He jumped up when she opened the door. His head sagged when he saw it was only Cecilia. "It's just you and me now," she told him. He lay down, resting his head between his paws. She sat down next to him and patted him on the head. "I'm not happy about it either."

Moments later, his ears perked up and twitched from side to side. He jumped up and began running from the front door to the side door. Cecilia first thought he had to go to the bathroom, but he always went to the door to the backyard for that need. Instead, it was his excited run when he knew Joey was almost home. For a moment, she got excited too, before reality hit it her. Joey was not coming home.

Ferris began pawing at the side door and she let him out. She stared as Joey's truck pulled into the driveway. Ferris's excitement doubled and he ran along the fence, as he waited for the driver to get out. Ferris growled when he did.

"Hi, Mrs. Chandler," the employee from Chandler

Construction said. "Hi, Ferris."

The two stared at him, as if they didn't know who he was. "It's Randy," he introduced himself, although he'd met Cecilia a few times. Cecilia nodded and Ferris growled again. "I thought you'd want the truck here."

"Thank you, Randy." She tried to smile but her face forgot how.

Cars began pulling up in front of the house and Cecilia cursed herself for not remembering. This is what happened after her father-in-law's funeral too. The mourners came to the house after the funeral to...she didn't know what. It wasn't to commiserate. Most had looked like they were having a good time, eating and drinking the food they had brought.

"Thank you," she told Randy again before returning to the house. It took several attempts to get Ferris back into the house. He continued growling at Randy.

Cecilia accepted condolences with as much grace as she could, with Ferris at her side. She recognized few of the mourners. They introduced themselves as friends, employees, and neighbors. She registered none of their names.

Her in-laws arrived with the masses. Jeremiah and Brittany Coleman lived in the neighboring county. Cecilia didn't know them well but felt Joey's sister, Brittany, was the one person in the house who could be as sad as her. Cecilia hugged Brittany, who lightly returned the embrace.

When the stream of mourners ended, Cecilia sat in

an armchair by the living room window, Ferris at her side. She watched as the strangers in her home ate, drank, and talked. A few tried to engage her in conversation. What was worth talking about? she thought.

There was one glaring absence, her sister Janna. She'd arrived late to the church and Cecilia hadn't seen her since. She checked her phone and found the excuse. "Had to get back to the city. Concert tickets tonight."

Cecilia shouldn't be surprised but she was. Her sister always put herself first.

Exhausted from the day, Cecilia headed upstairs. She doubted anyone would notice. She felt like a stranger in her own home. She jumped when she found two people in her bedroom.

"Brittany? What are you doing in here?" Cecilia looked from Brittany to Jeremiah before noticing the tape measure in their hands. "What are you doing?" she asked again.

Brittany stuttered and Jeremiah answered for her. "We're just taking some measurements. Making sure our furniture will fit in here. We figured you'd be taking your furniture."

Brittany found her voice and added, "But leaving Daddy's furniture, right?"

"Leaving it when?" Cecilia asked.

"When you move back to the city," Brittany answered.

Cecilia's only decision in the last few days had

been to breathe. No other decisions ever entered her mind. The thought of moving? Who would think about that today? In that moment, before even asking herself the question, she decided. "This is our home. I will not be leaving it."

"But, with Joey dead, it's not your home," Brittany told her. "It was Daddy's."

"This is our home. I will not be leaving it," she repeated. Ferris pushed himself against her leg. She scratched behind his ear.

Jeremiah started to argue but Cecilia cut him off. She cleared her throat but struggled to find her voice. "Get out," Cecilia told them.

They remained frozen. "Get out," Cecilia said, again and again. Each time, she was louder. By the fourth time, her raised voice could be heard downstairs.

As she followed Brittany and Jeremiah to the front door, she was yelling for them to get out. The mourners did not have to be told twice to leave and scurried out.

CHAPTER 26

VINNIE SAW HIS high school friend at the end of the bar. He pretended it was an accident.

"Hey, Randy!" he said, patting his former high school football teammate on the back. "Get us a round, will ya, Wendy?"

The bartender nodded and brought over two beers.

"Thanks," Randy said. He raised the beer and they clinked bottles. "How's work?"

Vinnie was grateful Randy had been the first one to bring up work. He didn't want him getting suspicious if he had. But everyone was interested in Vinnie's work these days.

"Busy," he answered. Randy seemed appeased by the answer. "How about you?" Vinnie asked.

Randy shrugged. "The same."

"Really? No changes at Chandler Construction?" Randy had been a foreman at Chandler Construction for the last five years.

Randy shook his head. "Not because of this." He took a sip of beer and then added, "I don't think anyone realizes Mrs. C runs it."

Vinnie laughed. "You call her Mrs. C?"

"Mrs. Chandler to her face. Mrs. C among the

guys."

"Not Cecilia?" Vinnie asked. This surprised Vinnie. They weren't too far apart in age.

"No. You call your boss by his first name?" Randy asked. He had a point. Vinnie couldn't imagine what the Chief would do if he walked up to him and called him Holden. "Things have gotten back to normal. I was a little worried there after Mr. Chandler died."

"Joey?" Vinnie asked to clarify. Both Chandler men had died while Randy had worked there.

"No, Mr. Chandler. The father. The son, he always told us to call him Joey. I think that was the problem."

"Really?" Vinnie couldn't see how that could lead to problems at the company.

"Too familiar. Too nice." Another former schoolmate entered the bar and they both waved to him.

"And Mrs. Chandler isn't nice?" Vinnie asked.

"No, she's fine." He took another sip of beer. "Mrs. Chandler is a lot like the old man. No nonsense."

Vinnie couldn't decide if Chandler Construction workers had positive or negative feelings for their newest boss. "So the workers don't like her?" he asked.

"Oh no, we like her plenty," Randy answered. "She's fair."

"How so?"

Randy finished his beer and signaled the bartender for another round, despite Vinnie barely touching his.

"Between us?" he asked. "I don't want this turning into a police matter." Vinnie nodded. "You know Kevin McNulty?"

"Sure. A couple years behind us in high school."

Randy leaned into Vinnie, not wanting the other patrons to hear. "Yep. Well, Joey found out he was stealing from the company. And he did nothing. Told him he'd give him another shot."

"That's very nice," Vinnie commented.

Randy leaned back and shook his head. "A new boss needs to set a tone. He set one that said he was soft."

"And Mrs. Chandler?"

With an eyebrow raised, he answered, "Well, this should come as no surprise—"

"Kevin kept stealing…" Vinnie completed the sentence.

"Of course. Mrs. C found out and fired him." The bartender dropped off the second round of beers. Randy waited until she was out of earshot before he continued. "She's hands off and a lot better than the alternative."

"Who?" Vinnie asked, pretending he didn't know.

"Mr. Chandler's son-in-law, Jeremiah. He'd have Chandler Construction bankrupt in a week."

Vinnie nodded, having already heard the stories about Jeremiah from him before. "Does Mrs. Chandler ever come by the construction sites?"

"Not usually." He took a sip from his second beer. "She did come once, though. To see where her husband died."

CHAPTER 27

Then

"I THINK THIS is a bad idea," Clayton said.

"You've said that," Cecilia responded. Clayton pointed to the upcoming turn and Cecilia made the right.

"I just—"

She cut him off. "I know, Clayton. If I could have found the place on my own I would have, but I needed you for directions."

"Well, I tried—"

"Your directions of turn left when you pass where the Garrison shop used to be weren't helpful. I've lived here two years, Clayton. I don't know where things are, never mind where they used to be."

"Okay, but—"

She cut him off again. "You are not going to win this argument, Clayton."

"I never win fights with my wife either. You'd think as a lawyer I'd argue better." He pointed again and she turned onto the dirt road.

Randy, the foreman, was waiting for them when they arrived. He met her on the driver's side door as she exited her purple Escort. Ferris jumped out after her.

Randy noted her clothing. It wasn't the usual attire she wore when he had seen her with Joey. When he had seen them in town together, she was always dressed up—skirts or dresses, something nice. His wife always commented on how fancy she was. Today, she wore no makeup and was dressed in black leggings and Joey's old jacket. "How are you, Mrs. Chandler?"

After her mother died, she learned that people did not want the truth when they asked. So she didn't give it.

"I don't want to take up much of your time, Randy. I assume we're behind on this project." He nodded. Most would have been surprised by her matter-of-fact tone. But he had seen her at the funeral. She was devastated by Joey's death. "Please just take me to where it happened."

Randy didn't bother to argue. He knew it was a terrible idea but Mrs. Chandler did not appear to be a woman to contend with. Plus, he did not want to argue with the new boss. Randy headed off to the accident site. Cecilia, Ferris, and Clayton followed him. When he stopped, Randy didn't speak and they both knew this was where Joey had died.

"Clayton, I'll meet you in the trailer. If you need anything from us, Randy, please be there when I get there." They knew they were being dismissed and left Cecilia and Ferris at the spot.

They stood at the site for a few minutes. She didn't

know why she had come. It certainly didn't make her feel better. And she certainly couldn't feel worse.

Ferris sniffed around the spot and then returned to Cecilia's side. She patted his head and doubted it helped him either.

As she headed to the trailer, she could hear shouting. Seeing the Mercedes parked next to the trailer, she knew the source.

"Jeremiah," she greeted him, as she stepped into the trailer. All three men stopped arguing when they saw her. "What can we help you with?"

"I'm here to take over the daily operations of Chandler Construction," Jeremiah announced.

"The business is not yours to run, Jeremiah," Cecilia told him.

"Well, now that Joey is dead, the business goes to Brittany." Cecilia winced when he said "dead," as if she had been slapped.

Cecilia shook her head. "This was established prior to JJ's death. The business went to Joey." Mr. Chandler was a fastidious man. He had ensured all his affairs were in order, even before his illness. When he first wrote his will, and then again when he was sick, he reviewed the will's stipulations with both of his children. They agreed with the terms. Joey would get the house and the business. Brittany would get the vacation home and a larger portion of his cash. JJ knew Brittany and Jeremiah would destroy the business, even if they had a small stake in it.

"Well, Joey is dead now." No one missed Cecilia

wince this time. She needed no reminders that her husband was dead, especially when she was where he died.

"Jeremiah!" Randy rebuked.

Jeremiah ignored him. "I'll be by the house later for the truck."

She kept her voice even despite her inner rage. "The truck is Joey's."

"And Joey is—"

She interrupted him before he could say dead again. "The truck is personal property. Not business. He paid for the truck out of our money and the Chandler Construction signs on it, as well." She looked to Clayton, who confirmed the private purchase.

"Whatever," Jeremiah answered, not having a comeback. "But the business—"

Cecilia looked to Clayton, who was clearly uncomfortable in the situation. Jeremiah was considerably bigger than him. And, as Clayton had stated earlier, he rarely won an argument.

"Per the stipulations in JJ's will, the business went to Joey. Brittany received an equal and fair share of the estate. The will was not contested." To give him a moment to catch up, she asked, "Agreed?"

"Yes, but—" Jeremiah started.

"Upon Joey Chandler's death, his will stipulates that all of his assets go to his wife, me. This is typical." She looked to Clayton for confirmation. He nodded. "You will not win if you attempt to contest

Joey's will."

Feeling defeated, Jeremiah's face became red. "Why would you want to stay?"

She ignored his question. "I think we are through." She opened the trailer door and signaled for him to leave. He stood motionless.

"Jeremiah, I think she's made her point," Randy said.

Feeling the weight of the three of them glaring at him, four if you counted Ferris, and having no recourse, he made for the trailer's door. He had never expected an argument. Brittany and he had expected she'd be out of the town once she could pack up her stuff. And leave it all to them.

He stopped inches from Cecilia. Puffing his chest out, he said, "You need to leave."

Cecilia held her own. "No, Jeremiah, it is you who needs to leave." Ferris growled.

They glared at each other until Randy interrupted. "Jeremiah, you need to go, now."

Jeremiah shot each of them a look before exiting the trailer. "You hate everything about here! Why are you staying?" he screamed as Randy slammed the door.

Randy and Clayton watched her, waiting for a response. Cecilia didn't speak but knew the answer. Joey loved his father. He never planned to move back to Folley to run the business. But his father's dying wish was that he would. So he did. Joey honored his father through maintaining the business.

Cecilia would do the same, for the both of them.

CHAPTER 28

THE CHANDLER HOUSE was the only place the Sewell team had found to work in peace. They had consulted the hotel about renting out their meeting space but the manager did not appear pleased at the prospect. He said any support of the defense was bad for business. The only reason the hotel's general manager hadn't evicted them was because he was afraid of Sewell and possible litigation.

They greeted Cecilia when they arrived and then went to their separate spaces. Cecilia to her office and Wyatt, Abigail, and Michael to their new office.

"What did you find out about Robert Gabbert?" Wyatt asked.

"Not much," Michael answered. "I don't understand the push for the information. Don't we have our hands full worried about Mrs. Chandler, without finding out about this Gabbert kid?"

"One, he's not a kid. He was eighteen," Wyatt corrected him.

"What could we do with the information anyway? You know bashing the victim never sits well with the jury," Abigail added.

"I know," Wyatt conceded "But I want to know

more. On the way here, one of the media reports said he didn't have a criminal record." Wyatt sipped his coffee. "And the mayor? The mayor's office only comment is 'no comment.' That's odd, isn't it? Shouldn't Mayor Townsend be using this publicity to further his career? Shouldn't he be the one holding the press conferences praising his nephew's virtues?"

"That's cold, Wyatt. Even for you," Abigail told him as she sat down.

"Briscoe really pushed the no criminal record as an adult. And he'd been an adult for exactly how long?" Wyatt asked.

Abigail scrolled through her paperwork, "Twelve days."

Wyatt smiled. "You know what that means…"

"Juvenile record," Michael answered.

"That is sealed," Abigail reminded them.

"Well, we'll get it unsealed."

"DANIEL BRISCOE, HERE to see you," the mayor's secretary said into her desk phone. Briscoe hovered over her desk while he waited to be led into Townsend's office.

She nodded and said "Yes, sir" twice, before ending with, "I'll tell him, sir."

She hung up the phone and looked at Briscoe. "The mayor is full today, Mr. Briscoe. He cannot see you." She made no attempt to reschedule the prosecutor, as her boss had instructed her.

Briscoe pointed to the empty calendar on her desk. "Looks like the day is open to me." He looked around the empty office. "No waiting appointments," he added, pointing to the empty chairs. "I think he can spare a few minutes for the man prosecuting his nephew's killer."

"No," she yelled as he marched for the mayor's office door. "I'm calling security," she called out as he opened the door.

Mayor Townsend was sitting at his desk, staring out the window. He knew he wouldn't be able to get rid of Briscoe so easily. "Don't call security, Mabel," he instructed her. "The media would love that," he mumbled.

"Has your schedule opened up, Mayor Townsend?"

"I'm a busy man, Briscoe. What—"

"Yes, I know you're busy." Briscoe pointed at the mayor's empty desk. "Too busy to make it to the press conference. Too busy to answer my phone calls. Too busy to take this meeting."

Mayor Townsend swiveled his chair from the window. "What do—"

"Too busy to answer any of the media's inquiries for an interview. Only time for your secretary to say 'No comment.'"

"What do you want—"

Briscoe sat across from him. "The media is going to start asking questions. They can only go with the grieving uncle supporting his distraught sister story for so long, Mayor."

Briscoe finally let him get out the full question.

"What do you want, Briscoe?"

"Your support," he answered.

"My support?" the mayor spat back. "You should have asked for 'my support' before you arrested Mrs. Chandler."

Briscoe glared at Mayor Townsend, indignant that the mayor would think he was Briscoe's superior. "I don't have to ask for the mayor's permission to arrest a killer."

"And you don't need my support for a trial."

"It will help." Briscoe couldn't understand the mayor's resistance. This could help them both. A high-profile trial could bolster both of their careers.

"Help who?" Townsend asked.

Briscoe leaned forward and smiled. "Both of us, of course."

"The best thing would have been to never arrest her. The best thing now, for *both of us*, is to plead this out. Come on, I read the file, it's not murder two."

Briscoe didn't think now, as he was trying to garner the mayor's support, would be a good time to point out the mayor was not a lawyer. "I have a good case."

"And what did Chief Owens say?" the mayor asked. "If he thought it was murder, he would have arrested her at the scene."

Another non-lawyer, Briscoe thought. "I will win

this case." He returned to his upright posture. "I would like your support. The whole town is behind the prosecution."

"The whole town wasn't called every time Bobby was arrested, or after every run-in with the law, when we swept it under the rug. That kid was a thorn in my side since he hit teendom."

Briscoe ignored him and continued to argue his case. "You and your sister sitting behind me is very powerful to the jury."

"Forget about it." Mayor Townsend shook his head. "My sister can do whatever she wants. You can talk to her yourself. She can look at his coffin and see the perfect boy she thought he'd be. I remember the monster he was becoming."

"Mayor—"

It was Mayor Townsend's time to interrupt Briscoe. "We're done here. I'm done with Bobby." He pointed Briscoe to the door. "I did all I could for that boy when he was alive."

BRISCOE PLODDED INTO the office, frustrated for not having gotten what he wanted with the mayor. He didn't say anything to Marcy as he walked past her desk. She kept her head down. Twenty minutes later, a motion was delivered to the office.

Marcy walked into Briscoe's office carrying the official paperwork. "Chandler trial," she announced.

"As if there were any of other cases," he said.

He knew there were plenty of other cases but he had no interest in any of them. He read the motion while she stood at his desk, awaiting orders.

"At least this one I expected," Briscoe said as he read the brief. "Juvenile record. Not going to win this one, Sewell." He smiled at the paperwork. "I know I can win this one. Juvenile record? What juvenile record?"

CHAPTER 29

CECILIA SAT AT the kitchen island, moving the peas around on her plate. She wasn't hungry. She looked out onto the patio. If Joey were here, they'd be sitting on those old patio chairs. Those old, uncomfortable, avocado green metal patio chairs. She had wanted to replace them since they'd moved in. But he'd said no. He liked them, nostalgia from his youth. So there they remained.

Her phone tinged with an incoming text. Glad for a distraction, she clicked on the attached link. She quickly regretted it.

A news conference began. She recognized the prosecutor, Briscoe, and his assistant, Marcy, standing on the courthouse's steps. She didn't know the woman who stood to Briscoe's left.

Briscoe started the news conference. "Thank you all for coming. We wanted to give an update on the case." He quieted the reporters, who were shouting questions, and introduced the woman by his side. "This is Peggy Gabbert, the mother of the innocent boy murdered in cold blood by Ms. Chandler."

Cecilia gasped but continued watching as he stepped aside and Peggy walked up to the podium. She pulled out a piece of paper from her pocket and started to read from it. "My son, Robert Gabbert, was a kind young boy." The tears started and overwhelmed her until she could only mutter, "My boy, my boy." She cried at the podium, photographers snapping her picture, until Marcy helped her away.

Briscoe returned to the podium. "I have promised Mrs. Gabbert I will seek justice for her boy." The reporters shouted questions at him. Most were about Sewell. He repeated one. "Scared of facing Mr. Sewell in the courtroom?" He looked directly into the camera and answered. "No, I'm not scared." Cecilia believed him. She was the one who was scared.

With the press conference over, the screen faded to black.

Cecilia sat at the kitchen counter, with her head in her hands, staring at the dark screen. She scolded herself for clicking on the link her sister had sent. She should have known better. Janna would not have sent her something to make her feel better.

A month after Joey's funeral, Janna had sent a link for an online dating site. "Not getting any younger, sis."

Thoughtless. Inappropriate. Cruel.

This link had been the same.

Ferris heard Holden before she did. He started running to the door before Holden gently tapped on the glass. She wiped her face before getting up to open the door. Ferris was licking the glass by the time she got there.

"Not as stealth this time," she told him.

"I was there a minute before Ferris saw me," he said. "You were crying." And he didn't know what to do. Holden stood watching her, wanting to comfort her but not knowing how. He had debated leaving but he didn't want to.

She shooed him off. "It's okay." She turned and he followed her into the house.

"No, it's not." He opened his mouth to ask what had caused the tears. The list was lengthy.

She answered before he could. "I...I watched the news conference."

"Which one?" Holden asked.

Ferris started running around the kitchen island. Cecilia pointed to his treat jar and Holden got one out and he gave it to Ferris, once he sat for it. "The one the prosecutor held. My sister sent it to me."

He sighed. The news conference had been days ago. What kind of person sends that to their sister? Cecilia had said she hadn't been watching any of the media accounts. She said she rarely watched news before, why start now. Holden had encouraged her news boycott.

"Try to forget about it," he told her.

"Forget about it?" She sat on a stool and looked at Holden. "How? If you know a way to forget this whole year, please fill me in." He squirmed. He had no helpful response. "Mr. Briscoe said I killed an innocent boy. That...that can't be true. He attacked me. He was going to rape me. I'm not making that up."

"Robert Gabbert was no innocent boy, Cecilia." Briscoe had wanted him at the news conference. "United force," he had said. But, like Mayor Townsend, Holden refused. He wouldn't have been able to hold his tongue while Briscoe spoke positively about Gabbert.

"Robert Gabbert. I didn't even know his name before the press conference." She took a deep breath trying to prevent an onslaught of tears. "Does that make me an awful person? I didn't even know his name."

"No, it doesn't make you an awful person Cecilia." He reached for her hand and gave it a reassuring squeeze. "You've had enough on your mind."

"His mother. His poor mother. Standing behind him, crying for 'her boy'." Cecilia got up and started pacing. Ferris joined her. "I don't know what to do."

Holden reached for her but Ferris reached him first. He petted the dog and tried to calm Cecilia. "There's nothing you can do."

Her boy, what bull, Holden thought. The last time Gabbert was arrested his mother didn't even come down to the station to visit. She made no attempts to bail him out. She let him sit in jail. They all knew, the whole town knew, that was where he had belonged.

Ferris, bored with Holden, rejoined Cecilia's pacing. "Mr. Briscoe said he was a good kid. No criminal record."

Holden rolled his eyes. No adult criminal record

because he had turned eighteen the week before. His juvenile record was the largest he had ever seen.

She stopped and looked at Holden. "You believe me, don't you?" she asked. "He attacked me. They'll believe me, won't they?"

"Do I believe you? Of course I do. I saw you." Holden tried not to picture her bruised and beaten body. Her face's bruises were healing and had begun turning green. "I knew him." Holden couldn't expand on that. He didn't think she needed, or wanted, to know Gabbert's exploits.

Holden reached for her hand again but thought better of it. "I know you...I know you did what you had to." Ferris nuzzled against his leg and he got up to get him another treat. "Let's talk about something else."

"Something else?" she asked. "What else is there to talk about?"

Holden searched his brain for anything to change the subject. "Tell me something about your husband." He regretted his choice. After his divorce, after a string of bad dates, his sister had given him some dating rules. Dating Advice 101, she called it. Rule number one: never talk about the exes. He looked at Cecilia and tried to remind himself this was not a date.

She sighed. "You start. Tell me something about your...your what?"

"My ex-wife Annabelle?" He searched his brain for something nice to say. He searched for anything that might help Cecilia but came up empty. Instead, he told her, "She was good at putting people at ease. Far better than me."

"You're a police officer. Of course no one feels at ease around you." Cecilia laughed. Holden laughed in agreement. "Now you, something about Joey."

Her eyes drawn to the chairs again, she told him, "Joey loved those chairs."

"Those chairs?" Holden asked, pointing to the patio. "They're hideous."

Her eyes bulged, surprised he had agreed so heartily. "I know!"

Holden walked over to the sliding glass door for a better look. "They look uncomfortable."

"They are!" she agreed. "But he loved them. Something about them being from his childhood. He said sitting in them made him feel like a child again."

It was the first time she'd talked about Joey since his death and she was able to smile. She got up and got them Mountain Dews. She handed a can to Holden. "He hated Mountain Dew too," she told him.

"No!" Holden responded.

"Herbal teas and water only. Nothing with caffeine," she explained, shaking her head.

Holden sipped his soda. "I don't think I could make it a day without caffeine."

"Me neither!" Cecilia agreed between sips.

They returned to the kitchen island and drank their sodas, watching Ferris run around the kitchen with a tennis ball in his mouth. Holden tried to get it from him so they could play fetch, but Ferris wouldn't give it up.

When they finished their drinks, Holden stood to leave. Cecilia walked him to the patio door and said goodnight. "Thank you, Holden. You do put people at ease, you know." As he stepped outside, they both looked at the patio chairs.

"You want me to get rid of them?" he asked.

She looked at the chairs and then back to Holden. "You wouldn't be stealth lugging those with you."

"I'd find a way," he assured her.

"I'm sure you would," she agreed. "But, no, it's my job now. I'll take care of them."

CHAPTER 30

THE LAWYERS AND their assistants sat outside Judge Lowe's office. They maintained the same spots they had last time. They remained quiet until the judge signaled the two lawyers in.

"Juvenile record proceedings are confidential, Your Honor," Briscoe started. "Mind you, I'm not saying he has one," he added, turning to Sewell.

"You're kidding me, right, Briscoe?" Judge Lowe asked. "I couldn't count how many times I've seen that kid in my courtroom."

"Your Honor!" Briscoe snapped.

The judge ignored Briscoe and looked to Sewell. "You know I can't release the juvenile record."

"Your Honor, it will provide Robert Gabbert's history of criminal behavior."

"It's not relevant, Your Honor." Briscoe said. "Robert Gabbert is not on trial here."

"But he'll be on full display during the trial. I'm sure Mr. Briscoe here will paint Mr. Gabbert like he did during the press conference. As a good kid and 'with no criminal record.' I want the jurors to have the whole truth, and nothing but the truth," Sewell told the judge.

Judge Lowe turned to Briscoe for a response. "It's sealed for a reason, Your Honor. Robert Gabbert has his right to privacy."

"A dead man has no rights to privacy, Judge," Sewell retorted.

"It's inflammatory, Your Honor," Briscoe snapped.

"I tend to agree," Judge Lowe said. "No juvenile record release." Briscoe's smile of victory was short-lived. The judge continued, "But I won't let you tell the jury he doesn't have a criminal record either."

Sewell assumed there was a juvenile record after the press conference. It was confirmed by Judge Lowe once he arrived in the office. But now he knew it must be good.

"Thank you, Your Honor," Briscoe said. Feeling victorious, Briscoe strutted out of the office.

"You didn't really think you'd win, did you?" he asked Sewell.

"Juvenile record release? Doubted it. Always good to see the judge, though." Sewell put his briefcase down on the bench and put his overcoat on. Fall was in the air today. "What could I do with it anyway?" Briscoe didn't understand. "No lawyer is going to bash a victim, would they?" Briscoe shook his head no but couldn't figure out Sewell's end game. "No one's arguing she wasn't viciously attacked on her own property, are they?" Briscoe shook his head no. "I just would like to know what kind of man would do that to a young widow."

Briscoe had ordered Marcy to compile a file on Wyatt Sewell. He wanted to know everything he could on his opponent. As much as he didn't like to admit it, Sewell was a worthy adversary.

The pretrial proceedings, and the trial itself, was like a game of chess to Briscoe. This move made Briscoe scratch his head. No longer feeling victorious, he followed Sewell to the exit. Their assistants trailed behind.

Sewell paused at the door, after peeking out. "Oh the media. They just follow us everywhere, don't they?"

Briscoe seethed, finally understanding the move. The media was the pawn. Briscoe started to blame Sewell for the setup but thought better of it.

The proceedings were a matter of public record. Anyone seeing him and Sewell arrive at the courthouse could have made a call. He doubted Sewell would be forced to call them himself.

"I bet they'll find out, *if* Gabbert had a juvenile record." Before Briscoe could argue, Sewell continued, "The town doesn't like to talk to outsiders, right? I doubt they'd tell anyone on my staff the real truth about Gabbert. But I bet if there was a camera and a possibility of being on television, they'd talk." Sewell held the door open for the ladies to exit. "I even bet they'd tell the truth."

CECILIA WAS BEGINNING to look forward to Holden's visits. She often found herself listening for the gentle knocking announcing his arrival.

She noticed Ferris did too. His ears perked at any noise that could be Holden. He probably missed people more than she did.

Ferris heard something and ran to the patio door. Cecilia followed but she was disappointed. More disappointed than she thought she should be.

Drenched in the last rays of sunlight stood a middle-aged woman in the middle of her yard. Cecilia stepped out, pushing Ferris back to keep him in the house. "Hello. Can I help you?" When the woman turned, Cecilia recognized her. "Mrs. Gabbert...I don't think you should be here."

"And where should I be?" she asked. Cecilia shrugged. She didn't know, but she knew she shouldn't be here. "I needed to see where my boy died."

Cecilia could understand that. She'd needed to do the same. But in the end, it didn't help.

Mrs. Gabbert turned to face Cecilia. "Where you killed him."

Cecilia didn't look away from the woman's glare. She wondered if it was easier to have someone to blame. Cecilia had heard the platitudes—"accidents happen" or "When it's your time, it's your time." She decided it didn't matter. Grief was pain, regardless who was to blame.

Cecilia searched the yard in hopes of seeing Holden. But it was too early. It wasn't dark enough for his stealth arrival. Regardless, his arrival would be hard to explain to the grieving mother.

"Please, Mrs. Gabbert, you need to leave."

"He's in a cold grave and you're in this nice big house. Plenty warm, I'm sure."

"Mrs. Gabbert, you're trespassing. I don't want to call the police." Cecilia took her cell phone out of her pocket.

"That's all my boy was doing. Trespassing."

"That's not..." Cecilia started to explain but thought better of it. "You need to go."

"Why don't you shoot me?" Mrs. Gabbert asked. She stepped toward Cecilia.

"Why don't you shoot me? I'd be better off."

Cecilia wanted to disagree with her but couldn't. She understood the grief. A young woman shouldn't bury a husband. A mother shouldn't bury a child. Before Cecilia could ask one final time for her to leave, Mrs. Gabbert conceded. "It's getting dark. I better head home."

From the patio, Cecilia watched the grieving mother leave the yard and walk down the driveway. She got in her car and drove away. Searching for a distraction, Cecilia and Ferris went into the office. She opened her laptop and stared at emails. She felt the pictures, the framed ones on the desk, staring back at her. She looked at Joey. "I should have left," Cecilia conceded. "I should have given Brittany and Jeremiah the business, the house, everything." Ferris barked. She looked down at him and patted him on his head. "No, not you. I wouldn't have given them you." Looking back at Joey, she admitted, "I stayed for you. Just to stay close to you. But you're nowhere close."

She stared at Joey's photo until she heard the three light taps on the glass. "That's our buddy, this time, right?" she asked Ferris. He took off to the kitchen. Ferris beat her to the door.

Holden smiled as Ferris lumbered to the door, smacking his face against the glass, trying to reach him. Cecilia followed close behind. With her body now healed from the attack, her litheness had returned.

Cecilia unlocked it and let Holden in. "No alarm set?" he asked.

She'd taken to not setting the alarm until they were headed to bed, in the hopes Holden would stop by.

He handed her a case of Mountain Dew. "Figured you must be getting low."

"Must have made your *stealth* dash here harder," she said, as she opened the case.

"No, but you might not want to open one of those just yet. They may have gotten a little jostled." He mimicked an explosion and Cecilia laughed. She placed the full case into the refrigerator.

Ferris tapped Holden's leg. He patted him on his head and went over to his biscuit jar. Ferris sat, took a treat from him, and ran to his bed.

Holden sat at the kitchen island. Cecilia slid him a soda.

"Cheers," he said, holding his can up until she did the same. "It must be hard living here."

It was, for many reasons. But Cecilia wouldn't admit that. "I really don't have a choice," she answered, pointing to the ankle monitor.

"No, I meant before the attack, living in this town, Joe's town, after he died. It's hard to be an outsider here."

She laughed. "And what would you know about that?"

"I haven't always lived here," he answered, surprised she didn't know. "It's been...ten years. Moved here after college."

Cecilia wondered if that's why they connected. Two outsiders in a small town. Their mutual love of Mountain Dew could not be their only bond.

"Where would I go?" she asked.

"Anywhere. You work from home. You could live anywhere and still make a living."

Cecilia nodded agreement. "But...this is where we lived. This is where I lived." She took a sip of soda and stared at the can. "I don't remember life before him. I...I don't know how to live without him."

"So you stay here?" Holden asked.

"Yep." She stared at her half empty soda. "But I'm going to have to find a way to live without him. Because he's not coming back."

"When this is all over, do you think you'll stay?" he asked.

Cecilia was struggling to make it through each day

after Joey's death. It had been worse since the attack and subsequent arrest. She couldn't think about tomorrow, never mind what happened after the trial. It was one day at a time while under house arrest.

"It might not be my choice whether I stay or go." Smiling, Holden looked up at her, mistaking her meaning. "A conviction would force me to stay here or wherever you imprison someone."

"Oh, right." He shook his head. "They can't convict you."

Cecilia wanted to agree with him but couldn't. "Did you think it would get this far?"

He hadn't. All of this had gone much further than he expected.

"Why are you asking if I'll stay?" she asked.

"Because...I hope you do."

CHAPTER 31

MOST PEOPLE ARE habitual. In a small town, a good police officer can easily figure out a resident's habits. The time they usually leave for work, where they get gas, where they get coffee. It took Vinnie only a day to figure out Clayton Hindel's.

Vinnie arrived at Glinton's convenience store five minutes before Clayton arrived. Vinnie was pouring milk into his coffee when Clayton reached for the jumbo cup to pour himself a coffee.

"How are you, sir?" Vinnie asked.

Not a morning person, Clayton mumbled "fine."

Vinnie leaned in and asked, "You still working on the Chandler murder trial?"

This perked Clayton up. His association with Cecilia made him a popular figure in town. "Oh no, that's all Sewell."

"Oh," Vinnie replied. He stirred his coffee. "Got your hands full with Chandler Construction, right?"

"No more than any of my other clients," Clayton answered, while adding sugar to his coffee.

Vinnie leaned against the counter and sipped his coffee. "I'm surprised Mrs. Chandler still runs it. You'd think someone in Mr. Chandler's family would take over. Isn't there anyone else? A sister or a brother?"

"Joey had one sister, Brittany. She married a man from Covington." He added milk and stirred his morning caffeine boost.

"Oh, the big guy, right? I saw them at the funeral. He looks like a bully."

Finished with fixing his coffee, Clayton looked at Vinnie. "Ha, that's for sure. He tried to get rid of her after Joey died. That woman can hold her own."

Vinnie laughed. "I think the whole world knows that now." Clayton didn't join in and Vinnie stopped laughing. "Anything recent from Jeremiah? You'd think he'd try a hostile takeover now?"

He nodded agreement. "Cecilia was just saying that. But we've been fortunate. He's been real quiet."

They walked up to the counter and Vinnie paid for the lawyer's coffee. They parted and Vinnie knew his next stop.

Guilt was the only motive to keep a man like Jeremiah quiet.

After a quick Facebook check, he headed a county over and was waiting for Jeremiah when he left work.

"Mr. Coleman?" Vinnie asked. Jeremiah nodded. "We have a few questions for you."

"Me? Why?" Jeremiah's eyes darted to look anywhere but at Pugliese.

"It's about the murder of Robert Gabbert," he explained.

"Me?" he asked again, looking around and checking to see if any of his co-workers could hear. "Why do you want to talk to me?"

"We're interviewing anyone who knows Cecilia Chandler, in preparation for the trial."

Relieved, he took a deep breath. "Oh, sure."

"Just follow me to the station. Won't take long."

Vinnie smiled as he watched Jeremiah, at ease, go to his car and follow Vinnie to the station. Part of him would have liked to have Jeremiah sweat it out in the patrol car's backseat in the twenty-minute ride, worrying about what they knew about him and Gabbert. But he could refuse to cooperate. Vinnie had no leverage. Better for Vinnie to hit him with his relationship with Gabbert when he wasn't expecting it.

If Vinnie was right.

PUGLIESE ESCORTED JEREMIAH into an interview room. He put a file on the desk and pointed Jeremiah to a chair. He signaled another officer from the doorway. "Monty, can you get the Chief? Ask him to go into the viewing room."

She peeked into the room. "Who's that? What's going on?"

"Just go get the Chief," he ordered. He had no seniority over her and he was surprised she went.

Pugliese left the interview room door open. He wanted Jeremiah to feel free to leave. "Thanks again for coming in. So you're married to Joe Chandler's sister?"

"Yes. I still don't understand why I'm here."

"We don't want any surprises at trial. We want to know all we can about Mrs. Chandler."

Jeremiah nodded. Vinnie leaned in and asked, "You think if she goes to jail you'll get the business?"

"Really?" he asked. He smiled at the prospect of getting what he wanted.

"I'm surprised you haven't tried to get the business already," Pugliese commented.

"We've been trying to keep our distance from her," Jeremiah explained. "We don't want people to know we're related."

Owens entered the observation room with the female officer. "What is Pugliese doing?"

Monty shook her head, not taking her eyes off the interrogation.

In an effort to build more trust, Pugliese agreed. "Understandable that you'd want to keep your distance from Mrs. Chandler."

"Oh no," the Chief mumbled.

Pugliese opened the folder and readied his pen over the blank paper. "How well did you know Bobby?" Pugliese asked.

"What?" Jeremiah responded.

Both officers noticed he didn't ask who. The news referred to him as Robert Gabbert. Only people who knew him called him Bobby.

"Bobby Gabbert," Pugliese clarified. "The man

who was murdered. How well did you know him?"

"I never said I knew him." Jeremiah glanced at the open door.

"That's funny." Pugliese took a page from deeper in the file. He looked at the second page and dragged his finger halfway down the page. "Because your name is in his contact list on his cell phone."

Jeremiah slammed his hands on the desk. "Son of a—"

"You've got to be kidding me," the Chief mumbled. How could the bluff have worked?

"Look, I never told the kid to hurt her." He ran his hands over his shaved head. "Jeez, I only wanted him to scare her."

Pugliese turned to the two-way mirror and looked at where he expected Owens would be. He winked.

Jeremiah held his head in his hands. "Brittany's going to kill me. She told me not to do it."

"So your wife was in on the plan too?" Pugliese asked.

"No, it wasn't a plan. I thought if she got scared living in that house by herself she'd want to go back to the city. She'd leave. Like she should have done months ago."

Pugliese slid him a legal pad and told him to write down his story.

"What am I going to be charged with?" Jeremiah asked.

"I don't know. But you've seen the prosecutor on the news. He does like to go for the max, doesn't he?"

Pugliese answered, before leaving the room.

He strutted into the observation room. "Aren't you going to congratulate me?" he asked Owens.

"For what?" Owens answered. "Why are you doing this? Do you think Briscoe is going to drop the charges?"

"Oh no. Huh...I didn't think about that. I still think she's guilty." Eyebrows furrowed, he was deep in thought, until he remembered his motivation, which had nothing to do with Cecilia. "I wanted to prove I'm right. She wasn't his typical victim. Never thought about the effect on the case."

"I'll tell you what you should be thinking about, Briscoe." Owens looked back at the interrogation room. Jeremiah was slowly writing on the legal pad. "Briscoe is going to be furious."

As HOLDEN PARKED his car, he reminded himself he shouldn't be here. He got out of the car, took a quick glimpse around to ensure he was alone, and hopped the fence.

He flipped his headlamp on and slinked through the yard to the patio.

Ferris was waiting at the door when he tapped on the glass. Cecilia handed him a Mountain Dew when she opened the door. He wondered if she had been waiting for him too.

"It's hard work being that stealth," she said.

He nodded agreement and took a sip of the soda. He froze as he was slipping his backpack off when she reached for him. For his cheek, for his lips, he didn't know. Instead, she reached toward his forehead and flipped the headlamp off. "You don't have to be stealth in here."

"Oh, yeah," he agreed and removed the headlamp. He put it in the backpack and pulled out a bag of Doritos.

"Doritos?" she asked.

"I thought hackers liked snacks like this."

"One, I'm not a hacker. I am a computer genius. Two, I don't even think that is a stereotype anyone has. All that cheesy stuff would get on my computer." Before he could fear she was really angry, she smiled. "Should I have donuts here for your next visit?"

Relieved she wasn't mad, and that she expected another visit, Holden sat on his usual stool. Ferris sat next to him. Holden rubbed behind his ears and Ferris leaned into his leg.

"You'd think you didn't get any attention all day," Cecilia told Ferris. "Between me and the defense team, someone is always petting him, or throwing a toy for him, or giving him a treat." Ferris barked at the word "treat."

Holden got up and reached for the biscuit jar. Ferris sat, his tail brushing against a stool, as Holden gave him the treat. "He's got you trained well," Cecilia commented.

The ding on an incoming email came from the

office. Cecilia got up to check. "Looks like someone has you trained too," he said.

She smirked at him and he followed her into the office. He'd been in here before, the night of the attack, but he hadn't noticed the framed photos on the desk. He looked at them. Cecilia and Joey. Jeremiah and his wife.

"That's my in-laws," she said.

"I'm surprised you keep their photos."

She'd kept everything the way Joey had left it.

"They look nice, don't they?" she asked. They did but they both knew they weren't. Holden stared at Jeremiah and wondered how someone could be that greedy. A career in law enforcement should have parted him from his naivety by now.

She caught him staring at the wedding photo. "You know Brittany?"

"No," he answered, thankful she hadn't asked about Jeremiah.

He couldn't tell her about Jeremiah. It wouldn't help her cause. It would only cause her more pain.

"I tried reaching out to Brittany a few times after her father died. That's what I thought I should do. I thought I could help. I know it's hard to lose a parent." She looked at Holden to confirm. "But she wanted nothing to do with me. Never even returned the calls, emails, cards."

"Joey doesn't have any other siblings?"

"No. Just Brittany." She stared at their wedding photo. "Joey said they liked me. They seemed happy with me when Joey first brought me around. I could fix their computers or set up their televisions or WiFi." She looked up at Holden and shrugged. "Now, they'd get rid of me if they could."

She didn't know how true that was.

CHAPTER 32

"**W**HAT ARE YOU doing here?" Owens asked, when he pulled into his parking spot at the station.

Briscoe was illegally parked in the fire zone, next to his spot. Owens fought the urge to give him a ticket. He got out of his car and headed into the station.

"We need to keep this quiet," Briscoe demanded.

"And what is 'this'?" Owens asked.

"You know darn well what this is." He leaned in and whispered, "Coleman."

Owens had no idea how he could have found out so soon. He thought he'd at least have the morning to figure out a plan. To deal with Coleman and Briscoe.

"You arrested him. Did you think I wouldn't find out?" Briscoe asked.

"I didn't arrest him." Because I didn't know what to charge him with, Owens didn't add. "We only took his statement."

"Don't arrest him," Briscoe ordered.

"Don't?" Owens asked.

A pair of officers walked past. Owens waved a greeting. Briscoe waited to answer until they were out of earshot.

"You heard me!" he shouted. Briscoe held his tongue until another officer walked past. He lowered his voice before adding, "I don't want the media finding out about Coleman."

"They're going to find out about him. You know that," Owens said. He paused, waiting for Briscoe to argue. He didn't, so he continued. "We have to do something with him. What he did was wrong. It's a crime."

More people were coming and going from the station. Briscoe took Owens by the elbow and directed him to the front of his car, far enough away from prying ears. Owens stood still and glared at him.

"I know that," Briscoe admitted. His conciliatory statement prompted Owens to move out of bystanders' earshot. "Just not yet. Bury it for a while. Misfile the paperwork. Wait until the trial is over and we'll do something. Maybe the media won't find out. If they do, we'll say small town station overwhelmed with all the press in town."

Owens didn't like his continual use of "we." Coleman was not their problem. He was Briscoe's problem. "How about I write the headline? How about small town prosecutor realizing he shouldn't have arrested a woman for protecting herself?"

"I'm not having this argument with you again."

Owens stepped toward Briscoe and looked down at him. "And now he's too scared to back down."

Briscoe had never won a physical fight in his life.

Not even to his younger brother. He knew he would never win one against the police chief. Plus, an altercation between the prosecutor and police chief would make any town's paper.

"Owens, calm down." Briscoe stepped back and leaned against the car. "I don't want Sewell finding out about this."

Owens stepped back as well and leaned against the building. "Don't you have to tell the defense?"

"I have to tell them about anything related to this crime," Briscoe conceded.

"And you don't think this is?" Owens asked.

Briscoe shook his head and answered, "No," without hesitation.

Owens threw his hands in the air. "It's the reason Gabbert was there."

Briscoe motioned for him to calm down. "It doesn't matter why he was there," he explained. Owens shook his head and headed into work before Briscoe continued, "She killed him. It's a murder trial. That's all the jury needs to know." He got back in his car. "And get the autopsy report. Today!" he shouted as he drove away.

CHIEF HOLDEN OWENS walked into the morgue. "I'm here for the paperwork on Gabbert, Robert." The young man at the front desk looked up with a blank look on his face. It had been a trying twenty-four hours, except for his short visit with Cecilia. He wanted to retrieve the file quickly and drop it off at Marcy's desk. "The shooting victim," he clarified.

"Oh, the young dude." The clerk squinted and tapped a few keys on his computer. "Doc cut him up yesterday."

"Yes, I know," Owens responded. His patience was waning. "Can you get me the paperwork please?"

He made a phone call and a few moments later a woman in green scrubs and a white lab coat came out.

"I'm Dr. Landry," she introduced herself. She held her hand out to shake his hand. Owens hesitated, knowing where that hand had been. "I performed the Gabbert autopsy."

"Chief Owens," he said, holding out his hand. He tried not to cringe when he shook her ice-cold hand.

"Sorry it took so long. I couldn't get here before this." She should be apologizing to the Gabbert family not him, Owens thought, for delaying the funeral. "Follow me," she said before turning to go back where she had come from.

When she turned, he squirted some hand sanitizer from the bottle on the desk and scrubbed his hands furiously. "Why?" he called out. "I just need the report."

Dr. Landry turned and looked at him. He was still rubbing the hand sanitizer in. "You do know I wash my hands after an autopsy, right?"

"Of course..." he answered.

She continued before he could feign an excuse for

the sanitizer. "Usually the detective in charge wants a full explanation. I like to do that over the body."

With the hand sanitizer worked in, he didn't know what to do with his hands. He crossed them over his chest. "I'm the chief of police, not a detective." He told her again, "I just need the report."

"Well, send the detective over and we'll go through my findings."

"There is no detective assigned," Holden explained. "We already arrested the shooter."

She removed her glasses and looked at him closely. "I think you would find it helpful. Are you sure you don't want to go over the body with me?"

"I do not." Owens had seen Gabbert enough times in life, always in a bad situation. He didn't need to add dead on a slab to the list.

"Oh, I'd like to know," Pugliese announced as he entered.

"What are you doing here, Pugliese?" Owens asked. He checked his watch. He wasn't on duty yet.

"I'm dating a nurse. I came to see her before my shift. I heard you were down here with the dead doc."

"Forensic pathologist," Dr. Landry corrected him.

"Yes, ma'am." Pugliese grabbed some gloves from a box and put them on, snapping them at the wrists "Can we go back now?"

Glad to have someone to go over the body with, Dr. Landry went through the door. "Okay, follow me."

She handed Owens a pair of gloves and each of

them a mask. They put them on. Owens was glad the mask would cover Pugliese's smile and his own disgust.

She pulled open one of the silver compartments and pulled out Robert Gabbert's dead body.

"Eighteen-year-old man. Manner of death: shot to the head." She pointed to the gunshot wound as if they needed direction. "No other abnormalities. I'm still waiting for the toxicology screen. That'll take a week or two. I doubt that will affect your case."

Owens stared at the dead body. Other than the autopsy incisions, and the body being naked, Gabbert looked no different than he did when Owens had arrived on the scene in Cecilia's back yard. He had no idea why Dr. Landry forced them to come back into the lab. He only needed the file and he was still waiting for that.

Dr. Landry looked up from the corpse. "That was some shot. You have a marksman on your hands."

Owens shook his head. "Not even close."

CHAPTER 33

CECILIA CLAIMED JJ'S, and Joey's, office as her own. It was her refuge while the defense team worked. Her old desk sat barren in the corner. She considered removing it from the house. As she waited for Clayton's arrival, she noted the large antique mahogany desk otherwise remained the same. The only difference was her laptop now lay on it.

Ferris adjusted to the change and sat at her feet, same as he always did in the office.

Clayton arrived, extra-large coffee in hand, and they held their regular meeting on Chandler Construction without incident. Clayton made to leave but Cecilia stopped him.

"Do you know the prosecutor? Briscoe?" she asked.

"Seen him at legal events. But don't know him personally," he answered, still organizing his paperwork.

"Joey have any trouble with him?" she asked. Clayton shook his head. "JJ? Mr. Chandler," she corrected herself.

"No." He put the paperwork in his briefcase and looked up at Cecilia. "Why?"

She shrugged. "I just don't understand. Why the push for this trial? I wondered if it was a personal vendetta against the Chandlers."

"You watch too many movies," Clayton told her.

She ignored him. "I've lived here a couple years. I don't remember there ever being a murder trial here before."

He put his coat on. "There has never been a murder here."

She stared at Clayton, fearing this was what all the residents thought. That she had murdered the intruder. "Okay, see you later," she dismissed him.

Her fingers tapped her laptop's keys. For the first time, she googled something related to the trial, Daniel Briscoe. She was not a hacker. She would only look in public files, as tempting as it was to go where she wasn't legally allowed to go. But she was in enough trouble. She didn't need to add hacking to her list of crimes.

She had one motivation. The more she knew about her enemy the better, she thought.

She dismissed the articles on anything related to her trial, anything dated after the incident. She perused all the articles on his previous cases and trials. Most of them ended in plea bargains. Nothing pointed to a vendetta against the Chandlers.

She checked out his college paper and read any articles where he was mentioned. There was nothing related to any of the Chandlers or her. She regressed through his life until she found what she needed. A vendetta of sorts.

Sometimes you just have to know where to look.

CHAPTER 34

"HOW ARE YOU dealing with the house arrest?" Holden asked, once settled on his barstool, soda in hand.

Cecilia shrugged. "Not real different from life before the arrest. Not since Joey died anyway. I didn't leave the house much since the funeral. I work online. I shop online. Anything I need I have delivered." Ferris walked back to Cecilia and she patted him on the head. "Except Ferris's walks. Can't do that now. But he hasn't been in the mood. I let him run around the yard for exercise. Seems to appease him." She rubbed his neck before he plodded off for a toy. "The daily routine is the same. Wake up, feed Ferris, work, feed Ferris, go to sleep. Repeat."

"You're still working?" he asked.

"Of course. Why wouldn't I?" She spun her soda around in her hand.

"No negative repercussions on your job after the arrest? With all this media attention?"

She shook her head no. "I work online. I'm an independent contractor. None of my clients could pick me out of a lineup." She smiled at her joke but Holden didn't. "Come on, that was funny! A little arrestee humor? 'Pick me out of a lineup.' Get it?"

Holden didn't smile at the joke, but he did smile at Cecilia. He loved Cecilia's smile but he rarely saw it. He could only hope he'd see more of it in the future.

"But your name? Cecilia Chandler. It's been on every news program, local and national. No one's even asked?"

"I had the business before I got married. It's under my maiden name, Corrigan. It's the beauty of working online. They don't know when times are bad. The clients didn't know when I got married, when I was widowed, when I was arrested. In that world, I can still be alright. Not fighting to stay out of jail. Not fighting for my life. I can still be CeCe."

"CeCe," Holden said.

"Yep, just CeCe." She missed being called CeCe. Joey always called her it. As did her friends and sorority sisters. Since moving to Folley, it was only Joey calling her CeCe. "You can call me CeCe. That's what my friends do." She needed to change the subject before tears started to form. "But the ankle monitor itself. That's an annoyance."

She reached down and pointed to the red skin around the ankle monitor. "I'm trying not to scratch it but the skin is so dry. I think I'm scratching it when I'm sleeping." Her hand hovered over the red skin as she considered scratching the itch. The impulse to claw at her leg becoming overwhelming, she pulled her hand back and crossed her arms firmly across her chest. "I wish I could soak it and put some lotion on it. But they said I can't get it wet." She looked down at the leg, the urge to scratch the red skin her only thought. She looked away from the leg, hoping to push the itchiness out of her mind. Looking at Holden, she added, "I'm taking a bath with my leg hanging out of the tub. I must look ridiculous."

Holden tried not to picture Cecilia, naked in the tub, but it was too late. He'd already seen her half naked while taking the photos of her bruised body. He often found himself seeing those images in his mind. This image, of a now healed Cecilia's naked body, would be much harder to push aside.

"Do you have any alcohol?" he asked.

She briefly wondered if it was a test. "No. That's part of the bail restrictions. No alcohol in the house."

He smiled. "No, I meant rubbing alcohol."

"Oh, okay." She got up and went to the master bathroom. Ferris followed her. In the medicine cabinet, she collected the bottle of rubbing alcohol and some gauze pads. She returned to find Holden, gazing out the sliding glass door into the dark backyard.

"Is this what you wanted?" she asked.

He shook the image of her naked body in the tub out of his head when she spoke.

What he wanted was her naked in the tub, with him joining her. He settled for touching her in a different way.

Holden cleared his throat and answered, "Yep. Just sit." Holding out his hands, she handed him the bottle and gauze. He knelt on the floor as she sat on

191

the stool. Ferris ran over and licked his face. Not the kiss he was dreaming of, but the only one he'd be getting tonight.

He took her foot and placed it on his knee. He gently cleansed the irritated skin around and under the ankle monitor. He flossed the gauze between the monitor and her skin and ran it around her ankle. He held her calf softly as he inspected the skin. His mouth inches from her skin he fought the urge to kiss her.

She softly moaned. "That feels so much better. Thank you."

Afraid of what he might do next, he said, "I better go," and shot up.

"Okay, thanks," she yelled out as he closed the sliding door.

She marveled at the leg, which was for the first time in weeks not itchy. She didn't notice the abrupt departure.

THE BEEPING ON his phone disturbed Vinnie from his late-night snack, a cup of green tea and a banana. It wasn't the beep of an incoming text or voicemail. It wasn't a beep he recognized at all.

He picked up the phone with his left hand, still holding the banana in his right. Unconsciously, his hands clenched, causing the banana to squirt out onto his lap.

"Crap!" he exclaimed in response to the mess and

the phone's alert.

He got on the patrol car's radio with his banana-smeared hand. "Get to Chandler's now!"

Vinnie flipped on his lights and sirens and threw the car into drive. Tires squealing, he pulled out of Glinton's convenience store's parking lot and sped toward Cecilia's home.

As he pulled onto Cecilia's street, he turned off the sirens and lights for a stealthy approach. His fellow officer, driving in from the opposite direction, followed suit and they both pulled up in front of Cecilia's. Each jumped out of their car, leaving the car door open.

"You really think—" Officer Rango started to ask.

"Tech doesn't lie, my friend," he answered, pointing to his phone. Pugliese could not hide his smile.

Another police car pulled up as Pugliese and Rango approached the front door, guns drawn. The house looked the same as the other nights Pugliese had driven by. He had made a habit of driving by, at least twice, each shift he was assigned. Just to make sure. He checked the app on his phone regularly, even when he wasn't working. Some would say he was obsessed. Pugliese would say dedicated. He knew computer-savvy Chandler would do this. She'd waited until the media trucks had left plus a little more time. He wasn't surprised she had waited until everyone else had put the case in the back of their minds.

Pugliese banged on the door. He signaled for the third officer to go around back. "Make sure the car is in the garage." Officer Landings nodded understanding and did as he was ordered.

"Police! Open up!" Pugliese yelled as he banged on the door again.

Cecilia was still sitting in the kitchen, enjoying the rest of her soda and marveling at the itch-free leg, when she heard the banging. Ferris and Cecilia looked at each other. They got up before the second knocking. Before she could get to the door and ask who it was, the door flew open.

She screamed at the sight of the two officers, with their guns drawn.

"Hands up!" Pugliese ordered.

"What's the—" Cecilia started to ask.

"Shut up!" Pugliese ordered. "Rango, clear the house. Make sure she's alone." Gun leading the way, Rango walked up the stairs and checked each of the rooms.

Landings came in the front door, gun holstered. "Car's still there, Pugliese. Truck too."

"Clear the first floor," Pugliese ordered Landings. He nodded understanding, pulled out his gun, and started walking through the first floor.

Cecilia stood as still as she could, hands in the air. She could feel Ferris's shaking body on her leg. Her eyes the only part of her that moved. "What's going on?" she asked.

"Down!" Pugliese ordered. Cecilia knelt down, hands still in the air, and Ferris laid next to her, his shaking intensifying.

"I—" she started to speak again but Pugliese interrupted.

"Shut up! I already told you!"

Cecilia pursed her lips and remained quiet. She heard someone coming up the porch and looked over Pugliese's shoulder. She smiled when she saw Holden. As he entered, he tipped his hat at Cecilia. "Mrs. Chandler."

Ferris, happy to see a friend, jumped up from Cecilia's side and ran to Holden. Ferris jumped on him, expecting the usual petting. "Down, boy," Holden directed him. Surprised by the sharp tone, Ferris sat.

"What seems to be the problem, Pugliese?" the chief asked.

Pugliese took a few steps back, in order to see Owens. His gun remaining trained on Cecilia. "What are you doing here, Chief?"

"Heard on the radio there was a problem at the Chandler house. Can you explain?"

"Mrs. Chandler here has been removing her ankle monitor."

Holden stepped to the side to look at Cecilia's ankle. "Looks like it's still on, Pugliese."

Holden held his hand out to Cecilia to help her up. "Don't touch the suspect, sir!" Pugliese yelled.

"Put the gun away," Holden ordered him. Rango and Landings returned from the inspection of the house, shaking their heads at Pugliese. "Put your guns away too," Holden ordered.

"What'd you find?" Pugliese barked.

"Nothing," answered Rango, after he holstered his gun. "House is clear."

Pugliese looked to Landings, hoping for better news. "Nothing but two open sodas in the kitchen."

She glanced at Holden before answering. To Holden, it felt like minutes passed. To the others, just seconds. "I like my Mountain Dew. Is that a crime?"

"Get back on patrol," Owens instructed the two officers. They did so, both giving Pugliese a stern look for getting them in trouble with the Chief.

"She disarmed the ankle monitor, Chief." He pointed to the monitor, which was untouched. "Probably using some tech stuff so she can escape the jurisdiction."

"Mrs. Chandler," Holden said again, his hand still held out. She took it and stood.

She looked down at the ankle monitor. "I'm not a hacker, Officer."

"Can you please have a seat, Mrs. Chandler?" Holden pointed to the kitchen.

Cecilia noted the use of her full name again. "Yes, Chief Owens." She did little to hide her annoyance.

They walked into the kitchen and she sat on the same stool she had when he cleaned her skin. The bottle of rubbing alcohol and used gauze remained on the kitchen counter.

Ferris tapped his leg, and Holden gave him a biscuit from his treat jar. "Have you been cleaning around the monitor?" he asked.

Cecilia always knew Holden snuck in her back

door for a reason but she had never put much thought into it. She was glad for the company, especially his company. The first night, he had said it was so the media wouldn't see him. But the media trucks had left weeks ago and he still snuck in the back door. As he stood in front of her, hiding their friendship from his co-workers, she was hurt.

He touched her leg softly, as he did before. She tried to ignore his gentle touch as he inspected her leg. "Skin's pretty irritated. Try to be more careful next time you're cleaning the skin."

She nodded but wouldn't look at him. Holden turned to find Pugliese scowling at the soda cans. Only one had lipstick on it. "Is the monitor back online?" Holden asked.

Pugliese pulled out his phone and opened the app. The monitor was back online.

"Yes. But she was fiddling with it, sir."

"She was cleaning irritated skin." Holden straightened up and tried to catch Cecilia's eye. She wouldn't look at him. "We apologize for the disturbance," he told Cecilia as he headed to the door. Pugliese huffed. Holden pushed Pugliese toward the front door. He inspected the kicked-in door and added, "Someone will be out tomorrow to fix the door."

Cecilia closed the door without speaking. Her only friend in this town didn't want anyone to know.

"Really?" Holden said to Pugliese, pointing to the door. "Was that necessary?"

"I thought she was trying to run."

"And where is she going to go? No passport. Her face has been all over the news. This isn't some serial killer, some lady who's a danger to society."

Holden escorted Pugliese to his patrol car. The other patrol cars were gone. The street remained appropriately quiet for this time of night. Holden was thankful the officers had made a quiet approach. He did not want to face the neighbors and have to explain the events.

"That dog sure seems to like you, sir." Pugliese looked at the Chandler home. "Strange for a dog that was attacked by an intruder fairly recently."

"We've been in the house before, Pugliese."

"He didn't greet me like he did you, didn't ask me for a treat."

"I didn't have a gun pointed at him and his owner," Owens reminded him.

Pugliese agreed. But there was something about the encounter that bothered him.

CHAPTER 35

T HE NEXT MORNING, Holden headed to his car and got out his tool kit. He waved at Pugliese as he was headed into the station.

"Where are you going?" Vinnie asked as Holden was getting in his patrol car.

"Going to fix Mrs. Chandler's door." He paused, before getting into the car. "Unless you want to do it?"

"I'm sure she could get it fixed."

"Yeah, and who in this town would take her calls?" Holden didn't wait for an answer, got in the car, and drove away.

"She owns a construction company, for goodness sake!" Vinnie yelled after him.

TOOLBOX IN HAND, he rang Cecilia's doorbell. The door stood slightly askew. He regretted not returning last night to fix it. He rang the bell again. He heard movement behind the door and Cecilia opened the door. "Hello, Chief Owens, how can I help you?"

Holden noted her frosty tone. "Good morning. I

came to fix the door."

"Oh, I figured it was official business with you coming to the front door and all." Her tone was not warming up.

"CeCe—"

"Oh, it's CeCe now, is it? Now that all your co-workers are gone."

"I'm sorry—" he started.

"Oh stop. You might have mentioned you were the one who at least told me I could clean the ankle monitor like that. They busted in here, guns out. It was terrifying."

"CeCe—"

"They're not as *stealth* as you are. Look at the door. He kicked it down!" She stepped back and pointed to a desk. "I had to put this against the door to keep it up last night."

"I know but I couldn't—"

"Yeah, I get you can't tell them you come over to see public enemy number one. But to treat me like a stranger, that was...cold. You know, Wyatt wouldn't be so thrilled to find out I've been talking to you without him present as my counsel. But I wouldn't pretend I didn't know you."

"CeCe—" Holden wanted to explain. But how?

"Shut up, he said to me. Twice in my own home. I'm treated like a criminal in my own home!" She looked down at the ankle monitor. "I am a prisoner in my own home because some dumb kid attacked me and Ferris in my own home!"

At the sound of his name, Ferris came in running from the backyard. He jumped for Holden, missing him by two inches, to greet him. His second try was successful.

"Ferris!" she rebuked. "Sit." He quickly obeyed. His tail tapped the ground while he waited to be released from the sit command. "Don't play with him. He's the enemy."

"I'm not the enemy, CeCe," he pleaded. Trying to change the subject, and return them to their pleasant relationship, he asked. "How's the ankle?"

"It feels much better, thank you!" she shouted at him as she walked away.

"HOW'S MRS. CHANDLER?" Vinnie asked when Holden returned to the station's parking lot.

"Pissed off."

"Well, you seem to have that effect on people today. Briscoe's looking for you."

Holden held his profanity until returning to his patrol car. His anger had not evaporated in the short drive to the prosecutor's office.

The chief walked into the office, slamming the door against the wall. Startled by his quick arrival and the door slam, Marcy smeared her lipstick across her face. Holden did not care.

He walked into Briscoe's office, finding him filling out some paperwork.

"Now what?" Holden asked.

"How are you, Chief?" Briscoe asked when he looked up. He looked happy. Owens didn't like meeting with an angry Briscoe, but a happy one was far more unsettling.

"What do you want, Briscoe?"

Briscoe returned to completing the paperwork. "I heard there was an incident at the Chandler house."

"It's under control."

"For now," Briscoe responded. Owens glared at Briscoe. "Do we need to revoke her bail?"

"No."

He signed his name at the bottom of a form and waved it at Owens. "I think we need to revoke her bail."

"Then why did you ask?"

"Because I need you with me." He got up and put on his jacket. He looked in the mirror, straightened his tie, and ran his hand through his hair. "Got to look good for the cameras."

"There's no cameras today." He was thankful the media had missed last night's events. He didn't want to have to answer the media's questions on the incident.

"Oh, there will be," Briscoe assured him.

"I think this is a mistake," Owens warned as they exited his office.

Marcy was still scrubbing the lipstick off of her face. Neither man noticed.

"All I need you to do, Owens, is tell the judge

what happened last night."

"Nothing happened," he tried to explain. "It was a misunderstanding."

"Bull," Briscoe spat.

They walked the rest of the way to the judge's chambers in silence. Sewell was sitting outside the office. His glare at Briscoe was as intimidating as Owens's. Briscoe didn't notice.

"What's going on?" Sewell asked.

"Where's Ms. Chandler?" Briscoe said, looking up and down the hallway.

"She's home. Where else would she be?" Sewell asked.

"Not for long," Briscoe answered. He smiled.

Disturbed by Briscoe's grin, Sewell turned to Michael. "Go get Cecilia."

Pulling up his contact list, Michael called Cecilia and told her to be court ready in five minutes. She asked why but Michael had already hung up. Michael ran to their rental car.

The lawyers and police chief were called into Judge Lowe's chambers.

"Aren't we missing someone?" the judge asked.

"She's on her way, Your Honor." Sewell looked at Briscoe and Owens. "My assistant went to get her."

Judge Lowe looked at Briscoe. "I'll give her ten minutes. If she's not here by then, we'll get started."

Holden leaned into Briscoe and whispered, "I really think we need to talk about this before you talk to the judge."

"No." Briscoe remained sitting, smile plastered across his face.

Sewell sat in another chair looking from Owens to Briscoe, trying to figure out what was going on.

With two minutes to spare, Michael and Cecilia ran into the judge's chambers.

Sewell rolled his eyes when he appraised Cecilia's attire. Holden smiled.

Cecilia's hair was pulled back in a ponytail. She was wearing black leggings, gray boat shoes, a T-shirt, and a blue blazer. When she caught the two men looking at her Beastie Boys To the 5 Boroughs concert T-shirt, she buttoned her blazer.

She wasn't fast enough.

"What's on your shirt, Ms. Chandler?" the judge asked.

She could feel Wyatt's glare. "It's a concert T-shirt, sir." She was overwhelmed knowing the four men were staring at her chest.

"The Five Boroughs?" he asked.

"Um...yes, New York."

With disdain, he said, "Oh...New York. Are you a fan?"

"The T-shirt was my husband's, sir. I apologize for not being properly dressed for you."

Wyatt nodded approval for her conciliatory tone.

"Oh...it's always the dead husband," Briscoe mumbled. "Can we get to the matter at hand please?"

"Get to it, Briscoe," Judge Lowe ordered him.

He stood, puffed out his chest, and told him, "Ms.

Chandler violated the conditions of her bail conditions and her house arrest last night."

"What?" Michael and Wyatt said in unison, while Cecilia was left speechless. They turned to Cecilia for explanation and she shook her head.

Holden hung his head.

Briscoe continued, "Last night, at eleven p.m., she left the confines of her home, triggering her ankle monitor's alarm."

"Your Honor—" Owens started.

Judge Lowe held his hand up. "Mr. Sewell, can you explain?"

"Can I have a moment with my client, Judge?" Sewell asked.

"No," the judge ruled. He pointed to Cecilia and signaled for her to step closer to him. She did as ordered. "Ms. Chandler, did you try to leave the jurisdiction last night?"

Cecilia looked from one man to the other, panicked, not knowing who to address.

"No," she answered, looking at the judge.

"Have you ever tried to leave the jurisdiction?" Judge Lowe asked.

Cecilia shook her head vehemently. "Not since you put the monitor on and ordered me not to."

Lastly, the judge asked, "Are you going to try to leave the jurisdiction?"

Relieved that her previous answers had met the judge's approval, she sighed before answering, "No."

Appeased with her answers, Judge Lowe looked at

Briscoe and Owens. "Who wants to explain to me why I am late for lunch at CB's Diner? If he runs out of the Sloppy Joes, someone is going to be in contempt!"

"Your Honor—" Briscoe started.

"Chief Owens, can you explain?" the judge asked.

"There seemed to be a malfunction of the ankle monitor last night. Setting off a false alarm. When my officers got to the Chandler residence, she was in her home."

"Malfunction?" Briscoe yelled. "Nonsen—"

Judge Lowe held up his hand. "And where was she when officers arrived?"

"The officers on scene reported she was in the house when they arrived. I arrived within ten minutes and she was in her foyer."

"Is this accurate, Ms. Chandler?"

"Yes, sir. My skin was irritated from the monitor." She swung her leg up and placed her foot on the judge's desk. Sewell closed his eyes at the offense. "I was trying to clean it. It's a little better now."

Judge Lowe inspected the area. "Okay, thank you, Ms. Chandler." He motioned for her to remove her foot from his desk. "Anything else you'd like to add?"

She looked at Owens. Both knew there was plenty that she could add. And cost two police officers their jobs. "No, sir. It appeared to be a misunderstanding."

Judge Lowe dismissed them all. Wyatt took Cecilia by her arm and guided her to a bench outside the office. "Nice outfit," he whispered.

"You gave me five minutes to get ready. You're lucky I'm wearing pants," she whispered back.

"Could you have told me it was a malfunction before I made an imbecile out of myself?" Briscoe said to Owens on their way out of the office.

"I tried," Owens answered through a clenched jaw.

Owens passed Wyatt and Cecilia seated on the bench. "Why didn't you tell me?" Wyatt asked her. "You have to tell me everything." She nodded understanding and avoided looking at the passing Holden.

Owens outpaced Briscoe and passed Michael down the hall, on his cell phone. "Calling in an order please...Sloppy Joe. Thanks."

Holden calmed down by the time he returned to the station, thankful Cecilia's bail had not been revoked. Sloppy Joe in hand, he headed to his office to have lunch. He passed Officer Pugliese.

"You owe Mrs. Chandler your job," he told him.

Pugliese huffed. "Please."

CHAPTER 36

PROMPTLY AT NINE, Cecilia opened the front door expecting to see her defense team. She only saw Wyatt. "Abigail needed another Starbucks run?" Cecilia asked when she let the lone Wyatt come in.

"A caffeinated Abigail is a happy Abigail."

Cecilia followed him to the defense team's office and she stood at the table while he unpacked his briefcase and flattened out his daily copy of the *Folley Press*. She usually went her own way after letting them in. He identified her hovering as a need to ask something.

"Why haven't you told them about Ferris? Why haven't you told the media I was protecting him?" she asked without prompting.

"Strategy."

"I...I'm not second-guessing you. I know you are a very experienced and skilled defense lawyer. I'm just thinking this would garner us support. There was that gorilla at the zoo a couple years ago. People went nuts when it was killed. I think animal lovers would support Ferris. That they'd support me for protecting him."

Cecilia thought public pressure might force Briscoe

to drop the charges.

Ferris plopped his head on the dining room table. Usually Cecilia would have scolded him for this. But she leaned down next to him and looked at him closely. "Come on, he's cute."

"I won't argue about that. Come here, Ferris." Wyatt nuzzled his ears. "We all know you're cute."

"But?" she asked.

"There's only one way to win this case and it's in the courtroom. We can't fight this case in the media."

"But—"

"Yes, I've used the media a few times. Held a few press conferences, for all my cases. Mainly to placate the media. I like to keep them appeased. In case I need them."

"But—"

"And I needed to use them to get Gabbert's juvenile record. I couldn't use it in court anyway. It looks a lot better when the media rips him to shreds than if I did it. It won't affect the trial but I think we're all glad it's out there."

"But..." She paused, expecting him to anticipate her question again and answer. He didn't and she continued. "...maybe Briscoe would give in to the pressure and drop the charges."

Wyatt nodded understanding. "I see what you're saying, but that's not Briscoe. He's not the hick country lawyer we all expect. He's quite shrewd. He graduated top of his class. I can see why he's hoping this case catapults his career. We've looked into him.

We've talked to area lawyers, co-workers, and classmates. If we cage him in, he'll strike back. Better to lull him to sleep. Let him think we're not going to use the dog issue."

"But you are?"

"Of course! If Ferris doesn't garner sympathy for you, I don't know what will!" He patted Ferris again, before Ferris ran off to find a toy. "I just have to wait for the right time." She nodded but wasn't convinced. "Trust me, Cecilia." She took a deep breath and tried to believe Wyatt was right.

She headed to the door so Wyatt could start his workday and she could start hers.

"If it makes you feel any better, I'm sure Briscoe's wondering why I haven't told the media yet either."

AFTER GETTING HER order, a double espresso, Abigail headed to the door and another long day at work. A familiar face caught her eye. "Hi, Dan," she said as she walked up to his table.

He took off his glasses and looked up from his tablet. "Hello, Ms. Hodson," Briscoe greeted her. He put his glasses back on and returned to reading the news on his tablet.

She sat down next to him and sipped her coffee. "There's still time, you know," she said.

"For what?" he asked, without looking at her.

"To drop the charges."

He put the tablet down. "Are you scared that your team can't win?"

She smiled. "No, we'll win. Wyatt will win. He always wins."

"Well, someone is bound to beat him and it's going to be me. I want to beat him."

"Don't we all," she said.

"Really?"

"You think I want to be his number two forever? One day I'll be on my own."

He nodded and took a closer look at her. He was surprised by her aspirations. He thought she was, and would always be, Sewell's lackey.

"You know we look into everything when we're preparing for trial." He nodded, not surprised. "Even things we know will never come up during the trial." He waited, knowing she wasn't done. "We look into everything."

"That doesn't scare me."

"It should," she said, in between sips.

"I looked into you too," he told her.

She laughed. "But we have better, and more, resources. What do you have, Marcy? Who is forty-one and still lives with her mother? And their three cats?" She expected a reaction from him. Outrage. Surprise. Anger. But he had no reaction. "I know why you don't like dogs," she revealed.

"I never said that," he said, returning to his reading.

"You don't need to. I know."

He noted her confidence but also her language. "Interesting, you said 'I know' not 'we know.'"

She smiled. Her research on him was accurate. It had surprised the defense team. Dan Briscoe was a formidable opponent.

Abigail asked one question before she got up to leave. "Is this what she would want you to do?"

WYATT WAS SCANNING the police's crime photos. It wasn't the volume of photos he was used to receiving in violent cases. But a small town like Folley wasn't used to a case, or a trial, of this magnitude. His eyes were starting to glaze over and his stomach growled. He knew he'd have to break for lunch soon. A mark caught his attention. He grabbed a magnifying glass and focused on the spot.

"Abigail, what does that look like to you?" he asked.

She got up and looked over his shoulder. She smiled. Wyatt didn't want her answer, only her reaction. "I'll send it off to the lab for examination."

The defense team broke for lunch and each was in a different part of her house. Ferris made a continual loop to each of them in hopes of getting a piece of their lunch. Or to clean up any crumb they dropped. Each was on their cell phones or tablets and would pat Ferris as he passed by.

In between projects herself, Cecilia also stopped

for lunch. She walked into her dining room. It had become defense team central. The table was littered with files. *Folley Press* copies were stacked on a side table. The floor was covered in filing boxes. They had commandeered a table from another room to hold a printer and scanner and a WiFi router. She barely recognized the room. Cecilia only came in when she was summoned.

"What's this?" she asked pointing to a folder marked 'R G'.

"Crime photos," Michael answered. "I don't think you should look at those."

Ignoring Michael, she flipped through the photos.

"So, this is him? Robert Gabbert." He looked so young and so dead. "What's that?" she asked, pointing to the mark in his forehead.

Michael looked over her shoulder. "That's the bullet mark."

"I only shot the gun one time. Just to scare him. How did I hit him in the head?"

"You're obviously some marksman." He took a bite of his sandwich. "All those hours at the gun range worked for you."

"Me? I went to a gun range once. With Joey." She thought for a moment. "That was over a year ago. I hadn't touched a gun between then and shooting him. I've only touched a gun twice in my life."

"Wyatt!" Michael yelled, his latest bite still in his mouth. "Say it again, Cecilia," he told her as Wyatt entered.

"I...I don't know how I shot that"—she started to say 'kid' but Holden told her she could not think of him that way—"intruder in the head."

"About the gun range," Michael corrected her.

"I only went once," she told Wyatt.

Wyatt looked to Michael, who was smiling and had mayo on his lip. He turned his attention back to Cecilia. "But you've been paying a monthly membership."

"No I don't."

"The business account still has a monthly membership to the local gun range. Don't you use it?" Wyatt asked.

"No, of course not! I didn't even know I had one. I don't pay the business bills. Clayton handles all that."

"Get Clayton on the phone," Wyatt directed Michael. "And find the gun range owner. And anyone who works at that gun range."

"Well, it was the luckiest—" Michael started.

"Or unluckiest shot," Wyatt corrected him, "anyone has ever hit."

CHAPTER 37

CECILIA STOOD AT the open sliding glass door and watched the sunset. She missed the nights sitting on the deck with Joey, while Ferris ran around the yard. On cold nights, like this, Joey would pull her in close and wrap them up in a blanket. Despite those terrible metal patio chairs, he made it comfortable. At least in the dark, she couldn't see the hideous green.

Lost in her thoughts, ten minutes ticked away. A gust of wind brought her back to reality.

"Ferris," she called out. He'd been out for a while now, she realized. He hadn't run around the yard wild for months. Since Joey had died, his escapades in the yard—running after squirrels, jumping at butterflies, chasing after blowing leaves—had diminished. He had taken to running out, doing his business, and running back in. She couldn't think of one time since the attack that she had to call out for him to return to the house.

The last bit of light was gone from the horizon. She pulled her gray hoodie—Joey's gray hoodie—across her chest as she stepped out into the yard. She glanced down at the ankle monitor. They'd assured her that its boundaries were the boundaries of her yard. She hoped they were right, as she stepped onto the patio. She did not want a repeat performance of police officers with guns storming into her home.

Cecilia hadn't been out in the backyard since the attack. She'd let Ferris out the kitchen door, wait a few minutes for his return, and then close the door. The motion light flicked on as she stepped out onto the patio. She scanned the yard but didn't see Ferris. "Ferris," she called out again. She prepared to be tackled by the golden retriever, his usual response when called while outside. She waited motionless but heard and saw nothing.

Cecilia gasped as the backyard's light shut off and the yard was engulfed in darkness. "Ferris!" she screamed. Oh no, she thought, where could he have gone? "Ferris!"

She waved her arms in a panic and the backyard light flipped back on. She ran the perimeter of the yard, along the fencing, continually calling his name. She cursed Joey for not replacing the fencing like he had talked about. This was too low, too easy for Ferris to jump. But he had never escaped the yard before.

Cecilia made a second lap of the yard. Each call for him was becoming more urgent, more panicked. Breathless, she ran into the house to the front door and out into the front yard. She prayed she'd find him sitting by the front gate, wondering how he'd gotten there. She ran the perimeter of the fence and saw no sign of Ferris.

Cecilia glanced at her watch. How long had he been missing? Five minutes? Twenty? She didn't know. All she knew was that it was too long.

Cecilia grabbed her cell phone as she ran through the kitchen, wanting to scan the backyard again. It was still empty. She stared at the phone and tried to think who she could call. She scanned her contact list and stopped at the listing for the service that had microchipped Ferris.

She called and shouted, "I lost my dog!" when the operator answered.

"What, ma'am?"

"My dog, Ferris, he ran away. Well, he probably doesn't realize he's run away. I don't know. Just gone. He's not in the yard." She kept scanning the yard but there were no signs of Ferris. "Can you track him?"

"Track him?" the operator asked.

"Use the microchip to track him. To tell me where he is." She didn't know what she would do when they told her where he was. She couldn't leave the confines of her property. She'd figure that out once they told her where Ferris was. One problem at a time, she told herself.

"Ma'am, we don't do that."

"What?" Cecilia asked. She hoped she had misheard the woman.

"When's he's found, someone with a microchip reader scans him to get his microchip number. Then they input the number in the website and your name and details will come up."

Joey had handled the microchipping. She had never thought about it until Ferris was gone. Had he only put in his cell number? The office number? Had he put in the business number? They didn't have a home phone. She had no idea. Like their business and personal accounts, she should have updated Ferris's microchip account when Joey died.

"Ma'am? Once someone finds him and scans him, they'll see you as the owner and call you."

Cecilia was now thankful that no one knew that Ferris was the reason she shot at the intruder. Ferris could be the victim of vigilante justice if he got into the wrong hands.

In typical customer service fashion, the operator asked, "Have I answered all your questions today, ma'am?"

She hung up before mumbling, "No, you didn't answer all my questions. I still don't know where my Ferris is!"

Cecilia scrolled her contact list again. There was no one she could call. The vet was closed for the day and if someone brought Ferris in, they'd recognize him. She ran around the yard again, calling Ferris's name to no avail. She ran to the front yard in the hopes of seeing anything.

She quickly regretted that hope.

OFFICER VINNIE PUGLIESE was making his regular

patrol pass by the Chandler home. He was disappointed each shift, until today.

Pugliese saw Mrs. Chandler running around her front yard. At first he thought she was going to run out the gate; instead, she ran along its perimeter. He pulled up to the curb and got out. When Cecilia saw him, her eyes bulged. He could see the panic on her face and smiled. He knew he had caught her doing something she didn't want to be caught doing.

As a police officer, he learned to recognize that look.

Because he saw it so often.

Cecilia dropped to her knees in the yard and held her hands above her head. "Officer, I didn't leave my property. I swear. I haven't been cleaning the monitor either. I don't know why the alarm went off."

Vinnie walked through the gate. She remained on her knees and she was thankful his gun remained in its holster. She continued scanning the front yard but could see no signs of Ferris. Finally, with a moment of quiet, the loss of Ferris hit her. Tears welled in her eyes. With her hands above her head, she couldn't wipe the tears that ran down her face.

This wasn't what Vinnie had expected. Through her arrest, her booking, and arraignment, she had been stoic. No signs of emotion. Even when he had first arrived at the scene, there had been no tears. He had attributed that to shock.

"What's wrong, Mrs. Chandler?"

"Ferris is gone. He got loose," Cecilia explained.

She could see he didn't understand. "The dog, my dog, Ferris. He got out of the yard. I can't go after him because of the monitor and...and I don't know what to do."

Pugliese waved for her to put her hands down and she wiped the tears away. He walked over to her and held out his hand to help her up. "Okay, one more time, tell me what happened."

Cecilia wiped her face again and cleared her throat. "I let Ferris out into the backyard, to...you know...do his business. He's usually back in within a few minutes. But he didn't come back." She looked at her watch. "It's...been over thirty minutes, I think."

Pugliese looked around the front yard and surrounding area. There was no sign of Ferris or anyone else. "Do you think someone snatched him?"

"What?" she asked. He instantly regretted asking. "No...I thought he started chasing a squirrel or something." She looked around the front yard again. "Do you....do you think someone came in the yard and took him?"

She couldn't imagine standing at the door, watching the yard and not hearing someone in the area. But Holden had proved, many times, that someone could sneak into her yard without her having an inkling of it. Just a little stealth was all they needed.

Vinnie didn't want to remind her that she was not a popular person in town. She had killed a town resident. "Let's check the backyard again."

He followed her through the front door through

the kitchen to the backyard. The floodlight turned on when they stepped onto the patio. They both scanned the yard but saw nothing. "Okay, he's not here. Any place he might go?"

Cecilia shook her head no. "I can't think of any place."

Pugliese headed back to his patrol car. "I'll put a call out and we'll look for him."

"Wait," she said. "Um...you think maybe you shouldn't broadcast *my* dog is missing?"

He nodded his head. She was probably right. "I'll find him."

"Thank you," she called out, as he walked away.

Pugliese got back in the patrol car and debated where to go to look for the missing dog. He hoped no calls came over the radio. He didn't want to explain he was looking for a dog. Never mind her dog.

He drove down the rest of the block, seeing no golden retriever. He turned the car around. Vinnie had no idea how far a dog like that could get. He passed the Chandler house again and could hear Mrs. Chandler yelling for Ferris. He made a left at the end of the block onto a small side street that went to the local reservoir. A half mile up the road, Vinnie saw the golden retriever sitting at the end of the clearing.

Hoping not to spook him, Vinnie got out of the car and walked slowly over to Ferris. The dog noticed him but remained sitting. It looked like he was waiting for someone. Vinnie walked over to him and patted him on his head. "You okay, boy?" The dog looked no worse for wear. Just a few leaves and sticks stuck in his fur from running through the woods.

Vinnie looked around the area and wondered why Ferris had run to this spot and why he sat here, as if waiting for something. Or someone.

A foot from where Ferris sat, Vinnie saw tire impressions. It looked like a truck had been parked here a few days ago, right after the last rain. The tire impressions remained in the dried mud.

"Let's go, boy," Vinnie said and lightly touched Ferris's collar. Ferris obliged and jumped in the backseat of the patrol car when Vinnie urged him to.

Vinnie pulled up to the Chandler home and got out. Cecilia came running out the front door when she heard the car door close. Before she could ask, he let Ferris out of the backseat and opened the gate. Ferris ran to Cecilia and she didn't try to brace herself from the incoming tackle.

"Oh, thank God!" she told Ferris, as he licked her face. "I love you, little one! What would I have done if you were gone? You can't leave me like that." After a minute of nuzzles, he ran into the house to his water bowl, parched from his adventure.

Cecilia got up and found Vinnie observing the scene. She went over to him, went to hug him, and thought better of it. She held out her hand and peered at his nameplate. "Thank you, Officer Pugliese. I can't tell you how much it means to me that you found him."

Vinnie could see how much it meant to her. He'd

once returned a lost child, at a strip mall, to a mother and had seen that same look.

HALFWAY THROUGH HIS shift, Vinnie headed back to the station. The chief's car was parked in the lot. The incident with Mrs. Chandler and Ferris had troubled him.

He leaned into Owens's office. "Working late, Chief?"

Holden withheld a smart aleck reply and asked, "What do you want, Pugliese?"

"To talk to you about the Chandler case," he answered, entering the office and closing the office door.

Owens sighed and placed his pen down. "There's nothing to talk about. We arrested her. Briscoe's prosecuting her. We won't agree about it."

"Maybe we will..." Pugliese said. Holden furrowed his brow, surprised by the possible change in opinion. "I think I may have been wrong about Mrs. Chandler."

Owens leaned back in his chair and observed his patrolman. "Why this sudden change in heart, Vinnie?"

"She lost Ferris."

Holden shot up. "What! Oh my God! CeCe must be out of her mind." He went to grab his jacket and head out to Cecilia's. She might be mad at him but she'd accept his help for Ferris's sake.

"She was."

With one arm through his jacket, Holden turned and asked, "Was? What do you mean?"

"I found him. He's fine."

Holden flopped back in his chair, glad Ferris and Cecilia were alright. He shoved away the small part of him that was disappointed he didn't have an excuse to see her.

"Found him on that side road by their house. The one to the reservoir, you know?"

Holden nodded yes. He concealed his surprise that Ferris had found the spot he had parked his truck when he went to the Chandler home. Holden guessed he wasn't the only one missing his visits.

"There were tire tracks there. Pretty recent. You think Jeremiah hired someone else to scare Mrs. Chandler?"

"I think Jeremiah learned his lesson," Holden said, knowing the cause of the tracks.

"Okay...but Ferris. He was just sitting there, like he was waiting for someone. It was kind of sad. But not as sad as when Mrs. Chandler thought he was gone. They only have each other now that Mr. Chandler is gone."

Holden nodded agreement and they sat in the office, silent, for several minutes.

"What'll happen to Ferris if she goes to prison?" Vinnie asked.

To Holden, the better question was: What would happen to Cecilia if she went to prison?

CHAPTER 38

CECILIA WAS SUMMONED into the defense team's office for trial preparations. Michael sat at the head of the table and she sat next to him, feeling like a guest in her own dining room.

Wyatt was at the other end of the room, talking to someone on the phone. She couldn't tell if it was related to her case.

Michael slid over a piece of paper, titled Witness List. "Tell me what you know about the following people."

She nodded understanding.

"Do you know Sydney Soloway?" Michael asked.

"No, don't recognize the name," Cecilia answered.

"He lives down the street," he told her.

She shrugged. She could recognize neighbors' faces but not their names. That was more Joey's realm than hers. He could have probably told Michael everything about the neighbor—how long they had lived in Folley, their children's and pets' names and ages, what car they drove. Cecilia would be lucky to match the neighbor with their house.

"Think about it," he said, tapping his finger on the name. "Think if there's any reason he'd be testifying against you."

She nodded understanding.

He sighed and continued, "Fine. Dr. Kinney."

"Ferris's veterinarian."

"Any reason he's testifying for the prosecution?" Michael asked.

"He stitched Ferris up after the attack."

"And before the incident, was he Ferris's vet?

"Yes, but Joey always handled that."

Michael's cell rang and he slid the paper to her. "Go through the list. Tell me anything you know about each," he said before answering the phone and leaving the room.

Cecilia ran her finger down the list. The police chief and Officer Vincent Pugliese were also on the list.

Her finger stopped at Chief Holden Owens. She regretted their last meeting. She had no way to contact him. She couldn't just call the police and ask to speak to him. And anyway, what would she say?

She tried to push thoughts of Holden, and their evenings drinking Mountain Dew in her kitchen, from her mind.

Vincent Pugliese was next.

She had information on both officers, about their visits to her house, that could be damaging to them. But they both were trying to help her, and Ferris, and she wouldn't use that against them.

Cecilia stared at the name Soloway, Sydney and tried to think who he was. She heard Michael curse from the kitchen and got up to see what the problem was.

Michael was using several paper towels to slop up spilled coffee. Ferris was at his feet trying to help, lapping up the spilled coffee from the floor. "Sorry, Cecilia. Ferris jumped and bumped my arm."

"No problem," she said, grabbing a few paper towels. She got down on the floor and nudged Ferris away. "You have enough energy. You don't need caffeine." He licked her face before trotting away.

With the floor cleaned she stood up and found Michael attending to the spilled coffee on his dress shirt. "I'm going to need to change this." He checked his watch while taking off the shirt. "I'll never get to the hotel and back and get everything Wyatt wants done by the end of the day."

Cecilia took the shirt and checked the size. "You can wear something of Joey's." She headed toward the stairs and the master bedroom. "Come on."

Michael hesitated. "I do not want to wear a Beastie Boys T-shirt."

Cecilia smirked at him. "That is not all your options. It's the best option but not your only option."

Begrudgingly, Michael followed and prepared to spend the rest of the day in a ridiculous shirt. Abigail and Wyatt would tease him unmercifully.

He followed her into her bedroom and to Joey's closet. She slid the door open, revealing an organized closet. Suits, dress shirts, and jackets hung grouped by color. The T-shirts and jeans were folded and stacked on shelves.

"You still have all his clothes?" he asked, marveling at the closet.

"Yes. It's just like he left it."

Michael turned to her, finding that hard to believe.

"Well, I picked up the dirty clothes he'd left on the floor but the closet…it's the same as when he left for work that day."

She remembered being mad at him that day that he hadn't packed yet. They were going into the city for a long weekend. He assured her he'd pack in five minutes after work. If he had packed, she knew she would have left the bag just how he would have left it.

She sat on the bed while Michael perused his options. "I had no idea he'd have suits like this." He checked the labels and said, "Nice."

"He wasn't always in construction. When we met in the city, he was wearing a stunning blue suit, crisp white shirt, pocket square that matched his tie. I'd never seen a more handsome man."

Michael chose a white dress shirt with light blue stripping. As he buttoned it up, he asked Cecilia, "When did he die?"

She could have answered with the exact day and time but roughly answered instead. "Ten months ago." Michael nodded but could think of nothing to say. He returned downstairs and to work.

Cecilia was left looking at the closet and remembering the man it belonged to. She smiled remembering him, and how handsome he was.

MAYOR TOWNSEND WAS online trying to find cheap airfare to escape Folley for the next few weeks. The trial was getting closer and he wanted to get away. Far away.

His desk phone buzzed. "Your sister, sir."

"Tell her I'm busy."

Peggy Gabbert walked into his office. She was dressed in mourning black. "Busy with what?" she asked.

He closed the browser before she got to his side of the desk. "Business." He pointed to a chair, on the other side of his desk. "What can I help you with?"

"I called Stewart. The hotel has plenty of rooms available. No media plans to attend the trial." She sat and crossed her legs. "That darn defense team is still there. He hasn't found a way to kick them out yet."

"Peggy!" he scolded her. "You can't get them kicked out of the hotel."

"Why not? I don't want them here. I don't want them helping that woman!"

Townsend didn't bother to remind her of Mrs. Chandler's legal right to counsel, something her son was afforded countless times. At his expense. He paid for it with his money and his hair. He blamed Bobby for the premature loss of his hair.

He glanced at the computer. Maybe he would take a medical vacation and get hair plugs.

Noticing his lack of interest, she yelled, "George!"

"What do you want from me, Peggy?"

"You have to get more involved."

"Haven't I done enough?" While he was alive, he didn't add.

"Tsk," she scoffed. "We need the media back."

"This town does not need the media back."

"More coverage is good for both of us."

Townsend glanced at his reflection in the computer monitor. More coverage would mean more hair loss.

"More coverage means more visitors to the town. More visitors means more money to the town's businesses. More business means more taxes," she explained.

This was not the tourism he wanted for Folley.

"Ask around, I'm sure your voters want the revenue. And they want to see you stand by your family."

At first, Townsend would have agreed. Everyone had rallied behind her. Bobby's funeral was heavily attended. But it was hard to stand by her after the media reports of his juvenile record surfaced.

Townsend had waited for a backlash after the reports of the many dropped charges, the minimal sentences, and incomplete community service, but it never came. Briscoe dealt with the media briskly, reporting he was too busy preparing for the trial to address them. They quickly lost interest and moved on.

The backlash Townsend feared never arrived. He'd always been careful with Bobby and Briscoe. He'd made sure his dealings with Briscoe were always observed. He was obliged to help his sister but he liked being mayor and didn't want to lose the job because of his nephew's antics.

"The town does not need more media attention," Townsend said.

"It'll help," she assured him.

The situation frustrated him. He couldn't win either way. He'd pull out his hair if he had any left. "How?" he asked, knowing he wouldn't like the answer.

"Keeps my boy in the news. Keeps him alive," she pleaded.

He loved his sister and her pain hurt him but there was nothing more he could do. "Peggy, I've done all I could. I kept him out of jail."

"You didn't keep him out of the morgue," she cried.

"Peggy...I think we should stay quiet. We don't want to bring more attention to him. Other...incidents may come to light."

She wiped the tears off her face.

"Bobby hurt that woman," he continued. "If he had lived, there was nothing I could have done for him. He would have gone to jail. Maybe it's better—"

"What!" she yelled. She stormed out of his office.

His secretary looked in. "Well, that went well."

It went better than he expected. She was gone.

He opened the internet browser and booked a trip.

CHAPTER 39

"CECILIA!" MICHAEL CALLED from the dining room.

She finished the email she was typing and sent it. He yelled again as she worked on one more email before she answered his calls.

Wyatt peeked in the office. "I'm sure you can hear him."

"I can. Sorry. I'll be right there."

Wyatt walked into her office and looked around. "This is how Joey set up his office?" he asked, surprised by the classic feel. It had the air of an older man.

"No, his dad."

He walked around to Cecilia's side of the desk and looked at the two framed photos. He recognized Cecilia and Joey, on their wedding day. He pointed to the other wedding photograph. "Who are they?"

"Joey's sister and brother-in-law, Brittany and Jeremiah."

It could be a coincidence but he didn't know too many Jeremiahs. "What's their last name?"

"Coleman," she answered after sending the last email and closing the laptop.

Wyatt nodded. They headed to the other home's office.

Michael yelled again for her, with even more urgency, as she entered the doorway. "Oh, sorry. Didn't see you."

Wyatt headed over to his stack of *Folley Press* newspapers and started flipping through to the one he needed.

Abigail spoke. "We're completing the witness list, and would like a character witness. We might not call him or her but it would be good to have a couple on the list."

"A what?" she asked.

"A character witness. Someone who could vouch for you. Vouch for your good moral conduct and background."

"Umm..." She stalled, trying to find an answer.

Without looking up, Wyatt said, "Please don't say your sister. She's a social media nightmare. Briscoe would devour her on the stand."

Cecilia laughed. Janna never entered her mind. Only Holden.

Wyatt found the paper he was looking for. He held his finger over a name. "Your brother-in-law, Jeremiah Coleman, you said?"

"Yes," she answered. "But he wouldn't be a good character witness. You can't call him."

"Oh, no." Wyatt handed the paper to Abigail and pointed to the article. "Anyone else you can think of as a character witness?" Cecilia bit her lip. Wyatt interpreted the silence correctly. "Okay, don't worry about it. Sometimes character witnesses backfire anyway."

"You know that new study agrees—" Michael started.

"Jury selection starts tomorrow," Wyatt interrupted. "Abigail..."

"I've got some clothes for you. This is the first time jurors will see you. First impressions and all that."

"Clothes?" Cecilia asked. "I have clothes."

The defense team exchanged a look. "We've seen your clothes," Abigail answered.

"Abigail picked you up a few things. Things that would be more appropriate than tight jeans and your husband's old T-shirts and sweatshirts." Wyatt signaled for them to leave. "She'll also explain accessories."

Wyatt handed Michael the paper after the two ladies left. Pointing to the name he recognized, he told Michael, "Get me everything on this that you can."

Abigail headed upstairs to the master bedroom, reviewing the elements of making a good impression. "Demure makeup. Simple hair. Small accessories. No watch. Nervous people look at a watch and jurors think they're bored. Not good." Cecilia nodded at each order. "Nothing flashy. Nothing sexy. You need to be a simple grieving widow. Can you do that?"

"I'm guessing you'll tell me how."

Cecilia couldn't remember anyone shopping for her since she was a child. She also couldn't see how jurors could decide her fate, based on her fashion.

"Isn't it a little...sexist that Wyatt has you doing this?" Cecilia asked.

"Do you want Michael doing this?" Abigail answered. Cecilia shrugged. She didn't want either of them doing this.

Abigail pulled out a few of the items she had purchased and held them up for Cecilia to see. "Trust me, I'm better at this than Michael." Cecilia shrugged again. "Oh...I'll show you what happens when Michael does this." She pulled out her cell phone and pulled up a photo.

Cecilia's eyes bulged at the image. A woman in a mini skirt with a colorful tight shirt and big hair. Cecilia didn't know where to look and only wanted to look away.

"Wyatt doesn't see color, sex, religion. He only sees ways to win."

THE NEXT MORNING, Abigail picked Cecilia up at her house and drove her to the courthouse. Other than hellos when she got in, they didn't speak. Cecilia realized she didn't know anything about Abigail, other than she was a lawyer. But now was not the time for small talk. She stared out the window, not taking in any of the scenery, and not noticing when Abigail parked and got out of the car.

"Cecilia, let's go," she said, tapping on the glass.

Cecilia jumped and got out of the car.

Abigail cringed when she looked Cecilia over. "Jeez, you have dog hair all over the new suit."

"I have a dog, Abigail."

Out of her briefcase, Abigail pulled out a lint roller. She manhandled Cecilia and removed the golden hairs.

There was one media truck outside the courthouse.

"People have lost interest, I see," Cecilia commented.

"Yes, those reports on Gabbert really decreased the sensationalism of the story. Now to them, it's just a self-defense case."

Cecilia didn't know if she should be relieved or worried. Abigail seemed neutral.

They entered the courtroom. Wyatt and Michael huddled over a legal pad. Wyatt appraised Cecilia. "Very nice," he said to Abigail.

Everyone stood when the judge entered. Judge Lowe signaled for everyone to sit. He called the first twelve potential jurors to the jury box.

"Your Honor, to spur the process, I gave the potential jurors here a short questionnaire," Briscoe announced. He pointed to the over thirty people in the room. Briscoe cued Marcy to get the filled out papers from them.

"Your Honor," Sewell interrupted. "I did not have advance notice of this."

"Just standard stuff, Your Honor," Briscoe said before handing a copy to the judge and the defense team.

Sewell looked over the list. A list of twenty questions. Some standard—name, occupation, age. Some that Sewell would agree to: Do you know anyone associated with the case? Do you have any family members in law enforcement? Have you heard of this case? Wyatt couldn't imagine anyone in this county, or in the state, not knowing about the case. Mixed in with the innocuous questions was the one Briscoe wanted answered most.

"Are you allergic to domestic animals?" Sewell read aloud. He looked to Briscoe. "Really? I would not consider this standard, Your Honor."

Cecilia saw the lone newsperson scribble in her pad.

They all knew Ferris would come out sooner or later but all parties thought it would be the defense team that raised the issue.

"Are you trying to have a jury with no dog or cat owners, Mr. Briscoe?" Wyatt asked. Briscoe mocked shock but didn't answer.

Wyatt returned his attention to Judge Lowe. "Your Honor, the prosecutor is actively trying to weed out pet owners from the jury pool for obvious reasons."

Out of the corner of her eye, Cecilia saw the newswoman scribble more on her pad. Her initial boredom in being assigned coverage to jury selection on a case everyone had lost interest in was gone. She would be on her phone, calling police contacts and her producer within seconds of exiting the courtroom.

Sewell glanced at the paper Abigail handed him. "Your Honor, Mrs. Chandler has the right to a jury of her peers. According to the American Pet Products Association, thirty-seven to forty-seven percent of all households in the United States have a dog, and thirty to thirty-seven percent have a cat. We can't have a jury of no pet owners."

"I agree, Mr. Sewell. Briscoe, your questionnaire here is out."

THE JURY SELECTION lasted through the day, with twelve jurors and two alternates selected. Wyatt, Abigail, and Michael seemed pleased by the group. Briscoe wore his usual stern face. Cecilia had no opinion on the group, except they looked at her too much.

As the defense team, with Cecilia, exited the court-house, the newswoman ran up to them. "Mr. Sewell, why the questions about domestic animals?" she asked.

"You'll have to ask Mr. Briscoe. He was the one with the questionnaire." Sewell pointed to Briscoe as he exited a doorway away.

She ran after Mr. Briscoe. Marcy trailed behind, scribbling down the orders he barked at her.

"Mr. Briscoe, why the questions about animals?" the newswoman asked.

"No comment," he answered.

She reworded the question and asked again. "Are animals an important part of this case?"

"No comment."

"Do you have a dog or cat?" she asked.

"Good God no," he muttered. "No comment," he corrected himself. But the cat was already out of the bag, as they say. She had her sound bite for the evening. She'd have until Monday when the trial started to learn more.

She directed more questions at him while he descended the stairs. He muttered "no comment" after each of them. Briscoe hailed Owens, who was standing by his patrol car. "Do something about this, will you?"

Holden smiled at the newswoman and escorted Briscoe to his car, in silence.

The defense team resumed their walk to their car. "I do like to see him squirm," Wyatt told them.

Cecilia tried to catch Holden's eye as they got to the parking lot but thought better of it. She watched Briscoe and Marcy depart, leaving Holden behind. Cecilia watched him give a little wave to the departing vehicle.

No one heard him mutter "you're welcome" as they drove away.

Holden snuck a look at Cecilia when he didn't think anyone was watching.

CHAPTER 40

HOLDEN SAT AT the bar and drank a beer. *Liquid courage*, he thought. It might be the last evening he could sneak over to Cecilia's. When the trial started he didn't know what chaos would ensue.

"I thought a police officer should never have his back to the door," a woman said, from his right.

Holden pointed to the bar's mirror, which gave him full view of the bar and both entrances. He hadn't missed the newswoman's arrival five minutes ago and had watched as she scanned the crowd, looking for someone. When she sat down on the barstool next to him, he feared she had found her target.

She stuck her hand in front of his mug. "Cheryl Milson, KRTV." He ignored it and took a sip of his beer. "Interesting day in court, wasn't it?"

"I wouldn't know. I wasn't in the courthouse." Holden resumed his observation of the bar. Looking in the mirror, he saw the townsfolk he usually saw here during his brief visits.

"But I'm sure you heard what happened. Small town. Small courthouse. Only one case going on." She watched him watch the mirror. "This is big news," she added, making eye contact with Holden in the mirror.

Holden shrugged and took a sip of beer. The bartender walked up. "What can I get your lady friend, Owens?"

"She's not with me. She's with the media," Owens explained.

Cheryl leaned into Holden to view his beer. He leaned away from her. "I'll have what he's having. And another one for the chief here too," she instructed the bartender.

She returned with one beer and handed it to Cheryl. "The chief wouldn't take a beer from you, honey. You freshened your makeup and opened an extra button on that blouse for the wrong target."

Holden tried to hide his smile while Cheryl tried to hide her embarrassment. She took a sip of her beer and grimaced. She called the bartender back over. "White wine, please."

Holden finished his beer, paid his tab, and got up to leave.

"Come on, Chief. Give me something," she pleaded before he walked away. "I'm stuck in this small town. I have nothing to do. Give me a story. Any story. Please make my time in the boonies worth it."

"That strategy won't work either, Ms. Milson," Holden said before departing.

The beer hadn't worked but the conversation with the reporter had. She was desperate enough to go to Cecilia's house to get a story. One more glass of wine and she'd probably realize that too. He couldn't be caught over there. That was a story his career couldn't survive.

Holden grabbed his coat and waved goodbye to the bartender, leaving Ms. Milson with her glass of wine and empty barstools on each side of her. She was blonde and pretty and the flirting approach probably always worked for her. Especially on a small town cop.

As he left the bar, he waved to Vinnie, who was getting out of his car and heading toward the bar.

HOLDEN AWOKE SATURDAY morning to a text from Marcy. A summons to Briscoe's office.

Owens didn't bother to ask why and headed over to the prosecutor's office. When he arrived, he found Briscoe pacing. He regretted not stopping for coffee.

"What is this?" Briscoe yelled when Holden entered.

"A newspaper," Owens answered.

Briscoe slammed the paper down. "They found out about the dog! Who told them about the dog?"

It was a short list that knew about Ferris.

"Leaked from Sewell?" Holden asked. All Holden knew was that it wasn't him.

"Doubt it. Not his style. He wouldn't leak this." He shook his head vehemently and continued his pacing. "If he were going to leak this, he would have done it earlier. He would have done it right away." Briscoe stopped briefly, considering it, then resumed his pacing. "No, not his style. Not his style to leak this. He'd give an interview. He'd have the dog there. They'd have all these shots of the mongrel running around. The All-American dog, Ferris." He looked at Owens when he turned around. "You know he's going to use it in his opening statement. That'd have more impact for him."

Owens couldn't comment on attorney strategy. He picked up the paper and skimmed the article. It sourced KRTV as the first to report that Cecilia Chandler had killed Robert Gabbert in an attempt to save her dog.

"I want an investigation into this!" Briscoe ordered.

"It just as easily could be someone in your office as someone in the department," Owens told him.

"It wasn't my office!" Briscoe yelled.

Owens knew a yelling match about whose office had leaked the news was pointless. He kept himself from yelling back, "It wasn't my office!"

"What does it matter?" Owens said instead. "You said yourself this would have come out during his opening statement. That's Monday. So the media learned of it two days earlier." Owens thought Briscoe would like the renewed interest in the trial. And in the prosecutor.

Briscoe didn't look pleased when he answered. "We'll see Monday if you feel the same way."

CHAPTER 41

LIKE ANY GOOD son, Daniel Briscoe visited his mother regularly. He always arrived with flowers. Mother's Day. Her birthday. His birthday. All the big events. And in his life, the big events included a trial.

He rarely had cases that went to trial. He pleaded out most of his cases. Everyone won that way. Taxpayers didn't bear the burden of a costly trial. The victims weren't subjected to the stress of a trial. Marcy wouldn't develop an ulcer.

"Hi, Mom," he said when he arrived. "Big case, the one I told you about, it starts today." He sat down and commiserated with her over the trial. "I'll never understand how someone could choose an animal over a person." He looked away before adding, "But you of all people could explain it to me, couldn't you?"

His mother always loved animals. The Briscoes owned a beagle when he was growing up. Dan played with Pepper for hours after school each day. Every day after school they'd walk in the woods together. They'd play all day on the weekends. Except the day of his school play. After school that day, he went home and put on his costume. Even though the play wasn't until eight.

He'd earned the lead role, King Roland, in the school's play. He stood in front of the mirror, regaling his costume. His mother had spent hours making his golden crown, his long maroon cloak, and his black shirt with the family crest. She fashioned a scepter out of his father's golf club. His father hadn't been happy about it but smiled when Dan entered the living room, with all the regality of a king.

As he recited his lines again, his mother ran in. She put on her hiking boots and a hat. It wasn't the outfit he expected his mother to wear to his stage debut. "Mom, where are you going?"

"Pepper's missing," she answered, while tying her shoes.

"But, Mom, the play," he reminded her. "We have to leave. Pepper will come back. Sometimes he runs in the woods. He always comes back."

"Well, he's not home yet and it's getting dark." She checked her watch. "He's always home by now."

Dan couldn't understand her anxiety. Sometimes dogs ran away. Pepper would be waiting for them when they got home from his play.

"But, Mom, we have to leave." They didn't have to leave for another thirty minutes but Dan wanted to be early.

"Your father will take you." She kissed him on the head. "I'll be there by the time the curtain rises. I promise."

"But, Mom!" he yelled out as she walked down the driveway. Her calls for Pepper got softer as she made it to the end of the driveway. In the darkness, he couldn't see which way she turned onto the county road.

As Dan walked down the stage's aisle for the coronation scene, he looked out into the audience. He found his father. To his right was his younger brother. To his left, the aisle seat, where his mother should have been, was empty.

While Dan sang his first song, Pepper sat on their front doorstep, waiting for their return. Neighbors could hear his howls for his family.

During the wedding scene to Queen Anne, he watched his father keep looking over his shoulder and checking his watch. His queen had to prompt him his lines of "I do."

The police arrived on the scene of the accident as Dan belted out his finale. The driver never saw her. Focused on finding Pepper, she never heard the car's approach.

While Dan gave a final bow, the sheriff pulled up to their home. While his queen received flowers, he stood on stage staring out at the empty seat, hearing his mother's voice in his head. She had promised she'd be there.

"I'll never understand, Mom. How could you choose Pepper over me?" He got up, said goodbye, and placed the flowers on his mother's grave.

CHAPTER 42

As EXPLAINED TO her on Friday, the defense team would pick her up at her home and they would drive over to the courthouse together. She took an extra glance at herself in the mirror before going downstairs. Ferris made to jump on her and she sidestepped the greeting. "No fur on me today, Ferris."

She patted him on the head. He sat patiently at her feet while she got him a biscuit. "I'll be back later." There was a growing knot in her stomach. How many more goodbyes would she have to say to Ferris? Wyatt and the team were confident they would win but there were no guarantees.

Her cell phone dinged with an incoming text. She sighed when she saw it was from Janna. "You're quite the star. Hope you look pretty today." Attached was an emoji she couldn't decipher the meaning of. She forgot about it when she got the text from Abigail that they were turning on her street.

The knot in her stomach grew when she got in the car and no one responded to her "Good morning." They all nodded and returned to their phones.

As they approached the courthouse, Cecilia leaned

forward in her seat, between Abigail and Michael. Janna's text now made sense. She marveled at the crowd. "Why are there so many people?" she asked. There were even more than right after the shooting. She could count at least eight media trucks.

"They found out about Ferris," Michael answered.

"Found out what about Ferris?" she asked.

"That Gabbert was threatening Ferris and that's why you shot him," Michael clarified.

Cecilia had no idea if the increased news coverage, the renewed interest in her trial, was a good or a bad thing. Wyatt's face remained neutral.

The driver pulled up to the courthouse. Wyatt turned from the passenger seat.

"You two," Wyatt directed Abigail and Michael. "Go out that door"—he pointed to the back driver's side door—"and stay on both sides of her. Hustle her up the steps. Do not talk to anyone." He looked at each of them. "Agreed?"

He waited until each of them had nodded agreement.

The defense team, and Cecilia, ran up the courthouse steps, flanked by media on all sides. The reporters shoved their microphones and cameras in their faces. They spat questions at them. The defense team, and Cecilia, said nothing. Cecilia only prayed she wouldn't fall, running up the stairs in the new high heels she wasn't used to.

Wyatt opened the courthouse door and closed it once Abigail, Michael, and Cecilia were inside. Wyatt stayed outside to talk briefly to the media.

"You're going to need to get more security, Briscoe," Wyatt told him as they entered the courthouse together a few minutes later.

"What? For this?" Briscoe asked. "I thought you'd love this. These are your people."

Marcy and Briscoe didn't look like they loved it. Their faces were red by the exertion of running from the media and the stress of the media's onslaught of questions.

"It's dangerous, Briscoe, and you know it," Sewell continued.

Briscoe shrugged and walked into the courtroom. Wyatt glared at him as he followed him in. It was the most emotion Cecilia had ever seen from Wyatt. Both teams headed to their respective tables in the courtroom, trying to ignore the overpacked gallery.

"Quiet," the bailiff commanded as they entered.

After a few moments to settle in, Judge Lowe arrived. He could not hide his shock of the size of the crowd.

Wyatt remained standing after everyone else was directed to sit. "Your Honor," he began, "may we speak in chambers before you call in the jury?"

Briscoe stood. "Your Honor," he said, "he's stalling. The state is ready to begin its case."

There was a bristling in the crowd. "Quiet!" Judge Lowe commanded after slamming his gavel down. "My chambers now."

The three men gathered in Judge Lowe's chambers.

He had feared the publicity about the trial in the initial weeks but it had all died down. Jury selection had been quiet. Only one reporter had even attended. Now, it was back to the circus he had feared. And one to which he didn't want to be the ringmaster.

"This is his doing and now he's complaining," Briscoe started.

"How is this my doing?" Sewell asked.

"He did this on purpose to get a continuance, Your Honor."

"I did not tell that reporter about Ferris. If I wanted to I could have, but I didn't."

Judge Lowe interrupted the dueling lawyers. "Fine, well now you can't. I'm putting a gag order in effect now. Neither of you will speak to the media."

"Fine with me. I'm not fighting this case in the media. I don't need to convince them. I only need to convince those twelve jurors." Sewell turned to Briscoe. "Although it does seem that the press is on my side, Briscoe."

"You'll address me and only me in this office, Mr. Sewell," Judge Lowe said.

"Yes, sir."

"And wipe that smirk off your face, Dan," Judge Lowe instructed, as the corners of Briscoe's mouth edged up.

With any hint of pleasure gone from his face, Briscoe said, "Your Honor, the state wants to continue this case."

"As does the defense, Your Honor," Sewell quickly

added.

The judge ignored them. "I'm postponing the case for a day. We need to get security. We need to limit the number in the gallery."

"Your Honor, I request that the jury be sequestered," Sewell asked.

"That's it, Your Honor," Briscoe balked. "He doesn't like the jury. He did some rethinking over the weekend and now he wants a mistrial."

"That is not what I said"—Sewell turned to look at Briscoe and then, remembering his earlier rebuke, turned his attention to Judge Lowe—"Your Honor."

"They'll blame me for the sequestering and take it out on the prosecution," Briscoe explained.

"No, they won't," Judge Lowe answered. "I'll explain I'm mandating it. And I'm neutral."

Briscoe shook his head in disgust at the loss.

While the two lawyers waited to be dismissed, Judge Lowe called the station. "I need Chief Owens in here *now*."

A CALL DIRECTLY from a judge, during the biggest trial this county had ever seen, got Chief Holden Owens in the courthouse in minutes. He had been around the courthouse all morning, helping the officers direct traffic and corral the media.

Part of him feared the judge would also want to know who leaked the story. Owens had put no effort into an investigation and hadn't planned to. Now, with the renewed media attention and subsequent traffic, he knew he'd have no time to.

He didn't notice Cecilia sitting outside the judge's office with the rest of the defense team as he entered.

Owens found the three men sitting in silence. He remained standing as he greeted the judge. "Yes, Judge Lowe, you called?"

"Yes." He looked up from the paperwork he was working on. "We need more security."

"Yes, sir," Owens agreed. "I've called in everyone I can for today. We seem to have it under control now." With the day's proceedings cancelled, the media had become more manageable. But he knew that was temporary. Tomorrow would be a repeat of the day, unless his department was better prepared. "My next stop is going back to the station to call in the auxiliary officers for the week."

Judge Lowe nodded approval. "Can you be ready tomorrow?"

"Yes, sir."

Judge Lowe signaled to dismiss him but Owens paused. "Are you ready in here, sir?"

"What do you mean?" the judge asked.

"I can control the crowd outside but what about inside? The court officers and courthouse security can't let everyone in like they did today. I heard the gallery was jammed. The fire marshal has already called me about it."

Owens looked to Sewell. Of the three, he was most

accustomed to these types of proceedings.

Sewell said nothing. He wouldn't speak until asked. He couldn't tell Judge Lowe how to run his courtroom.

Judge Lowe rolled his eyes. "You're right. I'll make some calls." He mentally went through his list of colleagues who would have had experience with high-profile cases. "I'll let you all know later what the plan will be."

He waved them all out.

CHAPTER 43

CECILIA SAT IN her office, staring at an empty inbox. She had told all her clients she'd be on vacation this week, with limited access to emails and the internet. Some vacation, she thought.

Her vibrating phone broke her trance. She didn't know who would be calling. The defense team was in her dining room, working. They would yell if they needed her.

Cecilia cringed when she saw her sister's name on the phone's screen. Three missed calls. Three waiting voicemails. She didn't want to hear her sister's voice today. Then a text appeared on the screen. "Where can I pick up my ticket?"

Her initial thought was her sister must have contacted her by accident. But three voicemails and a text could not be a misdial. Cecilia tapped to listen to the first voicemail, continuing to hope Janna had meant to call someone else. Maybe she had met a new friend named Cecilia. That hope was quickly dashed.

"What time does the trial start tomorrow? I'm not sure if I should leave tonight or in the morning."

"Oh, God," Cecilia mumbled.

She tapped on the second voicemail. "I can stay

with you, right? If you're under house arrest can you have visitors? Or would I be under arrest too?"

Cecilia tapped on the third voicemail. "What should I wear? You looked pretty meh today."

Wyatt had said he didn't want Janna at the court proceedings. She never thought it would be an issue. Now the trial was an event and Janna wanted an invitation.

Cecilia quickly typed three short messages to her sister, answering all of her questions and hoping to prevent her arrival.

"We do not know when the trial for my freedom starts tomorrow. Thank you for your interest in my well-being."

"No, you cannot stay here."

"There are no tickets for the trial."

Janna's response appeared within seconds. "But I'm sister to the defendant. There must be a ticket for me."

Cecilia got up and headed to the defense team. Another text pinged as she entered their office. "Are there *tickets* to the trial?" she asked.

The three were huddled over their computers, busy working. Only Abigail looked up. "Yes, Judge Lowe sent an email a few minutes ago regarding court proceedings for tomorrow. Are people asking you for tickets?"

Before Cecilia could answer, Abigail's phone rang and she answered it. It was a one-sided conversation. She tried to interrupt several times but the caller wouldn't allow it. The call ended with Abigail saying, "Yes, I'll call Judge Lowe if I have any questions."

Wyatt and Michael looked up at the mention of Judge Lowe. "Cecilia, can you give us a few minutes?" Abigail asked.

Cecilia knew that couldn't be good and she left. She let Ferris out into the backyard and watched him run around for a few minutes before he ran back into the house for a treat. As she took a biscuit out of his jar, Michael yelled, "We'll be right back." They left through the front door.

Cecilia watched from the front window as the three of them, arguing, got into their car.

WHEN CECILIA PACED the house, Ferris paced it with her. She had closed all the shades in the front of the house after they left, fearing the media trucks would return.

The doorbell rang and she froze. Ferris walked into her, then froze as well. The doorbell rang again and Wyatt called out, "Cecilia, it's us."

She and Ferris walked to the front door.

Wyatt, Michael, and Abigail stood on her front porch. Their suitcases next to them.

"This is unconventional but out of our hands. The hotel kicked us out," Wyatt explained.

Cecilia stepped to the side and let them in.

"The jury has been sequestered and they needed

our rooms," Wyatt continued.

"Judge Lowe told them they could have our rooms. *Our* rooms," Michael said. "I still say we could fight it."

"Do you really want to fight Judge Lowe?" Wyatt asked. "Is that in *our* best interests?" He looked at Cecilia for emphasis.

Michael looked up at Cecilia and agreed. "I'm just saying…"

Abigail walked up the stairs, dragging her large roller case behind her. "I'll take the front bedroom." Cecilia smiled, knowing the men did not know that was the guest bedroom with the attached bathroom. "You boys can have the other ones…" Her voice trailed off as she added, "And share the bathroom."

Ferris followed Michael as he headed to his new bedroom. He carried a much smaller garment bag compared to Wyatt's. She realized he probably couldn't afford as many suits as Wyatt could.

"I'm sorry about this," Wyatt said as they stood in the entryway alone. "It is unusual."

Wyatt laughed when she asked, "Does your room and board fees come off my bill?"

CECILIA FOUND IT difficult to sleep. She wasn't surprised considering the mounting stresses over the past year. From the bed, she stared at Joey's closet and realized it was silly to keep his clothes when someone else could wear them. She jumped out of bed, glad to have something to distract her racing mind. Ferris jumped out of bed, as well. He watched as she grabbed the hangers of all his fine suits, shirts and ties. He followed as she carried them to the guest bathroom. It took three trips and she hung them on the bathtub's rod. She left a note, "For Michael."

Cecilia had hoped the work would tire her and she went back to bed. Ferris sat on the floor, staring at the empty closet. Cecilia gazed at the ceiling, still unable to find sleep. Frustrated, she got up again and went downstairs to pace the main floor. Ferris paced with her. She looked out the front windows, admiring the Christmas lights her neighbors had put up. Three doors down, she saw the Jewish family's home. One candle lit on the menorah for the first night of Hanukkah.

Joey would have put their Christmas lights up by now. But not this year. There would be no Christmas lights. No decorations. There was nothing to celebrate.

As she paced, Ferris at her feet, she contemplated the reason for her insomnia. Was it the stress of the trial? Or the three other people now living in the house with her? For the last year, she had lived in the house with only Ferris. Before that, it had only been her and Joey, and Ferris.

The evening had been uncomfortable. She had become accustomed to the defense team's presence in her house during the day. But her only nightly visitor had been Holden. And that had been too long ago.

She had grown used to seeing the defense team in their work clothes. Now she saw them in their nightclothes. And they in hers. It seemed too familiar. Cecilia sensed they felt the same uneasiness with the situation. They were used to retreating to their own rooms at the hotel each night.

Ferris checked on each of them as they prepared for bed, until each said goodnight and closed their bedroom's door. Cecilia called Ferris into her room and closed the door before getting into bed.

The morning light started to drift into the house and she knew she should shower and get ready for the day. The others would be up soon.

When Abigail came downstairs an hour later, she found Cecilia staring at her coffee cup. Cecilia pointed to the waiting coffee and coffee cups for Abigail and the others. They sat in silence until Michael came in the kitchen.

"Whew! Look at you! Is that a new suit?" Abigail asked, looking him up and down. "Very nice. Did Wyatt give you a raise and not me?"

Michael laughed and looked at Cecilia. She was surprised that Michael had chosen to wear it. As the night had worn on, she thought maybe he'd find it creepy that she'd given him her dead husband's clothes. But it's not as if he died in them.

"It looks good on you," Cecilia told him. "Joey would be happy."

"Thank you," he answered before pouring himself

a cup of coffee.

At eight thirty, the driver arrived and the defense team, with Cecilia, exited her home. They arranged themselves in the sedan as they had done the day before.

Cecilia stared at her shoes. The cobalt blue heels. The ones Ferris had attempted to destroy. The ones Joey had fixed. They weren't the shoes Abigail had set out for her to wear but she felt she needed Joey and Ferris with her today in court.

They arrived at the courthouse and the scene was worse. Pandemonium was the word that came to mind.

"Oh my word," Wyatt mumbled. Michael and Abigail just stared. Cecilia was shocked as well, but was most concerned that the defense team was surprised by it. They'd worked high-profile cases before hers. They were known for it. But the scene before them was not anything they'd ever expected or seen before.

In addition to the news trucks, there were now protestors. Hundreds of them.

The police were doing the best they could to keep them apart. To Cecilia, it looked like the protestors were winning.

The driver parked in front of the courthouse and waited for them to get out. "Let's go," Wyatt told all of them and got out of the passenger seat. Cecilia followed Michael out his side of the car, the back passenger seat.

Michael headed to the courthouse stairs but Cecilia froze. The chanting could be heard, but not understood, when she was in the car. Now, it was decibels louder and overwhelming. And also clear.

"Dogs are family. Set Cecilia free!"

"CeCe. Put her in jail where she should be!"

The chants went back and forth. Cecilia stood listening, shocked by what she heard. "Are...are they calling me CeCe?" she asked but no one could hear her over the chanting.

Only people who knew her called her CeCe. And these were all strangers who wanted her in jail.

"There she is," someone yelled.

"Murderer!" another yelled when they saw Cecilia.

She stood frozen as people pointed at her and strangers called her CeCe. Wyatt put his arm around her and pushed her toward the stairs. "Cecilia, move!" He kept his hand on her back as they hustled up the stairs. Michael and Abigail waited for them inside the courthouse.

"Well..." Wyatt started.

"That was worse than I expected," Abigail said.

"Worse than any of us expected," Michael added.

The four of them stood looking out the window onto the crowd.

CHAPTER 44

CECILIA WATCHED AS the jury filed in. They were male, female; tall, short; fat, thin; young and old. They were all neatly dressed. "Sunday best," her grandmother would have said. Especially the oldest man, who wore an old brown suit with a bowtie. She couldn't imagine they could agree on anything, never mind agree on her future.

Daniel Briscoe walked up to the jury and placed his hands on the jury box. He glared at each of them.

"You need to know one thing. Cecilia Chandler murdered Robert Gabbert. Yes, he did attack her. Yes, she sustained a few injuries. But she got away. She got back into her home. The safety of her home. She was inches from a phone. A phone she could have used to call for help. To call for the police. But that's not what she did.

"She ran back into her house.

"She ran to the safe.

"She got a gun.

"She ran by the phone *again*.

"She exited her home.

"She shot one time.

"She killed eighteen-year-old Robert Gabbert,

when he was no longer a threat to her.

"She killed Robert Gabbert with one shot.

"She is guilty of second-degree murder."

He held up a photo and showed it to each juror. A close-up shot of Robert Gabbert's dead face.

The jurors recoiled.

WYATT SEWELL STRODE to the jury box. Michael placed an easel to their right, by the witness stand. It held several placards. The first one was blank.

"Mr. Briscoe is right. Mrs. Cecilia Chandler killed Mr. Robert Gabbert.

"On her property.

"Her sanctuary.

"Mr. Briscoe said Cecilia sustained a few injuries.

"These are the injuries she sustained."

The jury and the courtroom gasped when he removed the blank whiteboard.

He slowly showed three photographs of Cecilia's beaten body. The first was the wide shot of her standing in her dining room. Her body riddled with bruises. The second was a close-up shot of her torso. Purple and black. The last was of her bruised and swollen face.

Cecilia looked away. It was painful to look at.

"Those are not a few injuries.

"That is a woman who was beaten.

"Without escape." He paused and looked again at

the close-up photo of Cecilia's beaten face. The jurors did as well.

"In this state, one is allowed to use justifiable force. What is justifiable?" He looked at each juror, knowing they were asking themselves that question.

"Mr. Briscoe is right. She did manage to get free. By fighting for her life, using every ounce of energy she could, she got free. And she risked her life to run back out.

"But Mr. Briscoe left out one thing.

"She ran back out to save her companion.

"Her best friend.

"Her dog, Ferris."

Sewell revealed a picture of Ferris. The golden retriever's head was tilted to the right and his tongue was hanging out.

The crowd "ahhed."

Briscoe rolled his eyes.

CECILIA LEFT THE courthouse with her defense team. The police had permitted the driver to park in front of the courthouse while he waited for his passengers to take them away for lunch.

The prosecutor was a few steps behind them. Wyatt held the door open for Cecilia and she was overwhelmed by the size and sound of the crowd. Their muffled chants could be heard as they approached the door. There was a roar as they exited the courthouse. It hit her as if it were a wall and she froze in the doorway. There were some boos, some hisses, and an equal number of cheers when they saw her. "Cecilia, move," Wyatt told her for the second time today.

Looking down at her feet, clad in the cobalt blue heels Joey had fixed, she willed herself to move. She was forced to tell herself "left, right, left, right" to walk. Focused on moving her feet, getting herself to the car, she was no longer aware of anything, or anyone, else.

Cecilia felt pressure on her back. She silently cursed, figuring it was Wyatt trying to get her to move faster. The pressure increased to a push. She heard someone yell, "Gun!" The push increased to a shove. She hit the ground hard. The pressure of someone's weight on her back pinned her to the ground. He kept her down, protecting her from the bullets, as the gunman emptied his clip.

When the gunfire ended, she opened her eyes to find Holden an inch from her face. "Are you okay?" he asked.

Unable to speak, she nodded yes.

Keeping his hand on her back to keep her safely on the ground, Owens looked around the scene. Pugliese had a gun trained on the gunman. Officer Margaret Monty was putting handcuffs on him. "Under control?" he asked Vinnie.

"Yes, Chief," he answered, his eyes never leaving the gunman.

Not knowing if this was a lone gunman, Owens instructed everyone to get up, but stay low, and get back into the courthouse.

Owens helped Cecilia up. He held most of her weight as they ran back into the courthouse, following Briscoe, Marcy, Abigail, Michael, and Wyatt.

He helped her to a bench. Owens appraised everyone. They all answered they were physically fine. The two teams retreated to separate corners.

Owens knelt in front of Cecilia. "Are you okay?"

She nodded, still unable to speak.

She looked down at her shoes. The pretty cobalt heels she bought that Ferris had broken and Joey had fixed. The heel was broken again. This time the left one. But Joey wasn't here to fix it.

"My heel...My heel broke," she mumbled, pointing to the broken shoe. She felt her body starting to shake.

He took off his jacket and wrapped it firmly around her, rubbing her arms and trying to warm her up. "It'll be okay. You're just in shock. I don't think anyone was hurt."

"Owens!" someone shouted from deeper in the courthouse.

He made to get up but stopped when she spoke and looked him in the eye. "Thank you."

He smiled, glad she was able to speak again. He stood and straightened his uniform. "Just doing my job, ma'am." He motioned for someone in the defense team to sit with her but they were too engrossed in their conversation to see.

Cecilia reached for his hand, lightly touching his fingers. Her fingers were soft against his calloused hand. He returned to her eye level. "I miss you," she whispered.

"I miss you, too," he whispered back.

Holden got up when they called his name again. He tapped Wyatt on his shoulder as he passed. "Can you go sit with her? I think she's in shock."

"I think we all are," Wyatt answered. He went toward her, noting her new police jacket.

"Nice job. I was almost killed out there," Briscoe snapped as Owens walked by.

"We were all almost killed out there," Owens reminded him.

"You are supposed to be protecting me," he yelled, pointing to himself.

"I'm supposed to be protecting the public. I am not your personal bodyguard."

"Judge's chambers now," the bailiff instructed them. "You too, Sewell."

Owens made sure to keep several feet ahead, avoiding further conversation with the prosecutor.

"Heard we had some lunchtime excitement," Judge Lowe said between bites of his tuna fish sandwich.

"It's under control, Your Honor," Owens said. "The suspect is being taken to the station. I'm headed over to question him soon."

"Under control?" Lowe asked. "My courthouse has been shot up. Do you know how expensive it will be to repair the marble?"

Surprised by the question, Owens looked at each attorney before answering. "No, sir."

"A lot. So, Chief Owens, this is *not* under control." He pushed the remaining portion of his sandwich away. "How did a gunman get in the courthouse?"

"He was outside, Your Honor. He didn't get in the courthouse."

"He fired at people exiting. Close enough," he retorted.

"We can't inspect everyone outside. Only the people entering the courthouse."

"Well, that needs to change," Judge Lowe ordered.

"They're on public ground, Your Honor. We can't stop and frisk everyone in the area."

"Why not?" he yelled.

Owens looked to the two lawyers for help. They remained silent. "Because it's illegal, sir."

Owens saw Briscoe smirk and knew he'd enjoy the backlash Owens was about to get from the judge.

The smirk quickly faded when Wyatt intervened. "But you could cordon off an area in front of the courthouse. Keep all the protestors in that area and anyone who wants in must be checked. Like Times Square on New Year's Eve."

"This is not a party, Mr. Sewell," Judge Lowe

snapped.

"No, but it needs to be contained," Owens interjected. "I'll call Sheriff Winkins at the State Police. See if he can help, send me some officers."

CHAPTER 45

"WHAT DO WE know?" Owens asked upon arriving at the station. Pugliese was waiting outside the interview room.

"We pretty much caught him red-handed," Pugliese answered.

"True. Why does he want to talk to me?" While on the phone to the sheriff, he'd received word over the radio that the suspect wanted to talk to him.

"Oh...he likes talking. Since he's arrived, he's been talking and crying and screaming and—"

"I get it," Owens interrupted. He held his hand out for the file Vinnie was holding. It contained everything they had on the gunman.

"It's Gabbert's older brother," Pugliese told him.

Owens looked up. He had gotten a look at the shooter, not a great look, but a look. He hadn't recognized him. "That wasn't Ray."

"Oh not Ray Ray of Ray's Motors." Vinnie started singing the dealership's jingle. Once you started singing it, you couldn't stop. So Owens gave him the thirty seconds to complete it. "It's his older half brother. He doesn't live here in Folley."

"You read him his rights?" Owens asked.

"Of course."

File in hand, Owens entered the interrogation room. He found the suspect, leaning on the table, his head in his hands. He looked up when he heard the chief enter. "Can we move this along?" he asked. "I need to be with my mother."

Owens sat across from him and glanced at the file. "You won't be going anywhere anytime soon, Nicholas Anhel."

"Really?" he asked. "They said I didn't hit anyone."

Owens looked at him. He couldn't be serious. "You can't go around shooting at people."

"I wasn't shooting at people," he tried to explain. "Just her."

Once Holden knew the shooter was a relation to Bobby, he knew Cecilia was the target. But he didn't like hearing it. Holden got up to leave. Nothing else could be garnered from the interview and he wasn't sure how long he could hold his temper across from a man who tried to kill Cecilia.

"I need to get back to my mother. She's distraught. She can't eat, she can't sleep. All she does is cry. I don't know what to do," Nicholas told him.

"And you think shooting at the courthouse is a good idea?"

"She wants the trial over. Put that woman away. Why isn't it first-degree murder anyway? She killed him in cold blood. He was only running through her yard. A shortcut."

Cecilia's home was not a shortcut to anywhere.

Owens returned to the chair and sat. "Where have you been getting your news on the incident?"

"Just what my mom tells me."

Owens sighed. He could only imagine the biased story she had told him. "Sir, when was the last time you saw your brother?"

"Last Christmas." Or, as Holden calculated it, six arrests ago.

"And what has your mother told you about Robert's run-ins with the law?"

"Youthful indiscretions. Boys being boys."

Holden shook his head at Nicholas's ignorance.

"Come on," Nicholas said. "Bobby was just being a teenage boy."

"I'm sorry, Nicholas, but you've been misinformed. I think you should have had an honest conversation with your uncle, the mayor." Owens got back up and walked to the door.

"Fine. Call him. He'll get me out of here and back to my mother."

"He can't help you now." Owens reached for the doorknob. "Did you honestly think you'd be leaving here tonight? Every media outlet has you on video shooting at police officers, the prosecutor, and a celebrity attorney."

"Well, I was aiming for the murderer," he explained.

"You're lucky you're not a murderer."

Owens left the interview room and thought, *If only*

Cecilia had been as good a shot as Nicholas, none of us would be here.

HOLDEN MADE A few laps around the neighborhood before turning down the small roadway to the reservoir. He parked his truck and got out, wearing his typical rendezvous attire.

Dressed head to toe in black, headlamp on, he hopped over the wire fence, marking the perimeter of the Chandler land, and jogged toward Cecilia's home. He deftly maneuvered around the fallen trees and mounting fallen leaves in the area. He checked over his shoulder to ensure he left no tracks.

As he got to the Chandler fence, he flipped the headlamp off and headed to the sliding glass door. The headlamp was no longer necessary. The home was well lit. Holden had found that when people were afraid, they put lights on. By the looks of it, Cecilia must be terrified. Every light in the house was on. He shouldn't be surprised. Being shot at was terrifying. Holden knew from personal experience.

Dodging the perimeter of the motion sensor light, he jogged toward the back door. Ferris made a short bark, which was out of character. Ferris was not a watchdog.

Holden typically found Ferris sitting, or standing, at the back door, waiting for him during his visits to see Cecilia. Tonight, he heard a large smack against the glass and Cecilia scream, "Ferris!" Holden quickened his pace to the door but stopped when he heard a man's voice.

"Geez, is he okay?" the man asked.

Standing next to the glass door, pinned against the house and out of sight, Holden saw Ferris looking for him. Cecilia rubbed his head. "Yeah, I think he's fine."

Michael, dressed in a robe and flannel bottoms, came into view and also checked the dog.

"What the," Holden whispered.

Michael looked out the glass door. "You think someone is out there?"

Holden didn't move.

"No, the light would go on if there was," Cecilia told him.

"Maybe he has to go to the bathroom." Michael went to open the door but Cecilia put her hand on his. Holden tensed.

"No, let's wait," she told him. "You want that cup of coffee?" She prayed she could get Michael away from the door. Cecilia knew the only reason Ferris would run to the door like that, and knew Holden wouldn't want to be caught in her backyard.

Michael made a final look out the glass door and answered, "Yes, please."

Holden counted to five and ran back the way he came. He ripped off his black T-shirt and put his flannel long-sleeved shirt back on. He slammed the car into gear and headed to the hotel. Sewell needed to know that his assistant was acting inappropriately with a client.

He made a left onto the Chandler street. Getting to the main road, he stopped. He couldn't go to the hotel. He couldn't tell Sewell about Michael. He shouldn't know himself. He'd never be able to explain the inappropriate behavior without divulging his own inappropriate behavior.

He slammed his hand against the steering wheel. What would Sewell do with the knowledge? Remove Michael from the case? How would he explain it? The media was all over this case. It was a scandal Holden doubted Sewell could keep private.

Holden turned right, toward the station and away from the hotel.

Sewell, and his team, was Cecilia's best chance for freedom.

MICHAEL AND CECILIA were sitting at the kitchen island, drinking their beverages. Abigail was upstairs talking on her phone. Cecilia thought it was her girlfriend but Abigail was thin on details. Wyatt was also upstairs, taking a shower. She'd never met a man who took longer in the bathroom.

Ferris sat at her feet, looking out the sliding door onto the backyard. "I still think he has to go to the bathroom," Michael commented.

Cecilia glanced at her watch. Ten minutes had

passed since Ferris had crashed into the glass door. It was enough time for Holden to get away, if that was what had excited Ferris.

"Yeah, maybe you're right." She got up and let him out. Ferris stepped onto the patio and looked around.

"You're a strange dog," Michael told him. "Go make potty, or whatever." Ferris stood there and tilted his head to the right and then to the left.

Cecilia jumped when the doorbell rang.

"Who is that at this hour?" Michael asked.

"I...I don't know." They walked to the front door and Cecilia looked out to find Officer Pugliese. "It's okay, Michael. It's the police." He returned to the kitchen, trying to shoo Ferris to go to the bathroom.

"Everything okay?" she asked when she opened the door.

"It's not okay, if the police are here, Cecilia," Wyatt said, from the top of the stairs.

Cecilia motioned for Pugliese to enter. Pugliese did little to hide his shock as Wyatt strode down the stairs in his sleepwear.

"Don't you think it's inappropriate for you to visit Mrs. Chandler?" Wyatt asked. "You are on the witness stand tomorrow morning. That is, if you and your police department can keep Mrs. Chandler safe and get her into the courtroom alive in the morning."

"Wyatt," Cecilia said, "I don't think that'll happen again." She looked to Pugliese for confirmation. "You don't think that'll happen again, do you?"

"Well..." Vinnie answered, considering a response. Wyatt headed to the kitchen and Vinnie tracked him. "Is that a dressing gown?" Pugliese whispered to Cecilia.

"I don't know," she answered. "I was afraid to ask. I've never seen such an outfit."

"What is he—" Pugliese started to ask Cecilia. "Late-night strategy session?" he asked, hoping that was the answer.

"That is none of your concern, Officer," Wyatt answered. "Your concern should be that you should not be visiting my client without contacting me first."

"And you should not be sleeping with your client," Pugliese snapped.

Cecilia gasped and Wyatt laughed.

"They lost their rooms at the hotel to the jury," Cecilia told him. "That's why he's here. All of them are staying here."

"Oh good." Pugliese sighed in relief. "I did not want to report to the judge that you're sleeping with your client, Mr. Sewell."

Wyatt sat on a stool at the kitchen island. "What has you so concerned that you are visiting this late?"

"Ferris."

Ferris pawed at the glass door and Cecilia opened the door to let him back in. He ran to Pugliese, knocking over an empty stool in his route. Pugliese smiled and patted him on his head. Satisfied, Ferris ran to the counter that held his biscuit jar and waited until Cecilia gave him one, then he ran off to his bed.

"What are you concerned about with Ferris?" Cecilia asked.

"Has someone threatened Ferris?" Wyatt asked.

"No. I think we've all learned people are a little nuts about this case. Someone shot at you today. You think they'd be above poisoning Ferris?" he asked Cecilia.

Cecilia looked at the men in the room, hoping she had misheard. "He...he was shooting at me?"

"Yes," Pugliese answered.

"We were hoping he was aiming for Briscoe," Michael said. He went into his wallet. "I owe Abigail five bucks."

Pugliese ignored the inappropriate wager. "It's not private knowledge where you live. I'm afraid someone might try to hurt Ferris."

"Hurt Ferris?" she asked. She walked over to Ferris and patted him on his back. "How?"

The list that ran through Vinnie's mind was lengthy and he hesitated, hoping to give the least offensive answer. "I've seen neighbor disputes where someone throws poisoned meat into a yard."

"Jeez," Michael whispered.

Vinnie didn't want to cause a panic. He hadn't even mentioned his concerns to anyone in the department. He wanted them to be vigilant. "I'm just saying, keep a close eye on him. I wouldn't let him out loose. I'd walk him around. Make sure he doesn't get something he shouldn't."

Cecilia nodded understanding and mumbled

thanks. Pugliese made to leave, his objective completed. Cecilia started to speak but stopped. She bit her lip and considered telling Pugliese. But she didn't want to get anyone in trouble.

"Something you want to tell me, Cecilia?" Pugliese asked. "Have you had any unwelcome visitors?"

"Well..." she started.

"Cecilia!" Wyatt scolded her. "What aren't you telling us?"

"It was a few months ago," she tried to explain.

Through a clenched jaw, Wyatt asked, "What was a few months ago?"

She hesitated but found her voice before he could yell at her again. "Mrs. Gabbert," she told them.

Michael cursed and Wyatt threw his hands in the air. "And you didn't think you should tell us this?" Wyatt yelled.

Vinnie's jaw dropped. "Why didn't you call the police?" he asked.

Cecilia found the three men's glares intimidating. "I...I didn't want to get her in trouble," she tried to explain to Wyatt. "I didn't want to add to her problems." She looked to Vinnie. "I really didn't think the police would help me. You'd just arrested me."

Vinnie looked at each of them, realizing they probably didn't know. "It was her son who shot at you today." None of them were able to hide their shock. "Just keep a close eye on Ferris, okay?" They all nodded agreement. Vinnie made to leave again.

This time, Michael stopped him. "You know Ferris

heard something in the yard earlier. He attacked the door, trying to get out."

Cecilia couldn't think of a time Ferris tried to attack anything other than his dinner, but she didn't correct Michael. Maybe she was wrong and it wasn't Holden earlier.

"When was this?" Pugliese asked.

Michael glanced at the microwave's clock. "No more than thirty minutes ago."

"I'll take a look around." He looked to Cecilia and then Wyatt for approval. They both agreed.

Pugliese stepped onto the patio and the backyard light turned on, illuminating most of the yard. He walked the perimeter, using his flashlight as needed. He found nothing suspicious until he got to the fence bordering the left middle portion of the yard.

One boot print.

PUGLIESE RETURNED TO the station at the end of his shift. He was surprised to find the chief at his desk. It had been a long day and tomorrow would be a longer one. Both were scheduled to testify in court tomorrow. Plus, the chief would have to coordinate with the sheriff's office on the new security protocols.

Owens hovered over the day's paperwork. The gunman had confessed on the way to the station, plus again to him, and had already been shipped to the county jail. He shook his head in disbelief that he had gunned for Cecilia. Aiming for Briscoe he could understand.

"You are not going to believe what I saw tonight," Pugliese announced when he entered his office.

Holden was already annoyed from his visit to Cecilia's. He didn't need Pugliese to annoy him further. He hadn't heard about any peculiar calls during the night shift, so he doubted he could guess what Pugliese was referring to. He leaned back, waiting for Pugliese to explain, knowing he would need no prompting to do so.

Pugliese plopped down in a chair on the opposite side of Owens's desk and leaned in. "Mr. Wyatt Sewell, celebrity attorney, in a dressing gown."

"A what?"

"A dressing gown. A robe for rich people," he clarified.

Holden furrowed his brows. There had been no calls at the hotel. All his staff had enough sense to contact him if there were any issues with Mr. Sewell or any of the media.

"He was at Mrs. Chandler's," Pugliese added.

This reignited Holden's anger. He'd been at the station thirty minutes before he could put the image of the two of them out of his head. "You mean Michael," Owens corrected him. He regretted it the moment it was out of his mouth.

Pugliese shook his head. "No, Sewell was in the dressing gown. It was burgundy and silk. I think it had some pattern on it. I tried not to stare. Michael was wearing normal clothes. Some sweats, a robe."

"Why were they at CeCe's?" Owens asked. "What are you even talking about?"

Pugliese noted the reference to Mrs. Chandler as CeCe. "You know they got booted out of the hotel, right? They are all there. Too much media, the jury. No room at the inn," Pugliese said, pleased with his timely quote.

Owens could do nothing to hide his pleasure. He grinned and leaned back in his desk chair. He put his feet on the desk.

Pugliese recognized the tread.

CHAPTER 46

CECILIA SAT AT the defense desk, staring at her navy skirt. It felt too short, grazing her knees as she sat. Maybe that's what Abigail had wanted, to have her show a little skin. Cecilia gently pulled on the skirt to cover more skin but was unsuccessful. She pressed her fingers into her thighs, using all her willpower to not untie the bow on her pale pink blouse. She felt like it was choking her. Abigail had assured her it wasn't when she fiddled with it in the car.

Joey wouldn't even recognize her in a getup like this—conservative style, subdued colors. He'd always liked her proclivity toward bright colors and bold patterns.

Cecilia could feel every sensation on her body—the slight tightness at her toes from the pointed navy shoes, the pantyhose covering her legs, the clip pulling her hair back into a tidy ponytail. She wondered if this was what an anxiety attack felt like.

Her fingers were tapping her thighs, in no rhythm she could control. Wyatt put his hand over hers. "You look nervous," Wyatt said.

"I am."

He smiled at her and she waited for reassuring words. "Well, stop," he said.

He turned his attention from her to the jurors as they filed in. Most were well dressed again. The best-dressed juror remained the eldest, again wearing a suit and bowtie.

Briscoe wasted no time and called his first witness. "The prosecution calls Officer Vincent Pugliese to the stand."

After Briscoe established who Pugliese was, Folley police officer for seven years, he asked, "Can you please tell us what happened on the night you were called to the Chandler home?"

"I received a call from dispatch. Shots fired on Floral Lane." He maintained eye contact with Briscoe, afraid to look anywhere else. Pugliese found himself nervous. He'd been on the stand before but not in any case of this magnitude. Most of his testimony had been at traffic court. "I arrived on the scene at 2:23 a.m. and found Mrs. Chandler on the floor of the kitchen. She was in no immediate distress and I looked into the backyard. The deceased, Mr. Robert Gabbert, was outside."

"Why did you look outside?" Briscoe asked. "Is that where Ms. Chandler told you to look?"

"She didn't answer my initial questions. I looked out the door because the gun was lying by the sliding door."

"Was the sliding door closed?"

"Yes."

"What happened next?"

Cecilia listened as Pugliese recounted police procedures taken at her home—most of which she was unaware. The photos taken, the search of her home for other weapons, the removal of the body.

"Did you have reason to revisit the Chandler home later that day? With the chief of police?" Briscoe asked.

"Objection, Your Honor," Sewell said. "You've already ruled on this matter."

"Sustained," Judge Lowe ruled. He glared at Briscoe.

Briscoe's attempt to get the confession in thwarted, he walked back to the prosecutor's desk. "I'm finished with this witness," Briscoe announced, sitting.

Sewell got up to cross-examine Officer Pugliese. He stood at the podium, set up for either attorney to use for their questioning of witnesses.

"Good to see you, Officer Pugliese. How are your holiday preparations going? Shopping done?"

"Objection, Your Honor," Briscoe said.

"Sustained," Judge Lowe answered.

Pugliese laughed and answered without registering the judge's ruling. "I'm more of a Christmas Eve shopper." A few people in the gallery laughed.

"You said Ms. Chandler didn't answer your initial questions. Why not?"

Pugliese glanced at Cecilia before he answered. "She appeared to be in shock."

"But you said she was in no acute distress?"

"Yes."

Sewell pulled out a crime scene photo, an eight-by-ten photo, of the kitchen. The white floors and white cabinets were covered in blood. He walked in front of the jury, ensuring each juror saw the photo, before standing in front of Pugliese.

"Is this where she was sitting?" Sewell asked, pointing to an area on the floor with no blood.

Pugliese looked and nodded his head. "Yes, she was leaning against the kitchen cabinets."

"That's a lot of blood, don't you think, Officer?"

"Well"—Pugliese looked at the photo again— "yes."

"But you said she was in no acute distress."

"She was breathing but was covered in blood."

"Her own blood?"

"It appeared so. And the dog's." He turned to the jury, doing the best he could to defend himself. "The paramedics were there quickly and they attended to her. They took her to the hospital."

Sewell walked back to the podium and put the photo away. "Do you have a dog, Officer Pugliese?"

The officer swung his head from the jury to Sewell, surprised by the question. "No."

From the podium, Sewell asked, "Where did you find Mr. Gabbert's car?"

Pugliese was puzzled by Sewell's line of questioning. Briscoe's had been straightforward, sequential. Sewell was all over the place. "A few blocks away," he answered.

"And what did you find in it?" Sewell asked.

Pugliese rattled off the itemized list of the car's contents. None of it was of note, except the last, which Sewell asked him to repeat. "An overnight bag."

Sewell glanced as his paperwork on the podium before asking, "And what did that overnight bag contain?"

"Binoculars. Duct tape. Rope. A towel."

Sewell pulled out a photo of the bag found in Bobby's trunk. He showed it to the jury. "What did the officers at the station call that?"

"Objection," Briscoe said.

"Overruled," Judge Lowe ruled.

Pugliese could feel Briscoe's glare before he answered. "A two-six-one bag."

"Please explain to the jury what that means," Sewell asked.

Pugliese glanced at Briscoe for help. He had none to offer and was looking at his notes. "Two-six-one is police code for rape."

Sewell nodded and put the photo away. "Do you buy your mother a Christmas gift?"

Briscoe was fuming and didn't object fast enough. "Of course," Pugliese answered.

Sewell continued his cross-examination, returning to the far end of the jury box. He liked to take peeks at the jurors, to monitor their attention and reactions. "You said you received a call that 'shots' were fired."

"Yes."

Sewell began rapid-firing questioning. "How many shots were fired?"

"One."

"And how did you ascertain that?"

"Only one round was missing."

"Have you investigated any other shootings?"

"Yes."

"How many times do most people shoot?"

Pugliese shrugged and answered, "Depends."

"How many times are you taught to shoot an attacker?"

Pugliese straightened his posture, in preparation to defend his profession. Contrary to popular belief, police officers were not trained to shoot to kill. "We're not taught to shoot an attacker, sir."

"What are you taught?" Sewell asked.

"We are taught to stop the threat."

"So if you need to use your gun?"

"You use it until the threat is stopped."

"So, that could mean you use all the bullets in the gun?"

"Yes."

Sewell nodded and moved on. "Do you get called out on neighbor disputes?"

Pugliese found Sewell's cross-examination dizzying. He answered simply, "Yes."

"Are any of these shootings?"

"Sometimes."

"Any of them fire a warning shot?"

"On occasion."

"And how many times will they fire their weapon, as a warning?"

"Once."

"And again, how many times did Mrs. Chandler shoot?"

"Once."

Sewell nodded. "When you got to the Chandler residence, how did you get in?"

"Front door."

"Was it opened? Unlocked?"

"No." Pugliese pursed his lips. He despised Sewell's smug tone. He knew where Sewell was headed and answered before the defense attorney asked. "There was no answer so I kicked in the door."

"Do you do that a lot?"

Through a clenched jaw, he answered, "When necessary."

"I'm sorry, Officer Pugliese. I meant the Chandler house in particular."

"Objection!" Briscoe yelled.

Sewell smiled at Pugliese, before saying, "Withdrawn."

Mr. Sewell headed toward the defense desk and everyone waited for him to say he was done with this witness. Instead, he turned and asked, "Do you buy a Christmas present for your car?"

Officer Pugliese shook his head no while Briscoe yelled, "Objection."

Sewell was smiling when he sat down. Pugliese waited to be excused by the judge.

"Redirect, Your Honor?" Briscoe asked.

Judge Lowe nodded and ruled, "Go ahead."

Briscoe stood up and walked to the witness stand. "Where did you find the bag?"

"In the trunk."

"So this bag was not on his person?" Briscoe deliberately didn't refer to the bag as a rape bag.

"Correct."

"Typically when a person plans to commit a crime, do they not carry their tools with them?"

"Yes but—"

Briscoe stopped him from continuing. "Thank you, Officer. That is all for this witness."

"Redirect," Sewell said. Judge Lowe signaled for Pugliese to stay in the witness stand. Small beads of perspiration were forming on his forehead.

"But what, Officer?" Sewell asked.

"But if he were only casing the house, he wouldn't have the bag on him."

"Does Mr. Gabbert have a history of this type of crime?" Sewell asked. He knew what would happen next and he headed back to the defense desk.

"Objection," Briscoe yelled.

"He opened the door, Your Honor," Sewell retorted, as he sat.

"You've ruled on this matter, Your Honor," Briscoe reminded him.

"Sustained," the judge ruled.

Sewell smiled at Briscoe, who thought he had won.

CHIEF OWENS WAS standing on the courthouse steps monitoring the situation. He'd never seen so many people in Folley before.

"Judge wants to see you," the bailiff told him. Owens followed him to the judge's chambers.

Judge Lowe was sitting at his desk, drinking a cup of coffee. "Want some?" he asked, pointing to the half empty carafe of coffee.

"No, thanks," he answered. He didn't need anything else to get him hyped up.

"You're up next," Judge Lowe told him.

"Yes, sir." Owens didn't need the reminder.

Judge Lowe took a sip of coffee and looked out his office window. "How's it going out there today?"

"Still as crowded but more orderly. The sheriff sent a lot of officers to help."

Judge Lowe took another sip of his coffee. "You'll have them for the length of the trial?"

"Yes," he answered, nodding his head. "At a high expense."

"Mayor Townsend is going to flip about that."

"I left him a message this morning." He'd been glad Mayor Townsend hadn't been available. He would have more questions than Owens had answers. "Do you know how long the trial will last?"

"Based on the witness list, about a week." Owens nodded and breathed a large sigh of relief. "Tell me about it!" The judge was also thankful. His colleagues had presided over murder trials that extended months. "How's the town doing?"

"Pretty good. All the businesses are loving it. Selling more gas. All the area hotels are booked. Restaurants getting more diners. CB's Diner wanted to know if I had a reservation when I stopped by for breakfast this morning."

"Geez. I better not need a reservation later. I always have their Wednesday lunch special."

CB's Sloppy Joe's were legendary but not good for the uniform. For fit or for look. The sandwich lived up to its "sloppy" name. Holden only had it on rare occasions.

"Plus, it's bringing out people's entrepreneurial spirit," Owens added.

"What do you mean?"

"They're setting up stands outside their houses. Selling things."

"Like…"

"Placards, water, snacks. Some are renting out their garages or land to park." He laughed before telling the most unusual thing for sale. "I saw one charging to use their bathroom. He had quite a line too."

The judge laughed. "Is that legal?"

"Briscoe's too busy with the trial."

Judge Lowe nodded and his smile slowly faded. His mood turned sober. "You'll have extra security for the verdict, right?" Owens nodded. Sheriff Wilkins and him had already discussed it. "You know this could destroy a town. Right?"

Of course Owens did. But right now, he was only concerned that his testimony could destroy Cecilia's life.

CHIEF HOLDEN OWENS found Officer Pugliese seated on a bench outside the building, on the alley off First Street. It was likely the only quiet place in the area. The chants and murmurings of the crowd could be heard but it was light background noise here. Not the overwhelming pandemonium it was in the front of the courthouse. Owens had expected a smaller contingent of protestors today. He'd assumed people would be put off by the shooting. He was wrong.

Holden sat next to the glum officer and asked, "Was Sewell that bad? Or was it Briscoe?"

"I thought you said Mrs. Chandler didn't tell anyone what I did the night the ankle monitor alarm went off?"

It was Sewell then, Owens realized. "If CeCe told the lawyer, it was after the hearing with the judge. Most importantly, she didn't tell the judge."

Pugliese ran his hand through his hair. "I don't know what to do."

"Calm down. If Sewell was going to do something with it, he would have done it by now."

"Well, he just did something with it! If the media

finds out—"

"Don't worry about it." Owens's phone buzzed.

It was a text from Briscoe. "Where are you?! You're on stand in ten."

Owens got up to head inside the courthouse. "It's almost time for your shift. Just keep the peace out there, alright?" he told him, pointing to the front of the courthouse. Pugliese nodded.

Briscoe was standing outside the courtroom, arms crossed, when Owens arrived.

"Where have you been?"

"I've been working, Briscoe," Owens answered, but Briscoe had already moved onto his next gripe.

"I wanted to go through a few key questions again."

Once had been enough, Owens thought. "I got it. Keep the answers simple."

They entered the courtroom and Holden stood in the back. All the seats in the gallery were taken. The judge and jurors filed back in and, when the judge gave the signal, Briscoe announced, "The prosecution calls Chief Holden Owens to the stand."

Cecilia avoided eye contact with him as he walked to the stand in full uniform. She'd become accustomed to seeing him in his stealth attire. She'd seen him more often in that than in his police uniform.

She kept her head down, looking at the legal pad in front of her, and didn't notice the many women in the gallery who admired him, and checked for a wedding ring, as he took his oath.

Holden avoided eye contact with Cecilia as well. He felt all eyes on him, as he put his hand on the Bible, repeated the oath, and sat down in the witness stand.

Briscoe had the same line of questioning with Owens as he did with Pugliese. When had he arrived on scene, what had he found, what procedures were taken.

Owens answered each question succinctly. Cecilia, and the jury, did not hear one thing new. She, and the defense team, noticed more than one jurors' eyes glaze over by the monotone and tedious testimony.

Briscoe completed his questioning and turned to find his assistant, Marcy, smiling. He misinterpreted it, believing the testimony had been effective. It was a smile not intended for him, but for the witness.

SEWELL STOOD AND began his cross-examination from the podium. There was a pit in Owens's stomach as he waited for Sewell's first question. He'd never been nervous before on the stand but the stakes had never been as high.

With Briscoe, he'd known what was coming; with Sewell, he had no idea. Owens glanced at Cecilia, who was looking at the jury. She was in a pink blouse and blue skirt, not the usual tight pants and old band T-shirt he was used to seeing her in. Or that he had come to look forward to seeing her in.

He briefly wondered how much she had told Sewell about him. She had told him about Pugliese breaking down her door, only after Sewell's questioning after the hearing. Could she have told him what caused the alarm? That cleaning around the monitor had triggered it? And that he was the one who had been cleaning it? During one of his evening visits to her home?

Further questions evaporated from his mind when Sewell began his cross-examination. "Are you finished with your Christmas shopping, Chief Owens?"

Owens was startled by the question. He didn't have anyone to buy for anymore. Not since the divorce. He sent money to his sister and sister-in-law and they would buy gifts for his niece and nephews.

Briscoe objected before he could answer.

"Just making conversation, Your Honor," Sewell explained. "Did you know Robert Gabbert?"

"Yes."

"How did you know him?"

Owens looked at Judge Lowe. "Objection," Briscoe yelled. He scurried up to the judge. "You've ruled on this matter, Your Honor."

"Yes, Mr. Briscoe, I have. Mr. Sewell, I'm warning you. Bring this up again and I'll be forced to grant a mistrial." Through clenched teeth, he added, "I do not want a mistrial. I do not want to go through this mess again."

Mr. Sewell nodded understanding and returned to Chief Owens. "You didn't immediately arrest Mrs.

Chandler, did you?"

"No."

"Why not?"

Owens glanced over at Cecilia and contemplated his response. She was looking at her hands. He could feel Briscoe's glare. He answered as Briscoe had instructed him. They both knew this question was coming. "I arrested Mrs. Chandler when Mr. Briscoe obtained an arrest warrant."

Holden braced himself for Sewell's next question on why he would wait for an arrest warrant when he found the shooter, only yards away, from the deceased.

"Do you like dogs?" Sewell asked.

The question put him off balance and he answered, "Yes."

"Do you have one?"

"Not currently." Owens had been trained to answer all lawyer questions succinctly, yet he heard himself go on. "Baxter died a couple years ago." A chocolate Labrador who had loved the water and would spend hours with Holden at the lake.

"I'm sorry for your loss," Sewell said. Owens nodded, appreciating the condolences. He'd taken the loss hard. It was the last time he could remember crying. "Did you buy him Christmas presents?"

Owens smiled. "Yes. A big rawhide bone every year." The biggest he could find.

"Your Honor," Briscoe interrupted.

"Move it along, Mr. Sewell," Judge Lowe instructed him.

Sewell nodded and walked over to the jury box. The jurors were more engaged in his questioning than with Briscoe's. They sat at attention, waiting for his next question, most of them watching Owens, especially the ladies. "You have the ability to arrest someone at the scene of the crime, do you not, Chief Owens?"

With happy memories of Baxter floating through his head, it took him a moment to process the question before he could answer, "Yes."

"You do not need an arrest warrant to arrest someone, do you?"

"No."

"So, I'll ask again, why did you not immediately arrest Mrs. Chandler?"

Chief Owens looked at Sewell. He didn't want to look at Cecilia or Briscoe. He didn't want to waver. "I did not feel a crime had been committed."

With his point made, most defense attorneys would have ended the questioning there. Ask for a lunch break to leave this as the last statement in the jurors' ears.

Mr. Sewell was not most attorneys.

"Do you buy your couch a Christmas gift?"

Owens laughed and shook his head no, while Briscoe yelled objection.

CHAPTER 47

L UNCH HAD LULLED many of the protestors into quiet. Many sat talking to each other, no longer shouting at their opposition. Holden was leaning against his patrol car, enjoying the peace and hoping it would last.

Vinnie joined him and they watched the crowd for several minutes before Pugliese shattered the peace. "You look better than me after testifying."

Holden shrugged.

"I guess he wasn't as tough on you," Vinnie said.

Holden shrugged again.

"Mrs. Chandler looked very nice today, didn't she?"

Holden turned to Vinnie, not liking where the questions were going.

"So how long has it been going on?" Vinnie asked.

"What?" Holden asked.

"You and Mrs. Chandler." Vinnie smirked at the glaring Holden. He corrected himself. "Or should I say you and CeCe?"

Owens shook his head and asked again, "What?"

"I saw those looks between the two of you in the courtroom."

Holden had used every ounce of strength not to look at Cecilia while testifying. He'd only failed once.

"You weren't in the courtroom when I testified. You're not allowed in the courtroom in case they call you on rebuttal," Holden reminded him and resumed monitoring the crowd.

"Fine," Vinnie conceded. "But I know."

"You don't know anything."

Vinnie smiled. "You'd be surprised how much I know. I'm a detective."

"You're a patrol officer," Owens corrected him. He looked over at Vinnie. "Detective? I thought you wanted my job."

"After this mess?" He pointed to the circus in view. "No thanks. I want to transfer to the city and be a detective."

"Okay." This was news to Holden and hard to imagine. He couldn't picture Pugliese lasting a week in the city's police department.

"So back to you and Cecilia."

"There is no me and CeCe." Holden bit his lip on the slip. He now realized he'd made it before in Vinnie's presence.

Vinnie ignored him. "How long have you been seeing each other?"

"We are not seeing each other."

"Another term then? I don't know what your generation says."

"I'm not that much older than you, Pug."

Vinnie smiled broadly. "I have hit a nerve. That's

your tell. You only call me 'Pug' when you are annoyed."

"Yes, I am annoyed. You are implying I'm dating a defendant. It is a fireable offense."

Pugliese nodded and turned somber. He was disappointed that the chief thought he'd use the information against him. He was only motivated by one thing. The same thing that motivated him to find Jeremiah. To prove that he was right. "Let's talk in hypotheticals then."

"Talk all you want. I'm not listening to this nonsense."

"I'll tell you what I've observed." He cleared his throat. "Ferris likes you. Fearful of all the other officers, he ran to you. You know where his biscuit jar is. Your truck's tire imprint was on the side road by her house. The one to the reservoir. Where I found Ferris when he got loose. Because he was looking for you. Because you must have been visiting pretty regularly." Pleased with himself, Vinnie took a break before continuing. "Last night, your shoe print was on her property. By the fence, in the mud. You must have gone over there to check on her after the shooting. You must have seen Michael and gotten jealous, because you were in a mood when I got to the station. When I told you that the defense team had been kicked out of the hotel, you were relieved. You smiled."

Holden couldn't hide his surprise. He had grossly undervalued Pugliese's policing skills. Maybe he could make it as a detective in the city.

CECILIA SAT WITH Abigail at the defense desk, while Michael and Wyatt spoke over in the corner. Cecilia watched them and wondered what they were discussing. She couldn't tell if it was good or bad. For all she knew it could be about what to have for dinner.

The case was called back to trial and everyone returned to their spots.

Briscoe announced, "The prosecution calls Dr. Alfred Kinney to the stand."

Ferris's veterinarian walked to the witness stand. He was dressed in a gray suit, not his usual blue scrubs and lab coat.

"How long have you been Ferris's veterinarian?" Briscoe asked.

"Three years. Since Joe took him in."

"Joe?"

"Mr. Chandler."

Briscoe remained at the podium. He didn't wander the courtroom like Sewell did. He didn't want to distract the jurors. "You said Joe took him in. Not Joe and Cecilia Chandler?"

"No," he answered. He looked at the jurors and added, "I didn't meet Mrs. Chandler until Joe's funeral."

"So she wouldn't come to Ferris's checkups?"

"No," the veterinarian answered.

Briscoe didn't need to but he glanced at his list of questions. He'd reviewed all his questions so many times he knew them all verbatim. "Did Ferris have any emergency visits?"

"Yes. Three."

"Did she come to any of those?"

Dr. Kinney shook his head. "No."

"In your records, who is Mr. or Ms. Chandler to Ferris?" Briscoe asked.

"His owner."

Mr. Briscoe smiled. Dr. Kinney had been prepped well by him for his testimony. The doctor answered the questions quickly and briefly. Briscoe had made two of his points regarding Ferris and headed toward the remaining two.

"Do you carry malpractice insurance?" Briscoe asked.

"Of course."

"How much is it annually?"

"Four hundred and eighty-seven dollars."

"How much is malpractice insurance for a human doctor?"

"I don't know."

Briscoe walked over to the prosecutor desk. He'd prepped Marcy well also and she handed him the requested pieces of paper. He handed one to the defense team, one to the judge, and one to Dr. Kinney.

"Do you perform surgeries in your clinic?" Briscoe asked.

"Yes."

"Do you know the malpractice insurance for a surgeon who works on people?"

"No."

"Can you read the highlighted section regarding surgeon malpractice insurance in this state?" Briscoe held up the paper and pointed to the highlighted area, so the jurors could see.

Dr. Kinney put his glasses on and read, "Twenty to twenty-eight thousand dollars per year, based on coverage purchased."

"Why do you think your insurance is so much less for working on animals as doctors working on people?" Briscoe asked.

"Objection," Sewell interrupted. "Dr. Kinney is not qualified to answer questions on insurance premiums."

"Sustained," Judge Lowe ruled.

"What is Ferris worth?" Briscoe asked.

"He failed out of service training, so nothing."

There were a few murmurings in the crowd. Judge Lowe slapped his gavel. "Quiet." The side talk ceased. "Anything else, Mr. Briscoe?"

"No, Your Honor. I'm finished with this witness." Briscoe sat at the prosecution desk and exchanged smiles with Marcy. They were the only ones smiling in the courtroom.

Mr. Sewell got up to question the veterinarian. Briscoe's questioning had been effective. He noted several jurors taking notes at the high points. The bow-tied elder gentleman took notes at every good point Briscoe made.

"If Ferris hadn't failed out of service training, would he be worth something?" Sewell asked.

"Well, he'd have more value." Sewell didn't push for what that meant exactly. He didn't want a dollar figure placed on Ferris. Sewell already had one.

"Do you have any pets, Dr. Kinney?" Sewell asked.

"Of course," he answered. "Two dogs and a cat."

Sewell walked over to the jury box. "Do you buy them Christmas gifts?"

"No."

Mr. Sewell was surprised by the answer but didn't let the jury see. He noticed the veterinarian's wedding band. "Does your wife?"

"Yes," he answered.

"Do you buy your wife a Christmas present?"

"Of course." Although being taught by Briscoe to answer all simply, he couldn't help himself and added, "I'd be in the dog house if I didn't."

Mr. Sewell laughed at the pun. "Is Ferris in good health?"

"Yes."

"Has Mrs. Chandler brought him in for his regular checkups?"

"Joe...Mr. Chandler would bring him in for checkups."

"But since his death last year, has Mrs. Chandler maintained the appointments?"

"No."

Sewell turned and returned to the podium. With his back to the jury, Sewell shot Cecilia a look. She had sworn Dr. Kinney could say nothing to harm her.

The defense team had instructed Cecilia to remain neutral at all times at the defense team desk. If she needed to react, she would have to wait for a break and go into their room to do so in private.

"What appointment did she miss?" Sewell asked.

"The follow-up after the incident. When he was cut with the knife." Dr. Kinney turned to the jury and told them, "He had stitches."

Cecilia scribbled something on a piece of paper and slid it over to Abigail. She looked at it and slid it to the corner of the desk for Sewell.

"Did Mrs. Chandler bring him into the clinic after the attack?" Sewell asked, heading over to the desk.

"No, I made an emergency house call. It was three in the morning." He smiled, proud of himself for his dedication to animals. "Mrs. Chandler was not there."

"Because she was at the hospital," Sewell clarified, for the benefit of the jury. He took a quick peek at the note and slid it in his pocket. He initiated another round of rapid-fire questions. "Did she pick him up from your clinic?"

"Yes."

"Did she seem concerned about Ferris's well-being?"

"Yes."

"The stitches. They were absorbable?"

"Yes."

"So a follow-up wasn't really necessary?"

"Well, no. But I like to check."

"So you can collect the office visit fee?" Sewell asked. Dr. Kinney didn't answer and Sewell continued. "Do you know why Cecilia didn't make the follow-up visit?"

"No."

"Did you call to check on your patient?"

"No."

"Why not?"

Dr. Kinney stuttered, "I—I—"

"If she had called for a home visit, would you have gone?"

Sewell waited for an answer that would not come. Dr. Kinney did not want to answer that he wanted nothing to do with Mrs. Chandler. Her house was inundated with media the days after the attack and he would not have wanted to be seen entering her home. It could have negatively affected his business. "Well, she was under house arrest, so a follow-up visit was not possible," Sewell stated.

"Objection," Briscoe shouted from his desk. "Who's testifying here?"

"Sustained. Keep to asking the questions, not answering them, Mr. Sewell."

He nodded and walked over to Abigail. She handed him a folder. "You said Ferris is worthless?"

"Yes."

"But he's worth a lot to you, isn't he?"

Dr. Kinney looked from one lawyer to the next

and then to the judge. "I don't understand."

"In the time Ferris has been living with the Chandlers, how much money have you made off of Ferris?"

"Oh..." Dr. Kinney hesitated. "I don't know."

Sewell handed him the folder. "Here are the itemized bills for Ferris's care." Dr. Kinney nodded and scanned the pages. There were a lot of pages. "What is the total, highlighted in yellow, on the last page?"

Dr. Kinney pursed his lips before answering. "Your Honor, I...I can't know if this is an accurate amount."

The judge looked at the papers. "These look like your invoices, Dr. Kinney." The judge had gotten enough of those over the years with Fluffy. "Are you saying they aren't?"

"Well, no, but..."

"Just answer the question then."

Dr. Kinney cleared his throat. "Nine thousand, five hundred and sixty-three dollars."

The gallery gasped at the inordinate amount. Judge Lowe didn't command them to be silent because he gasped as well.

"And?" Sewell asked.

"Seventy-three cents."

"And over how long a period?"

Dr. Kinney looked from the first invoice to the last. "Three years."

"And you said earlier Ferris is in good health?"

"Yes, but—"

Sewell cut him off and continued, "How much do

you charge for a home visit?"

"Oh...I don't know offhand."

Sewell handed him the invoice for the night of the attack. "How much does it say you charged?"

"Five hundred dollars."

"What else did you charge Cecilia for?"

"Objection," Briscoe yelled. "How is this relevant?"

Sewell looked to the judge. "I'm getting to that, Your Honor."

"Overruled. Please read the charges, Dr. Kinney."

Dr. Kinney nodded and read down the list of charges, including vaccinations.

"Are Ferris's vaccinations up to date?"

"Yes. Ferris is up to date on all vaccinations."

"Have you ever see any signs of neglect?"

"No."

Mr. Sewell paused, allowing the jury to take in that Ferris was well cared for under Cecilia's care, before changing the line of questioning. "Did you know the veterinarian associations are fighting domestic animals becoming legally people?"

"Yes."

"Why is that?"

Dr. Kinney did little to hide his annoyance with the defense attorney. "You'd have to ask them."

"Is it because you like that legally a pet is worth 'nothing'?" Sewell asked, using Dr. Kinney's own words against him. "Nothing to sue over if something goes wrong. Keeps those malpractice premiums low, doesn't it?"

"Objection," Briscoe said. "As you ruled earlier, Dr. Kinney cannot answer questions about malpractice premiums."

"Sustained," Judge Lowe ruled.

"You and your colleagues want to keep pets as property yet, when clients bring their pets to you for treatment, you refer to these pets as their 'babies'. You refer to the owner as their 'mommy' or their 'daddy'. Don't you?" Dr. Kinney paused, contemplating an answer. "I'll bring some of your clients or staff in to verify if you don't admit it."

"Yes, I do."

With eyebrows furrowed, as if he didn't know the answer, Sewell asked, "And why do you that?"

"Because that's what the owner wants," Dr. Kinney answered. Briscoe smiled, glad Dr. Kinney had reiterated 'owner' as his clients' relationships to their dogs.

Mr. Sewell laughed. "Come on. How much do you make a year, Dr. Kinney?"

"Objection. Not relevant," Briscoe said.

"Sustained," Judge Lowe ruled.

Sewell continued, "Enough to keep a summer house in Mexico and a large home? One of the most expensive homes in Folley?"

"Yes."

"You have built a sturdy and very profitable practice exploiting the relationships of clients and their pets. You profit off a client viewing their pet as a child, a member of the family. They spend more money when they are trying to save the life of their dog or their cat, versus if they were trying to save a piece of property like an oven. If an oven breaks you get a new one. If a pet breaks, what do you do? Bring him to you...for a *sizable* fee." Sewell waved the invoices in the air.

"Is there a question?" Mr. Briscoe asked the judge.

The judge looked to Mr. Sewell.

"Thank you, Dr. Kinney." Mr. Sewell walked toward the defense table. "Oh, last question."

A juror tried to hide her smile.

"Do you buy your oven a Christmas gift?" Mr. Sewell asked.

Dr. Kinney paused before answering, "No."

CHAPTER 48

CECILIA HAD TURNED off her phone at night. The next morning, with Ferris next to her on bed, she turned it on.

Several texts from her sister, Janna, appeared. One was "Your phone is off." Momentarily, she thought maybe her sister had forgotten about the trial.

"Can't make trial. Can't get off work. Boss says sister on trial for murder not excusable absence."

"Oh thank God," Cecilia muttered.

"What's that about?" Abigail asked as she entered the room.

"My sister won't be coming to the trial."

"Oh, that is a 'thank God'." Abigail went to her closet and starting looking at options.

Cecilia read the last text from Janna. "You're dressing better. Abigail doing good job as always."

"She approves of your costume design work with me," Cecilia told Abigail.

"Thank you," she said, giving a small curtesy.

"She knows your name. Are you well known because of Sewell?"

"He encourages us to be active on social media."

Cecilia's eyebrows raised, fearing what she might

share about her.

"Nothing about our clients and never when we're at trial," Abigail added.

Ferris stood up and stretched before jumping off the bed.

"Looks like I'm going to need to find Ferris a new vet," Cecilia said.

"I would say so," Abigail answered.

Abigail laid out the day's outfit on the bedside chair. A pink sweater set and gray skirt.

"Can't I wear pants?" Cecilia got up and pulled out a few pairs of pants that would match.

"No. Skirts or dresses the whole trial. The women here expect you to wear a skirt or a dress. And the men want to see you in one."

"Fine." Cecilia acquiesced. "But I wore that skirt during jury selection," Cecilia reminded her.

"I know." She pulled out two-inch gray heels to match and placed them by the chair. "You want to appear neat, clean, and relatable. We can't have you in a new outfit every day."

Cecilia nodded, trying to push the notion from her head that she was being judged on her attire.

"We want you to look nice but not too nice. Repeating clothing makes them more able to identify with you." Abigail stepped back to appraise her work. "If you have a new outfit on every day, they'll think you're rich and un-relatable. Not one of them."

But I'm not one of them, Cecilia thought.

THE PRO-GABBERT PROTESTORS had noticed a lull in enthusiasm the day before. The pro-Ferris section was louder, more organized, and more populated than the pro-Gabbert side.

The Gabbert supporters knew they needed to bolster morale. They needed a larger crowd. They needed more media attention.

And only one person could do that.

The victim's mother.

Peggy Gabbert arrived at the courthouse and marveled at the scene. She was equally repulsed by the pro-Chandler side as she was pleased by the pro-Bobby side. As she had been each day of the trial.

She'd been pleased when a supporter, Ariika Johnson, had called her and asked her to speak before the day's proceedings. Once meeting arrangements were made, she hung up and called her brother.

The call went to voicemail. She left a message pleading for his support at the protest. She and Bobby needed him. She, and Ariika, knew the mayor's presence would garner even more attention than just Peggy's presence.

Ariika met her at her car and they headed to the cordoned-off area. "I'm sorry, Mrs. Gabbert," the officer said as she stopped her at the gate. "We have to search everyone." Officer Margaret Monty went through Peggy's purse and patted her down. She was glad Mrs. Gabbert didn't recognize her as the officer who had subdued her son, Nicholas, after the shooting.

Once in the protestors' area, Ariika escorted Peggy through the middle of their section. Pro-Gabbert attendees called out their condolences and their support to the grieving mother. Ariika assisted her onto a box so the crowd could see her.

Murmurings of "shh" went through the crowd. Peggy looked at the crowd of hundreds. Ariika's social media postings advertising a special speaker before the day's proceedings had worked. The crowd was larger than the day before. Much to her annoyance, even the pro-Ferris side was bigger.

Everyone quieted and waited for Peggy to begin. Even those on the opposing side.

She surveyed the posters that the crowd held. Some for her and some against.

Pro-life posters. Posters with Bobby's picture on it.

Every life matters posters. Posters with dogs, calling them their best friends.

She stood frozen. What was she doing here? She wasn't the public speaker. That was George. She didn't like the spotlight. That was George. She scanned the crowd hoping to see his face. She hoped he would save her once again, because that's what big brothers did.

But he wasn't there. He was hundreds of miles away, doing everything he could to forget the trial and bolster his hairline.

Nothing Peggy could say or do here could give her what she wanted. Nothing could bring her son back.

Someone yelled, "We love you, Momma!" and it woke Peggy from her trance.

"Good morning, everyone. My name is Margaret Gabbert." There were cheers. "You can call me Peggy." Many screamed "Peggy" in response. "I'm thankful so many of you are here, supporting me, my family, and most of all, supporting Bobby." She glanced at the pro-Ferris side and held her tongue. "My boy, Robert Harrison Gabbert, is gone. He was killed—murdered—by that Chandler woman.

"Now, the police have taken my other boy. They've arrested him for protecting his mother—"

The statement was met with boos and hisses from the other side. The opposing protestors yelled about her hypocrisy, but they were out yelled by the pro-Gabbert side.

Peggy raised her voice to be heard over the crowd. "Distraught with grief, my boy Nicholas was trying to do right by me, to do right for his brother."

The supporters began chanting "Justice for Bobby!"

The opponents began chanting "Justice for Ferris!"

She tried resuming her speech but was drowned out by the chants. They had lost interest in her and had returned to their interest in each other. Peggy looked at the courthouse and knew it was time for her to go. The attendees had begun filing in. She stepped off the box and made her way out of the protest area.

She made her way toward her waiting seat behind Briscoe.

The opposing sides didn't notice her departure. They were only concerned with their opposing views.

What good had it done? she thought. Bobby was still dead.

THE JURORS FILED into their section. Cecilia noted that more than one of the ladies wore a shirt they had worn previously. Being sequestered must be difficult, Cecilia thought. At least while under house arrest, she had access to all her usual items. How did one pack quickly for a trial that had no set end date?

The first juror caught her eye again, dressed in a suit and bowtie, as usual. He reminded Cecilia of her grandfather. He was a by-the-rules kind of man. Things were black or white. No areas of gray.

Briscoe stood and announced, "The prosecution calls Dr. Vanessa Landry to the stand."

In a navy business suit, cut slightly below her knee, she headed to the stand. She pushed her oversized black-framed glasses up the bridge of her nose when she sat.

"What do you do for a living?" Briscoe asked.

"I'm the state's medical examiner."

Cecilia recognized her name but had never met her before. She'd read the name on Joey's death certificate. She had performed his autopsy as well.

"What are your qualifications?" he asked.

"I have a medical degree with a specialization in forensic pathology."

Briscoe stood at the podium, asking his questions, as he did with the other witnesses. "How long have you been doing this?"

"Nine years."

"Do you work here in Folley?"

"As needed."

"How often is that?"

"Not often," she answered. "You don't get many homicides or suspicious deaths here."

"Did you examine Mr. Robert Gabbert?"

"Yes."

"Please tell us your findings."

Dr. Landry pointed to Marcy, who arranged the easel and stood next to it. She removed the first panel, a blank one, when Dr. Landry instructed her to do so. It revealed a wide shot of Gabbert's nude dead body on the morgue's table.

"I performed an autopsy on the deceased on the fifth." She signaled to Marcy, who removed the wide-shot photo for a close-up of Gabbert's head. "He died of a gunshot to his head." Dr. Landry pulled out a laser pointer and used the red beam at the gunshot wound.

"How close was Mr. Gabbert from the gunman?"

She signaled to Marcy again. Marcy removed the photograph of Gabbert's dead face, revealing a schematic drawing. The diagram had the Chandler's backyard, its trees, the fence, and the patio furniture. It also had Gabbert's dead body position and Cecilia's standing position.

"Based on the victim's and perpetrator's height, and gun type, I've established Ms. Chandler was approximately fifteen to twenty feet from the victim."

"So, not in immediate danger."

"Objection," Sewell said before she could answer.

"Withdrawn," Briscoe stated before the judge could rule. "Thank you, Dr. Landry."

Briscoe turned to return to the prosecution desk. He signaled to Marcy that the questioning was done. She placed the panels back onto easel. The close-up shot of Gabbert's face on top.

Mr. Sewell stood to cross-examine Dr. Landry. He headed to the easel knowing he wouldn't have the jurors' full attention until he removed the morbid shot.

"How are you today, Dr. Landry?" he asked, while he pulled out the crime sketch schematic and placed it on top.

"Fine."

"Are you preparing for the holidays?" He walked to the podium.

"Yes."

"Have you bought gifts for family and friends?"

"If we have agreed to do so and have established spending limits, yes."

Sewell pointed to the diagram. "Lovely schematic you have here."

"Thank you."

He walked back up to it and pointed at it. "I noticed it's not entirely accurate."

She glanced at it and asked, "In what respect?"

"The dog isn't in it. He should be right here." He pointed next to Gabbert.

"The dog is irrelevant to my calculations."

"Do you have a dog?" Sewell asked.

"No."

"Do you have any color photos of the autopsy?"

"No."

Mr. Sewell signaled to Michael, who delivered large color photos from the autopsy. Gabbert's face was not pictured.

"Is this Robert Gabbert?"

She took the photo, examined it, and answered, "Yes."

"What are these?" Sewell asked, pointing to colored areas on his trunk.

"Bruises."

"Do you know when they were sustained?" Sewell walked up and down the jury box so each juror could see the bruises.

"Shortly before death."

"And what does that tell you?" Ensuring all the jurors had seen the bruises, he placed the photos on the easel.

"That he had been in an altercation prior to his death."

"How big was Robert Gabbert?" Sewell asked.

"He was five-foot-six, weighing one hundred and sixty pounds."

"And what is Mrs. Chandler's height and weight?" Sewell pointed to Cecilia. Abigail poked her to stand. Cecilia stood and straightened her skirt.

"I don't know. I have never examined her."

Sewell looked over at the standing Cecilia and wished she would stop fidgeting. He gave her a sharp look and she stopped. "If you had to take a guess?"

"Objection," Briscoe yelled.

"She's a medical professional, trained in examining the human body," Sewell explained.

"Overruled," Judge Lowe ruled.

Sewell simplified the questions. "Is she taller or shorter than Gabbert?"

Dr. Landry appraised the standing Cecilia. "About the same."

"And does she weigh more or less than him?"

"Less."

Sewell removed the autopsy photos and replaced it with the schematic.

"Can you tell where Mrs. Chandler was aiming?"

"No."

"Lastly, do you buy your bed a Christmas gift?"

With her eyebrows furrowed, she turned to the judge. He nodded for her to answer. She answered, "No."

CHAPTER 49

THE DEFENSE TEAM had been granted a room in the courthouse for lunch. Judge Lowe had agreed with Mr. Sewell that the town did not have the security for Cecilia to enter and exit the courthouse for breaks and lunches.

Cecilia sat alone while the defense team prepared for the afternoon.

Holden was walking by and noticed she was alone. He made a short stop at the vending machine before returning. He peeked in the room, still ensuring she was alone, before he entered.

"Hi," he said, when he opened the door. "Waiting for lunch?"

"Not hungry."

"How about a soda? I have an extra." He slid it across the table to her. She smiled and reached for it.

Michael walked in. "Thanks, Chief!" he said, snatching the soda inches from Cecilia's hand.

Holden handed Cecilia his soda. "Thanks," she said.

"How's it going?" Holden asked.

Before she could answer, Michael interrupted, "What are you doing in here? I don't think Wyatt would like it."

"Better me than the press," Holden snapped at him. "You left her here alone. I was just checking on her."

Michael shrugged and turned his attention to his phone.

"I still have your jacket," Cecilia told him.

"I'll bring it to him tomorrow," Michael answered for him. He drank his Mountain Dew. "Is this a big drink here? She's got a ton of these in her fridge. How much of this stuff can one person drink?"

She looked up at Holden and smiled. "You never know when you might have a guest," she answered.

Holden returned the smile. "And I hear you have a few guests staying with you now. My officer told me about his visit and his concerns about Ferris."

A look of panic crossed Cecilia's face. "Do you think—"

"I doubt it. I don't know for sure. But I think he's right. Keep Ferris close." Holden glanced at Michael, who was busy with his phone, then back to Cecilia. He leaned in and whispered, "Why didn't you tell me about Mrs. Gabbert?"

"What'd you ask?" Michael said, looking up from his phone.

Holden straightened up in the chair and asked, "Have you seen or heard anything suspicious around the house?"

"Well, I thought someone was in the yard the night of the courthouse shooting."

"I doubt it was anything dangerous." Holden added, "Tomcat maybe? Friendly nighttime visitor?"

Cecilia covered her mouth to prevent a laugh. Holden wished they were in the room alone. He liked to see her smile.

"Yeah, the officer checked," Michael told Holden. "He didn't see anything."

"I'm sure there's no one in this town *stealth* enough to get in and out and Officer Pugliese not know," Cecilia said. She smiled at Holden, who smiled back.

"I doubt there is."

AFTER THE LUNCH break, Briscoe announced, "The prosecution calls Mr. Sydney Soloway to the stand."

A man in his sixties, dressed in tan pleated pants, a white long-sleeved button down shirt, and a brown sweater vest, headed to the witness stand. His tortoise-framed glasses sat slightly askew on his face when he sat.

"Where do you live, Mr. Soloway?" Briscoe asked.

"In Folley."

"More specific, please." Briscoe tried to hide his annoyance. The other witnesses were professional. He'd trained them well. Mr. Soloway was going to be more difficult to get the information he needed.

"Oh...On Floral Lane." He added, "105 Floral Lane," before Briscoe had to prompt him.

"Do you know Ms. Chandler?" Briscoe asked.

Mr. Soloway looked at Cecilia. Neither smiled at each other. "Yes. She lives three houses down."

"Have you ever seen Ms. Chandler with a dog?"

"Yes," he answered. Briscoe had instructed all witnesses to be specific and concise. Soloway was catching on. He added, "A golden retriever."

"Can you tell us what you saw?" Briscoe asked.

He cleared his throat and looked at the jury. Another instruction from the prosecutor. "One day, I saw her yelling at it in the front yard."

"What was she yelling?"

"I don't know exactly. Something about a shoe and she was waving a shoe around in her hand. I thought she was going to hit him with it." He motioned in the air, as she must have.

Briscoe used his eyes to signal Soloway to look at the jurors again. He did. Most of the jurors were looking at Cecilia.

Cecilia closed her eyes, remembering the incident. She was never going to hit Ferris. But she was mad. She didn't realize the neighbor had seen her. Up until a few minutes ago, she didn't even know Mr. Soloway's first name.

"That dog was really Joe's," he told the jury. She couldn't disagree with that.

"Why do you say that?" Briscoe asked.

"I used to see him playing with him, walking him all the time." Again, Cecilia couldn't argue. "I don't see her doing that." He paused before finishing. The galley gasped when he did.

"Mrs. Chandler doesn't like that dog."

WYATT SLAMMED HIS briefcase down on the table. Abigail and Michael huddled in the corner, on their phones.

"Why didn't you tell me you didn't like the dog?" Wyatt yelled.

"That's not true. I love him."

Wyatt raised his eyebrows. "Mr. Soloway tells a good story otherwise."

"Fine. I didn't always love him but—"

"But nothing, you should have told me."

"Told you what? How should I know a neighbor was spying on me?"

"It's a small town—"

"Who doesn't yell at a misbehaving dog? You think there isn't a witness or two of you yelling at your children? You think that means that you don't love them?"

Wyatt smirked, knowing she was right.

"I never abused him, never neglected him. Joey loved him so I lo—tolerated him. He was Joey's dog until—"

Wyatt glared at Cecilia for a moment before looking to his assistants. "Ideas?"

"Come on, Wyatt. We all know she loves the dog," Michael said. "We've been in her house for weeks. For goodness sake, we're living there now. If she didn't love the dog, we'd know."

"I know that," Wyatt relented. "I just didn't expect—"

Abigail interrupted him. "Jeez, Wyatt. Let's be honest. You don't care whether she loves Ferris or not." He didn't disagree with her and she continued. "You just have to prove to the jury she does."

SEWELL BEGAN HIS cross-examination from the podium. "The holidays are getting close, Mr. Soloway. Are you done with your shopping?" He didn't answer. "Don't want to admit on the record you still have to buy a gift for the wife?"

Mr. Soloway laughed. "True."

"Do you have a dog, Mr. Soloway?"

"Yes."

"Do you buy him a Christmas present?"

"No."

Wyatt nodded and turned, contemplating his next question. Cecilia scribbled something on a piece of paper and slid it over to Abigail. She nodded and then slid it over to the side of the table. She made eye contact with Wyatt, then to the slip of paper.

"Did you see these types of incidents a lot at the Chandler house?"

He paused. "No, I rarely saw Mrs. Chandler with the dog."

"Do you know the dog's name?" Sewell asked.

"Umm...no."

"So, you wouldn't say you and the Chandlers are close?"

"Well, I was pretty close to Joe," he told the jury.

"'Pretty close?'" Sewell asked. "But not so close that you know what his dog's name is? What does that mean, 'pretty close'?"

Soloway continually looked at the jury. Briscoe had told him that was his audience and instructed him to look there often. "I'd see him regularly in town or on our street."

Sewell walked from the podium to the jury box. He wanted to get Soloway's attention. "You ever see him yell at Ferris? That's the dog's name, Mr. Soloway."

"Not like—" he started, looking at Sewell.

"Yes or no, Mr. Soloway."

"Yes."

Sewell meant to keep Soloway's attention and began his rapid-fire questioning. "Did you ever see Mrs. Chandler hit Ferris?"

"No."

"Have you seen Ferris to be underweight?"

"No."

"Have you ever seen signs he was not cared for?"

"No."

"So, to the best of your knowledge, Ferris has been well cared for by Mrs. Chandler since Joe's death?"

"Yes."

"Are there dog shelters in Folley?"

"Of course."

"So, Mrs. Chandler could have gotten rid of Ferris?"

"Yes."

"Have you ever heard shooting from her house?"

"Yes, the night of the incident. I called the police."

"So she never held shooting practice in her yard?"

The quick series of questions threw Mr. Soloway and he forgot to answer the question with a yes or no. "Please, I can't believe she even knows how to hold a gun."

Wyatt walked over to the defense desk to look at the waiting note. A slow grin appeared on his face. He pocketed the note and returned to the podium. "Do you buy your dog a Hanukkah present, Mr. Soloway?"

He smiled. "Yes."

"Mazel tov. How about your desk?"

Soloway stared at Sewell, thinking he'd misheard the question. A few jurors were smirking so he assumed he hadn't and answered, "No."

BRISCOE AMBUSHED SEWELL as he exited the men's room. "I got your updated witness list."

"As you should have. That is the procedure. I provided it as soon as I updated it."

Briscoe hated Sewell's smug tone. "You can't call

Coleman."

"Why not?" Sewell asked. Briscoe pursed his lips. "Isn't Cecilia's brother-in-law a good character witness for her?"

Briscoe huffed. "Please, that is not the reason you are calling him to the stand."

"What? Is there another reason I'd call him to the stand?" Sewell asked. His eyes were wide in anticipation.

They both knew there was. "I can take this to the judge," Briscoe reminded him.

Sewell held out his arm. "Lead the way. I'd love to hear your case."

Briscoe hesitated. He knew Judge Lowe's reaction would not be positive. He'd have to do a little research to defend his actions before appearing before the judge.

"Just because he's on the list, doesn't mean I have to call him," Sewell commented as he resumed his walk to the courtroom.

"So you did this for show?" Briscoe asked.

Sewell shrugged. "It would garner a little more sympathy for my client if they knew about Coleman's and Gabbert's relationship, don't you think?"

Briscoe didn't know if he meant sympathy from the jury or the public. It didn't matter. He stormed off.

It was times like this Sewell really enjoyed his job.

CHAPTER 50

B RISCOE, STILL RATTLED from his conversation with Sewell, shuffled papers on the prosecutor's desk. His voice squeaked when he announced, "The prosecution calls Sergeant Paul Matthews to the stand."

In full uniform, the officer walked to the witness stand, took the oath, removed his hat, and sat down.

Cecilia looked at him and didn't recognize him as any of the other officers she had interacted with since her arrest. He had a different uniform from the Folley officers.

Briscoe stood at the podium and began his questioning. "Where do you work, Sergeant Matthews?"

"The State Police." His voice was deep and full of authority.

"How long have you worked there?" Briscoe asked.

"Fifteen years."

"And your specific duties with the State Police?"

"I'm a K-9 handler."

Briscoe referenced his notes. "Can you tell us what happened on April ninth of this year?"

"My K-9 partner, Marmaduke, was killed in the

line of duty." A few people "ahhed" in the gallery. Sergeant Matthews sat stoic.

Briscoe ignored the quiet murmurings and continued, "Was the responsible party arrested?"

"Yes."

"And what was he charged with?"

"A class A misdemeanor for criminal damage."

"And why was that?"

"Marmaduke is…" Sergeant Matthews cleared his throat. "I'm sorry…was regarded as property in the eyes of the law."

"And what was the sentence received?"

"Two years in the state penitentiary."

"Thank you, Sergeant Matthews, for your time and your service." Briscoe looked to Sewell, before sitting down at the desk.

Mr. Sewell got up to cross-examine the sergeant, with a folder in his hand. "I too would like to say thank you for your time and service to this great state."

"Thank you."

He stood at the edge of the jury box. "Last year, did you buy Marmaduke a Christmas present?"

"Yes." Sergeant Matthews didn't expand on the gift and Sewell moved on.

He walked up to the sergeant. "Can you tell me what this is?" Mr. Sewell asked, while handing him a copy of a newspaper article.

Sergeant Matthews waited to answer until he read the article. "It is a newspaper article about Marmaduke's death."

"Can you please read the highlighted portions?"

"K-9 officer Marmaduke was laid to rest today at the local pet cemetery. Marmaduke, Marmy to his fellow officers, was killed by a man who had just robbed the convenience store on Seventh. His K-9 handler, Sergeant Matthews, was also injured during the arrest." Matthews cleared his throat and continued. "The ceremony was attended by all the canine officers and their handlers from the department, as well as many from around the state. K-9 officer Marmaduke was laid to rest with full police honors."

Sniffles and murmurings emanated from the gallery. From the start of the trial, Judge Lowe had demanded a quiet courtroom. Disruptors would be forced to leave. Judge Lowe looked up to find the source of the noises emanating from the gallery. He saw more than a few reaching in their bags for tissues.

"What does 'full police honors' mean?" Sewell asked.

"A twenty-one-gun salute. His casket was draped with an American flag that the captain presented to me. He also received a K-9 salute."

"And what does that mean?" Sewell asked, before turning to the jury.

"It's ten seconds of controlled barking by other K-9 officers."

"And why were you presented with the flag?"

"Because he was my partner." Sergeant Matthews turned to the jury. "He was the best partner I ever had. Dependable. Loyal. Courageous." More than one juror wiped a tear from his or her face.

"And who is in the photo?" Mr. Sewell asked, pointing to the article again.

"Me."

"And what are you doing?" he asked.

Sergeant Matthews's jaw clenched. He glared at Mr. Sewell before answering. "Crying."

"I'm not trying to embarrass you, Sergeant. You lost your partner. I don't know a police officer, or for that matter a person, who wouldn't cry at the loss of their partner."

Wyatt pointedly looked at Cecilia and the jury didn't miss it. She looked down into her lap, hoping to stave off tears.

The tension eased out of the sergeant's jaw when he realized Mr. Sewell wasn't trying to attack him. In previous court proceedings, Sergeant Matthews had found cross-examination hostile.

Sewell began pacing in front of the jury. "I read you crashed your patrol car last year."

"Yes."

"Did you have a similar ceremony?"

"No," he answered incredulously.

This caused Sewell to stop and turn to Matthews. "But both your partner Marmaduke and your patrol car—I'm sorry, did you have a name for your patrol car?"

"No."

"Both are deemed to be property of the police department?

"Yes," Sergeant Matthews answered.

"Do you think that's right?"

"No," he answered, louder than Mr. Briscoe's objection.

Despite Sergeant Matthews's career-long disdain for defense attorneys, he was beginning to like Wyatt Sewell.

"Can you tell me what you think of the state's punishment of Marmaduke's murderer?"

"Weak." He turned to the jury. "If we'd been on loan to the feds that day, and Marmy was killed, that guy would have gotten a much stiffer penalty."

"Please explain."

"There's a federal law that has harsher fines for hurting or killing police dogs."

"Objection," Briscoe yelled. "How is this relevant?"

"I'll allow it," Judge Lowe ruled.

Mr. Sewell walked over to the defense table and Abigail handed him three pieces of paper. He handed one to the prosecution, one to the judge, and one to Sergeant Matthews. "Is this the law you're referring to?"

"Yes."

"Please read the highlighted portion."

"Under the Federal Law Enforcement Animal Protection Act, someone convicted of purposely assaulting or killing federal law enforcement animals could be fined at least a thousand dollars and spend up to ten years in prison."

"What do you think of that law?"

"Justice," he answered. Again, louder than Mr. Briscoe's objection.

"Can you tell me about the Fall Harvest Festival from last year?" Sewell asked.

"The local high school raised a thousand dollars for a bulletproof vest for Marmaduke."

"Do they hold similar fund-raisers for police officers?" Sewell asked, then turned to the jury before adding, "The two-legged kind?"

"No."

Sewell watched the jurors. The eldest juror who took notes of all the legal points had taken several notes during Briscoe's questioning. He took none during Sewell's. Sewell turned his attention back to the sergeant. "Why do you think that is?" Sewell asked.

"People like dogs more than police, I guess."

"Last year, did you buy your patrol car a Christmas gift?"

"No. Unless you count a deodorizer."

Mr. Sewell, as well as the rest of the room, laughed. Before returning to the defense desk, he said. "No, I don't think that's a gift for the car. That's a gift to the other people riding in the car."

THE DEFENSE TEAM returned to the Chandler home. Cecilia had thought they'd had a good day. But there was a tension in the car. It was coming from Wyatt.

She unlocked the door and Ferris jumped on her. "Missed you too, buddy." She hugged him, then followed him to the kitchen to let him out into the backyard.

"Office, now," Wyatt ordered his assistants. "Good night, Cecilia," Wyatt said before closing the dining room's glass doors. "Who is juror number one?" Wyatt asked the moment the door was closed.

"The foreman?" Michael asked.

"Yes," Wyatt snapped back.

Michael glanced at Abigail, surprised by the tone. He flipped through his notes and found juror number one. "Donald Derby, sixty-two, retired."

"And..."

Michael looked back at his notes. "Accountant."

"Jeez..." He paced the dining room. "Why didn't we get rid of him?"

Abigail answered, "No credible reason."

"Why didn't we use one of our—"

Abigail shook her head. "We were out of exceptions by the time he came up. He was the last juror chosen."

"What else do we know?" Wyatt asked.

Michael shrugged.

"Does he have pets?" Wyatt asked.

"You got that question excluded, remember?" Michael answered.

Abigail cringed, waiting for Wyatt's backlash. Through a clenched jaw, Wyatt answered, "Yes, I remember everything about this case, like all my cases. Abigail?"

"We don't know. I couldn't find anything else about him."

"No Facebook? No social media?" Wyatt asked.

"He's a sixty-something grandpa. There's no social media," Michael answered.

"My ninety-year-old aunt is on Snapchat, Michael," Abigail told him. "But Mr. Derby, no social media accounts."

"How'd he get to be foreman?" Wyatt asked.

"Who knows," Abigail answered. Foreman selection was performed in the jury room. "I thought they'd pick juror six." She grabbed Michael's folder and flipped until she found the juror's information. "Mrs. Welby. Former teacher. Retired as an administrator."

Wyatt sighed. He pictured the white-haired, seventy-year-old woman. She had reminded him of his second-grade teacher. Tough but loving. He feared Mr. Derby would have too much weight with the other jurors.

"What's the problem?" Michael asked.

"Haven't you noticed him?" Wyatt asked, looking at both of them.

Michael shook his head. Abigail didn't answer. All the jurors had arrived in their Sunday best on the first day. As the days progressed, their attire began to slack. But not juror number one.

"He's precise. Every day, he shows up neatly

dressed. Suit, bow tie, pocket square. He sits with perfect posture. He keeps precise notes." All the jurors had notepads. Some never touched them. Some wrote down everything. Some doodled on their pads. Not juror number one. He recorded each legal point made.

"And precision is bad?" Michael asked.

"In this case, yes." Wyatt plopped in a dining room chair. "He's a letter of the law kind of man."

"And?" Michael asked.

"And that means we're in trouble."

CHAPTER 51

THE DEFENSE TEAM arrived at the courthouse the same as they arrived every other day. In quiet, the driver drove them from Cecilia's and dropped them in front of the courthouse. The scene was the same as the last few days. Organized chaos with protestors and media being monitored and contained by the police.

Cecilia pulled her coat close over her chest as she exited the warm car into the chill December air. She had learned the defense team's skill of tuning out, and ignored the shouts as she headed up the stairs into the courthouse.

Briscoe stood and announced his last witness. "The prosecution calls Judge Harry Olsen to the stand."

A distinguished man with white hair entered the courtroom. Cecilia expected him to be wearing a judge's gown but instead he wore a black suit, white dress shirt, and a red tie. He took the oath and sat in the witness box.

From the podium, Briscoe asked, "Can you please tell us about a case you ruled over two years ago, Carlson versus Carlson?"

"It was divorce proceedings," he answered. He turned to the jurors and added, "A particularly acrimonious divorce."

"And what did they fight over in particular?" Briscoe asked.

"Flambo."

With eyebrows furrowed, as if he didn't know the answer, Briscoe asked, "And what is a Flambo?"

"A six-year-old Pekingese."

Briscoe nodded and asked, "And what did you rule, Your Honor?"

"The Pekingese went to Mr. Carlson."

"And how did you decide on awarding Mr. Carlson with the dog?" Briscoe asked.

"I decided as I always do." He looked to the jurors. "I took in the accounts of both parties, reviewed the overall value of the estate, and determined the value of the contested property."

"Are you saying the dog is property?" Briscoe asked.

"The law says the dog is property," Judge Olsen answered.

Briscoe paused to allow the jurors to let that sink in. "And what did you ascertain a Pekingese is worth?"

"The original cost of the dog was four thousand dollars plus training costs of over one thousand dollars. I approximated Flambo's value to be five thousand dollars."

"So, if Mr. Carlson got Flambo, what did Mrs. Carlson receive?"

"The used Mercedes."

"How did you come to this ruling?"

"Their assets were dispersed equally between the two parties. Each received one vacation home. Their main home, with its contents, were sold and the proceeds evenly divided. Each kept the car they called their own. That left one additional car, which had the same value as Flambo. Mrs. Carlson got the Mercedes. Mr. Carlson got the dog."

Briscoe remained at the podium but glanced at the jurors before asking his next question. "And why not the other way around?"

"Mrs. Carlson reported the Mercedes was hers before getting her new Mercedes."

"Why do you think the Carlsons fought over this particular item, this dog?"

"Objection," Sewell yelled.

"The judge sat on this trial. He's clearly capable of surmising why they argued over this asset in particular," Briscoe explained to the judge.

"Overruled," Judge Lowe ruled.

"To cause pain," Judge Olsen explained. "It was a dog when they went to the breeder to buy it. It was a dog when they boarded it in a cage when they went to Europe for six weeks. But when they knew keeping it from the other one would cause pain, suddenly it was more than a dog. It was family. Under the law it's property and that's how I ruled."

"Your witness," Briscoe said to Sewell before sitting.

Sewell got up and stood at the podium, preparing

to ask his first question. Judge Olsen scowled at him.

"How are you today, Judge Olsen?"

"Fine," he answered. He glared at the defense attorney.

"Are you ready for the holidays?"

Judge Olsen looked at Briscoe and then to Judge Lowe. "How is this relevant?" He returned his attention to Sewell. "I'm a busy man, Mr. Sewell. Let's get on with this."

Sewell nodded and proceeded with his questioning. "Are you familiar with legislation in Alaska regarding pet custody?"

"No. I do not reside over cases in Alaska, so no. It bears no relevance here."

Abigail handed Sewell a paper, with yellow highlighted lines. He walked it to Judge Olsen and asked, "Can you read the highlighted passages?"

The witness read the lines silently. "No, I will not read into the record laws from a different state."

"Your Honor?" Sewell asked Judge Lowe.

"Why aren't you objecting?" Judge Olsen asked Briscoe.

"Objection!" Sewell yelled. "Judge Olsen can't order the prosecutor during my examination!"

Briscoe stood. "Your Honor, I see no reason why the jurors need to know Alaska law."

"Agreed." Judge Lowe ruled in favor of the prosecution. "Alaska law has no place in my courtroom."

Sewell nodded and moved on. "Did you take into account Flambo's best interests when deciding his new home?"

"No," Judge Olsen answered.

"Why not?" Sewell asked.

"Because Flambo is *property*." He looked at the jury and further explained, "I also do not take into account how they will treat the mahogany dining room table when deciding who gets it."

Sewell returned to his notes. "Did the Carlsons have children?"

"No."

"If they did, would you have taken in their best interests on their custody status?"

"If they had children, I would have."

"Then why not do that with Flambo?" Sewell returned to the defense table and Abigail handed him another piece of paper. He glanced down at it before asking, "Did they not each refer to Flambo as family?" He tried to hand the paper to Judge Olsen.

He did not take the paper and answered, "They can call Flambo whatever they want in court papers. The law says he's property and that is how he was treated." Sewell nodded and returned the paper to the podium. As he walked away, Judge Olsen added, "I also do not take into account the best interests of a 1968 Mustang even when a claimant referred to it as his 'baby.'"

"Objection," Sewell shouted. "Judge Olsen knows to only answer questions asked of him."

Judge Lowe hesitated, as Judge Olsen stared at him, and then ruled. "Sustained. Strike that from the record."

Sewell sat down. Briscoe smiled, glad to not have to hear a ridiculous question about Christmas.

HOLDEN SAT AT the bar, alone, drinking his beer. He didn't want to go to his home, where no one was waiting for him. He wondered if he should get a pet.

Pugliese straddled up next to him at the bar. He signaled to Marla for a beer.

"How do you think it's going?" Vinnie asked.

"The case?"

"Is there anything else going on in this town?" He looked around the bar. "Everyone in here is either media or someone wanting to talk to the media."

Holden shook his head. "I don't know. Briscoe's proven his case. Now it's Sewell's turn."

"But if you had to put odds on it, what would you choose?"

"That's inappropriate, Pugliese." He returned to his beer. Home was sounding better and better.

"How's it going with Cecilia?" Vinnie asked.

Holden looked around, glad no one was close enough to hear them. "Lay off about CeCe."

Vinnie ignored him and continued, "What's the saying, 'We got no beef with a happy chief'?"

Holden shook his head and tried not to smile. "I have never heard that saying."

"I'm just saying before I go to the big city I want

to see you happy."

Marla dropped off Vinnie's beer and he took a long swig. "Cecilia is a nice lady," he added.

"That you thought should be arrested for murder," Holden reminded him.

He shrugged. "Well, we all make mistakes." He grabbed a few nuts from the bar's bowl and popped them in his mouth. "That's why you are the chief. I've learned from you."

"Not enough," Holden said, watching Pugliese. Through the mirror, he was watching the reporter, Cheryl Milson, strut around the bar. "You shouldn't be carousing with the media."

Their eyes met in the mirror. With his eyebrows raised, Pugliese asked, "Need I remind you who *you* shouldn't be carousing with?"

Holden finished his beer and stood. "Don't speak her name to me again. Are we clear?"

"Or what?" Pugliese stood. Holden stood four inches taller but Pugliese did his best to not look intimidated.

"Maybe Briscoe would like to meet Ms. Milson. Could you arrange that? You met her when? The day before the story about Ferris broke?" Holden put his jacket on. "Who's the better detective now, Pug?"

CHAPTER 52

U SUALLY, CECILIA WAS the first one up in the house. Today, the first day of the defense's case, Wyatt was already in the kitchen. She poured herself a cup of coffee and brought the carafe over to Wyatt, offering to refill his cup.

He didn't look up from his paperwork, shook his head and mumbled, "No."

Cecilia returned the carafe to the coffeemaker and sat across from him. As he studied his papers, it was the first time she saw the deep lines in his forehead. After a few minutes, Wyatt felt Ferris and Cecilia watching him.

He looked up and she asked, "How do you think it's going?"

He paused and removed his glasses. "Briscoe's made some good points. There's no doubt about that. The judge...Judge Olsen was powerful stuff. He looked right at that jury." He paused. "He's done what I would have. I'd be impressed if—"

"If what?" she asked.

He tried to smile. "Don't worry. We'll be fine. I have a plan. We'll be fine."

Reiterating "we'll be fine" planted a pit in her

stomach. She felt he was trying to convince himself, not her. And if he needed convincing, she was in trouble. Big trouble.

"All the jurors have to find me innocent for me to be free?" Cecilia asked.

"To be found *not guilty*," Wyatt corrected her. "Yes, they all have to find you not guilty."

"And what if they can't agree on not guilty?" she asked.

"Mistrial."

"And what happens then?"

"Depends on Briscoe. He could refile the murder two charges and we go through this again. He could refile under a lesser charge. He could plead it out. He could choose not to refile the charges at all. I don't know."

"Why do you think he charged me with second-degree murder?"

"I don't know. I think his political aspirations, or his campaign manager, forced his hand. I think he overshot. And that's our best shot." Wyatt put his glasses back on and returned to his papers.

And not that I'm innocent, she thought. That was what I thought was my best shot. She swallowed hard and asked, "So, you don't think it's because of his hatred of dogs?"

Scowling, he looked up. "His what?"

"He doesn't like dogs. Do you think that's why he's prosecuting me? He seems like a hold a grudge kind of guy. The story...it seemed compelling," Cecilia explained.

Abigail entered the kitchen and Wyatt cut her off before she could greet them. "So, Cecilia here was telling me something very interesting about Briscoe." Abigail's good morning smile slipped off her face. "I was thinking maybe after this case is over, we should hire her. She seems to be pretty good at digging into people's past." He glanced back at Cecilia, smiling. "I always thought Abigail was the best, but maybe I was wrong."

"I told you everything that was relevant to the case, Wyatt." She headed to the coffee machine and poured herself a cup.

Smile gone, he whipped back to looking at Abigail. "I pay you to tell me everything."

Cecilia's head ping-ponged back and forth between the two lawyers. She'd never seen them argue before.

"It's not relevant," Abigail repeated.

"I'll decide what's relevant."

Michael walked in and sensed the tension. They bickered back and forth a few more times before they each left the kitchen.

"Jeez, I knew yesterday was a bad day in court but I didn't think they'd get into a fight over it."

Michael didn't see the horror on Cecilia's face. "Driver's here!" Michael yelled, startling Cecilia, who was lost in her thoughts.

She kissed Ferris on his head. "I'll see you later, boy." She got him a treat and threw it to him. He jumped for it, hitting it with his nose. The treat flew toward the sliding glass door and he chased after it, crashing into the door. She smiled, fearing it would be one of the final smiles she would have with him. She met the others in the foyer and walked out the door.

Abigail stopped her. "Cecilia, you need more than that blazer. It's getting cold. They're predicting snow today." Abigail grabbed a coat from the coat closet and handed it to Cecilia. She put it on, remembering the last time she wore it. A year ago. To Joey's funeral.

Cecilia felt she was heading to her own.

THE DEFENSE TEAM and Cecilia sat in silence at their table, waiting for the judge and jurors to come in. The silence continued until the first defense witness was called.

"The defense calls Martin Frasier to the stand," Sewell announced.

Mr. Frasier walked stiffly from the doors to the witness box. He was clearly uncomfortable by the large group watching his every step. His hand shook over the Bible as he took his oath for truth.

"Happy holidays," Mr. Sewell greeted Mr. Frasier. "Do you have a large list of people to buy for?"

The personal question distracted him from the stresses of testifying. "Two children, David and Tyler. Five grandchildren, Connor, Bonnie, Frances, Junior, and Alyson. And of course the wife."

Briscoe held his objection while the witness prattled on. Briscoe had given up on the objections on the ridiculous holiday questions. Marcy pointed out it annoyed the jury, and Judge Lowe, when Briscoe interrupted. Sewell was disappointed that he didn't. He wanted to move on as well.

"Any pets?" Sewell asked.

"Oh yes. Mr. Calico. Need to get him some catnip."

Sewell watched the strain drain from Mr. Frasier's face as he spoke about his family. He felt comfortable initiating the questioning. "Can you tell us what you do for a living, Mr. Frasier?"

"Please call me Boomer. Because of all the booms where I work." He looked at the jury, disappointed no one laughed. "I own the Frasier Gun Range on the outskirts of town."

"Have you ever met Mrs. Chandler?" Sewell asked, pointing to Cecilia.

"Yes." He looked at her and gave a little wave. "Once."

"And where was that?"

"At my gun range. A few months before Joey died." He turned to the jury. "Joey was a good man. He'd be—"

"Objection," Briscoe yelled.

"Sustained," Judge Lowe ruled. "Please answer the questions asked, Mr. Frasier."

"Yes, Your Honor. I'm sorry."

Sewell walked up to the witness stand in an effort

to calm Mr. Frasier, who was visibly shaken from the judge's rebuke. "Why did Joey bring Mrs. Chandler to your gun range?"

He cleared his throat before answering, "Joey brought her by to learn to shoot."

"Only the one time?" Sewell asked, ensuring the jurors got the point.

"Yes."

"And why was that? Did she do so well the first time, no further lessons were warranted?" Sewell remained in front of Frasier, hoping to keep his anxiety levels low.

Martin laughed. "No, the first lesson did not go well."

"How badly did it go?" Sewell asked.

"Mrs. Chandler returned to the car after a few minutes. She didn't look happy." He leaned toward Sewell, as if it were just him in the courtroom. "City girls usually don't like the guns."

Sewell took a few steps back and continued his questioning. "Do you know why Mr. Chandler brought her to the gun range?"

"He was worried about her. He wanted to teach her self-protection. He didn't like her being alone in the house when he got stuck at a job site at night. Joey was—" Frasier stopped and looked at the judge. "Sorry, Your Honor."

Judge Lowe signaled Sewell to continue.

"Why didn't he bring her back?" he asked.

Frasier looked at Cecilia and gave her a sad smile.

"I think he was embarrassed. Some of the other boys there were laughing."

"Objection. Speculation," Briscoe said.

"Sustained," the judge ruled.

Sewell went to the podium and glanced at his paperwork. "Did Joey ever tell you why he didn't bring her back to the gun range?"

"He said she refused. Some husbands shouldn't try to teach their wives some things. You know what I mean?" Mr. Sewell nodded, as did some of the male jurors. "I offered to teach her but he declined. Said she wanted no part of a gun."

"What did you think when you heard Cecilia had shot Mr. Gabbert?" Sewell asked.

"I couldn't believe it!" he exclaimed. Surprised by his volume, he lowered his voice. "I thought it was an accident. Or a misfire."

Mr. Sewell walked to the defense desk and Abigail handed him a folder. Returning to the witness stand, he pulled out the eight-by-ten photo of Gabbert. The same close-up shot Mr. Briscoe had showed the jury during his opening statement. Mr. Frasier recoiled at the photo of the dead man. Then he leaned in and inspected it. He held his finger over the gunshot wound.

"That girl made that shot?" he asked, pointing to Cecilia, then to the gunshot wound. "From twenty feet?"

"That is why we're here, Mr. Frasier."

He shook his head as he inspected the photo.

"Well, I doubt that was what she was aiming for."

Frasier held the photo out to Sewell and he retrieved it. "Why do you say that?"

"Because when she shot a few rounds at my place, she missed her target completely. The boys had never seen such a bad shot. Or had such a good laugh."

"Last question," Sewell started. A few jurors and a few people in the gallery smiled. "Do you buy your gun a Christmas gift?"

"Um...No," Frasier answered. He watched Sewell return to the defense table and sit. "Is that a thing?" he asked him.

Sewell smiled and shook his head. He looked to Briscoe. "Your witness."

Briscoe stood. "Do you monitor the gun range?" he asked from the podium.

"Yes."

"Twenty-four seven?"

"Well, no. We're not open twenty-four seven."

"But you monitor the gun range continuously during business hours?"

"Yes."

"Who watches it when you have to go to the bathroom? Or go in the back office for supplies?"

"No one."

"So there are times when the gun range is not monitored?"

"Well, yes, but—"

"So, Mr. Chandler could have brought Ms. Chandler and you wouldn't have seen her?"

"He would need more than the five minutes it takes me to go the bathroom to make her a good enough shot to do that," he answered, pointing in the direction the coroner's photo had gone. "Plus, a girl like that don't go anywhere in this town and not get noticed."

Briscoe ignored him and continued. "Does Chandler Construction, the company Ms. Chandler inherited upon Mr. Chandler's death, have an account with you?"

"Yes."

"So, Mrs. Chandler could have come anytime to shoot?"

"Yes, but—"

"Does every shooter need to sign in?"

"Yes."

"Is it possible that someone can come to the range and not sign in?"

"No. I see everyone. I make sure everyone signs in."

Mr. Briscoe huffed. "Do you have to go through your office to get to the gun range?"

"No."

"So someone could go straight to the gun range without signing in?"

"Well—"

"I'm asking, is it possible?"

"Yes. But—"

Briscoe cut him off before he could say more. "That's all for this witness."

CECILIA SAT ON a bench and waited for the trial to resume. The lawyers and their assistants were in with the judge. No media outlet was allowed in this area. Staff only.

Alone in the hallway, she felt she was in purgatory.

Alive but not living.

Free but not really free.

Holden busted through the stairwell door and plopped down at the end of the bench. He was muttering under his breath while fiddling with his phone.

"Good morning," she said, to get his attention.

"CeCe?" He looked up surprised. "I didn't see you." He scanned the hallway. "What are you doing here by yourself?"

"Waiting," she answered. He nodded, then looked at his phone and stared. "What's the problem?" she asked, pointing to the phone.

"The phone is frozen." He turned it toward her and tapped it several times. Nothing happened.

"Did you try turning it off and back on again?"

"I've spoken to enough help desks to know that is the first thing I should try."

She held her hand out. Remembering her day job in the tech field, he handed over the phone. She hesitated. "There's nothing on here I shouldn't see, right?"

"Like pornography?" he asked.

With eyebrows raised, she slowly answered, "No, like police business. This is your work phone, isn't it?"

Embarrassed, Holden nodded. "Sorry, yes, it's my work phone. Nothing confidential except in email."

"Okay, I don't have to go in there."

"Okay." He watched as she tapped the screen a few times. Same results as when Holden had tried. Frozen. She shut it off again, counted to ten and turned it back on.

"Put in your code." He did and she took it back. He looked over her shoulder as she tapped a few keys, went into settings, and scrolled through. She tapped a few more times, then opened a few applications, but not the email, and returned to the home screen. She declared, "Okay, looks good." She handed him the phone back. "You look. Make sure it's working right."

Holden opened his email and everything was up to date. All the applications were working at their usual speeds. "Oh, I could kiss you!" he exclaimed. Once he heard himself, he uttered, "Sorry."

He watched as her cheeks became rosy. He resisted the urge to lean in and kiss her. There was a commotion behind him and he turned to see the defense team returning.

"Thanks, CeCe," he said as he got up.

"CeCe?" Michael asked as Holden walked away.

"THE DEFENSE CALLS Dr. Dario Anderson to the stand," Sewell announced.

Cecilia didn't recognize him from their brief meeting the night of the attack. He was clean-shaven and was wearing a well-tailored suit and dark rectangular-shaped glasses. He looked different from the unshaven man in blue scrubs she had met.

"Merry Christmas, Dr. Anderson." Sewell waited for the greeting to be returned but it wasn't. "Are you done with your shopping?"

"No."

"A few more shopping days left, right?"

"Yes."

"Do you buy your stethoscope a Christmas present?"

Dr. Anderson glanced at the judge before answering, "No." He shifted in his chair, waiting for the official questioning to begin. He eased when Sewell started. "Can you please tell us where you are employed?"

"Folley General Hospital."

"And what do you do there?

"I'm an emergency room doctor."

"Is this how you met Mrs. Chandler?"

"Yes."

"Can you please tell us your assessment of Mrs. Chandler the night of the attack?"

"She had a mild concussion. Two broken ribs. Multiple contusions. A few cuts."

"Please be more specific." Sewell placed a diagram on the easel for Dr. Anderson to point to. On it were four body diagrams, each showing a side of the body. Cecilia's injuries were already marked, in color, on the whiteboard.

Cecilia tuned out, not wanting to listen to her injuries and a recounting of her time in the emergency room. She watched the jury, as Dr. Anderson tallied up her injuries. They were engrossed, or grossed out, by his testimony. Using a laser pointer, he pointed to the location, severity and type of each injury.

"Why didn't you admit her?" Sewell asked.

"She refused."

"Why?"

"She wanted to get home." He shook his head. "Something about a dog."

"Do you have a dog or cat?" Sewell asked.

"No, too many hours at the hospital."

Sewell returned to the defense desk. He noted that juror number one had taken few notes during his first witnesses. "I'm done with this witness," Sewell told the judge.

Briscoe stood to begin the cross-examination. "Did you examine Mr. Robert Gabbert?"

"No," the doctor answered.

"Because he was already dead? Because Ms. Chandler killed him?" Briscoe asked.

"Objection," Sewell shouted.

"Sustained," Judge Lowe ruled. "The jury is instructed to ignore Mr. Briscoe's last comment."

"Were any of Ms. Chandler's injuries life-threatening?"

"No."

"That is all for this witness," Briscoe announced.

"THE DEFENSE CALLS Sophia Wesson to the stand," Sewell announced and waited at the podium as she entered.

Abigail tried to catch the woman's eye as she walked down the aisle. She knew the young tech would be nervous. But Wyatt had wanted someone like her. He didn't want a stuffy expert to testify. He wanted someone the jury would like.

Ms. Wesson approached the stand, focusing on putting one foot in front of the other. Abigail wanted to remind her to smile and to breathe, but Sophia never looked up from her shoes. Each click of her heels echoed in the courtroom. Her hand trembled over the Bible as she was sworn in. She'd never testified in such a high-profile case.

"Happy holidays, Ms. Wesson," Sewell greeted her.

"To you as well, Mr. Sewell." She smiled, the tension leaving her body. Abigail had assured her Mr. Sewell would put her at ease. Abigail made no such assurances for the prosecution.

"Where do you work?" Mr. Sewell asked.

"UM Labs."

"And what do you do there?"

"I'm a bloodstain pattern analyst."

"What is your degree in?"

"Forensic science."

"How long have you been working in this field?"

"Nine years."

Sewell removed the blank placard on the easel, displaying the blood-covered Chandler kitchen. "Can you tell me whose blood this is?"

"Cecilia Chandler."

"All of it?"

"Objection," Briscoe said.

"I'll rephrase," Sewell told the judge before he could rule. "Of the blood analyzed, whose was it?"

"All the blood I analyzed was Cecilia Chandler's."

"And what is this?" He pointed to the corner of the island kitchen. He removed that photo and revealed a close-up shot of the kitchen. The crime scene photo Wyatt had first seen in Cecilia's dining room.

"A fingerprint."

"Whose fingerprint?"

"Robert Gabbert."

"And what does that tell you?"

"That Mr. Gabbert was in the house during the attack."

"So no one could claim he'd been in the home at some earlier time?" Sewell looked pointedly at

Briscoe.

"Correct. He would have had to put his finger in the wet blood in order to leave the print."

Sewell had succeeded in proving that at some point during the attack, Gabbert had been in Cecilia's home. He watched juror one make a note of it. Whether this was when Gabbert snatched Ferris, he didn't know—but it didn't matter. It only strengthened Cecilia's case of self-defense. Briscoe couldn't claim Gabbert was only in the backyard.

With his point made, Sewell concluded his questioning. "Do you buy your front door a Christmas gift?"

"Does a wreath count?" she asked.

Mr. Sewell joined the laughter of the gallery before announcing he was done with the witness.

Briscoe began his questioning with no pleasantries. "Were you ever at the crime scene?"

"No."

"So you didn't examine the fingerprint in person?"

"No."

"What did you examine?"

"A photo of the fingerprint."

"Were you given any other fingerprints to compare this one to?"

"No." The tension she had felt upon arrival was returning as Briscoe fired questions at her. She reminded herself to answer each question succinctly and not to ramble on, as Abigail had instructed her.

Briscoe walked up to the easel and looked at the

enlarged photo. "How many points of comparison are there in your analysis?"

"Twelve."

"How many characteristics are there in the average fingerprint?"

"Depends."

"What is the recognized average number, Ms. Wesson?" He returned to the prosecutor desk and Marcy handed him his research on fingerprinting examination. He expected her to dodge the question.

"One hundred and fifty."

It matched his research and he proceeded. "So you were able to find only twelve where there are as many as one hundred and fifty characteristics?"

"Twelve is sufficient."

"Sufficient?" Briscoe asked.

"There is no standard requirement."

"What is the accepted range of points of comparison?"

"Twelve to sixteen."

He referenced his research again. Not because he needed to but because he wanted the jury to know these were accurate numbers. "Do some agencies have points of comparison up to twenty?"

"Yes."

"So when you were presented with *one* fingerprint to compare to just *one* person's fingerprints, you found the bare minimum of twelve points of comparison?"

"Yes."

"That is all," Briscoe stated before sitting. Both he and Sewell saw juror one make a note.

"THE DEFENSE CALLS Jeremiah Coleman to the stand," Sewell declared.

Cecilia did her best to conceal her shock. The defense team had not shown Cecilia the updated witness list. Sewell had charged Abigail and Michael with assessing her reaction.

Cecilia watched as Jeremiah walked down the aisle. She scanned the gallery, not seeing Brittany.

Michael leaned over and whispered to Cecilia. "Don't scowl at the witness."

She nodded and tried to appear neutral. She could not think of any reason Jeremiah would be testifying for her defense. She briefly feared Sewell had called him as a character witness and wondered if she could object.

Sewell glanced at Cecilia. He didn't like clients who didn't tell him the whole truth. He needed to make sure she wasn't hiding anything from him before putting her on the stand.

"Why did you hire Robert Gabbert to scare Mrs. Chandler?" Sewell asked.

He'd been afraid she had concealed this, in a misguided attempt to protect Joey's family and therefore Joey.

He didn't miss her shock. Neither did the jury.

"No comment."

"That doesn't answer the question, Mr. Coleman."

"I was told by my lawyer not to answer," he responded. "I take...I take the Fifth?" He looked at the judge, who nodded he had chosen the right number. And the right amendment. He was asserting his Fifth Amendment right against self-incrimination.

"Why did you want to get rid of Mrs. Chandler?" Sewell asked.

"I take the Fifth."

"How much did you pay Mr. Gabbert to stalk Mrs. Chandler?"

"I take the Fifth."

Sewell started another question. "What did—"

"Objection," Briscoe said. "The witness has made it clear he will not be answering any questions."

"Sustained," Judge Lowe ruled.

"One more?" Sewell asked the judge.

"Proceed."

"Do you buy your patio furniture a Christmas gift?"

"I take the Fifth," he answered.

Sewell smiled, as did everyone in the courtroom, except the prosecutor.

"All yours," Sewell told Briscoe as he returned to his seat.

Briscoe ignored him. "No questions for this witness, Your Honor."

CHAPTER 53

JUDGE LOWE EXCUSED the jury for the day. The trial was winding down and the gallery knew it. Only one witness remained before closing statements.

The defense team left the courthouse, steps behind the prosecutor team.

"They seem louder today," Cecilia said, once secure in the car.

"There's a rumor you're testifying tomorrow," Wyatt answered.

BACK AT THE house, everyone went their different ways. Wyatt went to the dining room/his office to prepare for the next day's questioning. Abigail took the rental car, muttering as she left. "I could kill Wyatt. All this talk about the holidays. I have to do some shopping."

Cecilia went outside with Ferris. He ran laps around the yard until he was tired. He returned to the patio and rolled around on his back.

Michael peeked out the sliding glass door. "Hey, Cecilia, can I borrow the car?" CB's Diner was having

Sloppy Joe's for dinner.

Cecilia agreed. She went back into the house and grabbed her keys from her purse. Michael caught the tossed car keys. The weather was getting colder and she'd been intermittently starting her car using the automatic start fob. She never left the confines of her house to do it. She knew she wouldn't trigger the ankle monitor alarm if she went to her car or the garage but she didn't want anyone to get the wrong idea. It would be her bad luck if Pugliese, or that Soloway neighbor, happened to pass when she went to the car.

Michael looked at the keys. "Oh...I meant the truck." He'd been wanting to drive that F-150 since the first day he'd seen it in her garage.

"Joey's truck?" she asked, needlessly. There were only two cars on her property, and only one of them was a truck. She paused. "Well...I doubt it'll start. It hasn't been driven in..." She could have said since he died, but continued "...in over a year."

"Oh, those trucks are tough. 'Ford tough' is the slogan, isn't it?"

She shrugged.

"So can I borrow that?" he asked.

She could not think of a good reason to deny him the loan. The only reason was that it was Joey's truck and no one had touched it since his death. She went to the drawer. Her hand hovered over the keys, a small part of her not wanting to give Joey's keys to Michael. A larger part of her reminded her that a truck should be driven, not housed in a garage. She took the truck's keys out and threw them to him. It was a strong throw and Michael caught them. He yelled "thanks" as he ran out the side door.

Cecilia watched as Michael ran to the garage, like a child on Christmas morning. Cecilia smiled, having watched Joey run to the truck the same way when he first got it. The truck started on first try and Michael backed out the driveway.

He couldn't believe he was driving such a huge vehicle. It would never be practical for him to own one, but it was fun to pretend for an hour or two.

He'd driven less than three miles when he heard a siren behind him.

Chief Owens had been patrolling the neighborhood when he spotted the Chandler Construction truck. The truck had the company's green and yellow logo on both cab doors. There was no mistaking the gray F-150 Limited as Joey's. It was the newest one in the Chandler Construction fleet.

Michael pulled over and wished he'd taken Cecilia's car. Even though it was purple, it was far less conspicuous. "Everything okay, Officer?" he said as the officer approached.

Holden recognized the driver when he glanced in the side mirror. "What are you doing driving this, Mr. Bloomington?"

"Chief Owens? How are you?" Michael was relieved it was an officer who knew who he was and that he was part of the defense team.

Everyone knew and recognized Wyatt Sewell, but

few recognized Michael and Abigail away from him. He didn't want to have to call Wyatt from jail, arrested for stealing the Chandler Construction truck. Because he was craving a Sloppy Joe.

"Did CeCe tell you that you could drive this?" Owens asked.

"What?" he asked. "Of course she did. Did you think I'd steal it?"

"Where are you going?" he asked.

Michael knew he didn't have to answer these questions but he didn't want the situation to escalate. He'd heard stories about small town cops and how they felt about the visitors from the city.

"CB's Diner for the special, a Sloppy Joe," Michael answered.

"Okay, well just be careful. She'd be upset if something happened to the truck."

"You seem awfully concerned with *CeCe*. Anything I should—"

Owens interrupted him. "I'm concerned about all the citizens in my town."

"How small town charming," Michael said.

Holden ignored him and watched as another police cruiser approached. Pugliese stopped and yelled from the driver's seat, "Everything okay?"

"Yes, just leaving, Officer," Michael said and rolled up his window.

Pugliese made a U-turn and parked behind Owens's car. He got out and stood with Owens. "You pull it over because you thought it was Cecilia?" They watched Michael drive away. "You think she was trying to escape?"

"No." Owens was starting to doubt Pugliese's detective skills. "She wouldn't be headed *into* town if she were trying to flee the jurisdiction." Or use such a conspicuous vehicle. It literally had her name on it.

"Where's he going?" Pugliese asked.

"To CB's...something about Sloppy Joes."

Pugliese nodded and licked his lips. "You know what, why don't I keep an eye on him?"

Owens agreed, thinking it was a conciliatory offer. They'd barely spoken since their argument in the bar.

Pugliese ran back to his car and followed Michael.

As Vinnie drove away, toward the diner, Owens realized what he was really after.

A Sloppy Joe.

CECILIA WAS PACING the kitchen. Ferris matched her cadence.

Wyatt stood at the kitchen doorway for several minutes before interrupting. "You need to get some sleep, Cecilia."

"I don't want to testify," she said, continuing the pacing.

"You have to testify."

"I don't think it's a good idea." She stopped her pacing and looked at him. Ferris walked into her. "All your other cases, you never had the defendant testify. Why now? Why me?"

"We have no choice. Your testimony is the only way to prove to the jury it was self-defense."

"But you've told them it was self-defense. Hol—Chief Owens said he thought it was self-defense."

"They need to hear it from you." He walked up to her and held her shoulders. "Do what Abigail told you and you'll be fine."

She looked over at Michael, leaning on the kitchen island, drinking a bottled water. "He's worried too."

Michael swallowed and said, "It's just that you're kind of...kind of cold."

"Michael!" Abigail hissed.

Cecilia wasn't surprised by Michael's comment or even insulted by it. It's what Janna had told her on her wedding day. She couldn't believe anyone would want to marry the "ice queen."

"What?" Michael asked. "You know it too, Wyatt. We've not once seen her cry. I've never seen her show any emotion. At the trial or at home."

"So you want me to cry?" she asked them.

Simultaneously, they yelled, "No!"

"Fake crying is far worse than no crying," Abigail explained.

"Just be yourself," Wyatt added.

"But"—she didn't want to admit it, but it was the truth—"most people don't like me at first."

"Well, this isn't a first impression. They've seen you all week."

That did not make her feel better.

CHAPTER 54

"THE DEFENSE CALLS Mrs. Cecilia Chandler to the stand."

The chair squeaked loudly when she stood. She smoothed her blue wrap dress and took a deep breath before taking her first step toward the witness stand. Judge Lowe ran a tight courtroom. There was never any chitchat in the gallery. Today was so quiet, Cecilia didn't think anyone was even breathing. Everyone could hear every squeak of her shoes as she walked to the stand. She watched her shoes as she walked, not wanting to see every eye watching her.

As she passed the defense team desk, Abigail squeezed her hand. A subtle reminder to follow all the directions Abigail had given her. Cecilia took another deep breath, straightened her posture, and proceeded. She met the eyes of the jurors, tried to loosen her facial expression from what Abigail referred to as a scowl to something resembling neutral, but definitely not a smile.

She took her pledge on the Bible to tell the truth and sat in the chair.

Cecilia and Wyatt had never gone over her testimony together. He said it was so it wouldn't become routine. He'd use the same questions, in a different order, and maybe throw in a few easy ones of his own.

"Are you ready for Christmas?" Wyatt asked.

"Um...no," she answered. She couldn't see past this week, never mind two weeks away.

"Why not?" he asked.

"I've been a little busy." She waved her hand, referring to the courtroom. A few in the gallery giggled.

"Have you put up a tree?" he asked.

"No, I can't get out to buy one. House arrest and all."

"How about shopping? Have you gotten your dog a gift yet?"

"Of course. I got Ferris a big tennis ball." She turned to the judge, to clarify she hadn't broken the conditions of her bail. "I bought it online."

Wyatt smiled and she knew he had accomplished what he wanted—to get her at ease.

"Can you please tell us what happened the night of the incident?"

"Ferris woke me up. He heard something outside. I thought he had to go the bathroom. I got up to take him outside." She paused. "Ferris was acting funny so I went into the backyard. When the backyard light flipped off, the man attacked."

The memory of the attack hit her as hard as the intruder had months ago. She closed her eyes and reminded herself the attack was over.

"Did you recognize him?" Sewell asked.

"No. He had a ski mask on."

"Then what happened?"

"He hit me. He punched me. He was going to rape me. I fought him as best I could and ran back into the house."

"And then?"

"I ran to Joey's safe to get his gun."

"Why didn't you call the police?"

"Joey always said we lived too far out for them to get to our house quickly. He said I needed to learn to protect myself."

"And that was what you were doing?"

"Yes. I only wanted to scare him off."

"Then what happened?"

"I ran back to the door and found him holding a knife to Ferris's throat." She cleared her throat. "I begged him to leave. To let Ferris go. I told him I hadn't seen his face. I wouldn't be able to identify him. The police wouldn't be able to arrest him. He could just leave. He didn't need to hurt Ferris."

"Did he hurt Ferris?"

"Yes. He cut him with the knife."

"Is this Ferris after the attack?" Wyatt handed her, and the jury, a photo of Ferris a couple days after the attack. He had several stitches across his neck. "Is he okay now?"

"Yes. The skin has healed."

"So, what happened when the attacker slit Ferris's throat?"

Cecilia's eyes bulged at the term, as did many of the jurors. "I saw some blood on Ferris's fur and knew he would kill Ferris. So I shot. I was trying to scare him away."

"What were you aiming for?"

"For the large tree behind him."

"How far away from him?"

"It was about twenty feet behind him and ten feet to his right." She looked Wyatt in the eye. "I never meant to shoot him. I know I'm not good with guns. I know if I had aimed for him I could have hit Ferris and I wouldn't have done that."

"What happened next?"

"The attacker let go of Ferris and we ran in the house. I closed the door. I wanted to get to the phone, to a more secure area of the house. I wasn't thinking clearly and then my legs gave out."

"What happened next?"

"The next thing I remembered was seeing Chief Owens in the house." Cecilia looked at Abigail, who gave a subtle nod that she was doing okay.

"Dr. Kinney said Ferris is worthless. Do you agree?" Sewell remained at the podium. He wanted the jurors to remain focused on Cecilia.

"No."

"What is he worth to you?"

She hesitated. It was not a question she had prepped for with Abigail. But she didn't find it a difficult one. "He's priceless."

"Last question," Mr. Sewell started.

The jury and the gallery had come to look forward to Mr. Sewell's last question. She was the only witness to know this type of question was coming. When she was having difficulty falling asleep the last few nights, she would run through a list of possibilities. Abigail wouldn't tell her what specifically Wyatt would ask. She doubted Abigail knew.

"Do you buy your refrigerator a Christmas gift?"

"No."

Mr. Briscoe stood to begin his cross-examination of Cecilia. He licked his lips. He was going to enjoy this. He'd been looking forward to it since he'd seen the witness list.

Cecilia reminded herself of Abigail's instructions. She couldn't prepare her for the specific questions but she prepared her for how to answer them.

Keep your answers short and specific.

Keep your voice level.

Do not react.

Mr. Briscoe skipped the pleasantries and went right into the questioning.

"So, what I heard there is that you chose an animal over a human."

It wasn't a question but she answered anyway. "That night Mr. Gabbert was the animal. He attacked me. He was going to rape me."

Mr. Briscoe turned to Judge Lowe. "I object. She cannot tell us what he was thinking."

"Overruled," Judge Lowe ruled.

"Well, he's dead so we can't ask him, can we, Ms. Chandler?"

"Objection!" Mr. Sewell yelled.

"Sustained," the judge ruled.

"You said you weren't thinking clearly that evening?" Briscoe asked.

"Yes, the doctor said I had a concussion from the attack—"

"But you were thinking clearly enough to get a weapon?"

"Yes."

"Why didn't you get a knife? You had to go through the kitchen to get the gun."

"I'd have to get too close to him to use a knife. I didn't want to get close to him. Joey told me to use a gun."

"So you were thinking clearly enough to remember where the gun was, to get to the safe, and open the safe?"

"Yes."

"Do you need a combination for the safe?"

"Yes."

"You were thinking clearly enough to remember the combination for your *husband*'s safe?"

"Yes. It's our wedding anniversary. June 25th. 0625." Cecilia bit her lip. "I guess I should change that now." She smiled when a soft roll of laughter went through the room.

"You said Mr. Gabbert was going to rape you?"

"Yes."

"Did he tell you this?"

"No."

"How could you know this?"

Cecilia thought of Abigail's instructions. Be specific. "He had me pinned to the ground. He was ripping my clothes off. He was removing his belt. He had an erection."

"When you shot the gun did you think your life was in immediate danger?"

"Yes."

Mr. Briscoe raised his eyebrows. "Mr. Gabbert was twenty feet away from you."

"Yes."

"He had a knife to your dog?"

"Yes."

"Did he have a weapon on you?"

"No."

"Then your life was not in immediate danger, Ms. Chandler." Mr. Briscoe turned, pleased with the cross-examination. He had proven that her life wasn't in danger when she shot the gun. That was all he needed to prove.

Mr. Briscoe stopped in his tracks when he heard Cecilia say, "I wouldn't have a life if I lost Ferris too."

DAN BRISCOE STOOD to give his closing statement. During his career he hadn't had to give too many of them. Most of his cases, he pleaded out. He knew his cases. He knew his state's laws. He knew how to serve his state best.

And he knew this case, this jury, and this defense team. Sewell would dazzle them with a long-winding closing statement, based on sentimentality. Briscoe would dazzle them with the truth. Succinctly.

Seated in the jury room, they would be left with one thought.

Chandler killed Gabbert. And they would vote guilty.

Briscoe walked over to the jury box. He leaned onto the railing and looked at each of them.

"When we first met, I told you that you needed to know one thing for this trial. One thing to cast a guilty verdict. Cecilia Chandler murdered Robert Gabbert. I was wrong."

Mr. Sewell's eyebrows raised. Briscoe was not a man to admit a wrongdoing. Otherwise, he would have dropped this case months ago.

"You need to know two things. Cecilia Chandler murdered Robert Gabbert. She did so to protect property. That is not self-defense. That is illegal. That is murder in the second degree."

Mr. Sewell put his hand on Cecilia's. He, and most of the people in the courtroom, had seen her flinch when Briscoe had said Cecilia had murdered Gabbert the first time and then again the second time.

"Love your pets all you want. But, in the eyes of the law, they are considered property. If she'd shot the intruder for threatening a television with a knife, you wouldn't even be considering whether she was a murderer. You've heard the expert, that dog is worth less than a flat screen.

"The law says our pets are property. Can you go into a store and buy a baby? No.

"Can you go into a pet store and buy a dog? Yes.

"Baby, Human. Dog, property.

"You are not here to make new laws. You are here to judge on one case. That of the murder of Robert Gabbert by Cecilia Chandler." While speaking her name, he pointed to her and the entire courtroom looked at her.

Except Sewell, who was watching Briscoe.

Sewell hid his surprise when Briscoe sat down. But he'd used a good public speaking trick. Reiterating Cecilia murdering Gabbert three times.

The hick lawyer Sewell had expected when he accepted the case wasn't the one he got. Sewell smiled at his adversary, who did not return the smile.

Wyatt Sewell stood to present his closing argument. He buttoned his jacket and looked at Cecilia. He gave her a reassuring smile before turning to the jury.

"First, I'd like to thank all of you for your time and attention in hearing Cecilia's case. We know it has been difficult for you to be away from your family during the trial. Especially since it's the holidays. But we'll come back to the holidays, in a minute."

He walked over to the witness stand and leaned against it. "You've heard Mr. Briscoe and the police.

Cecilia shot and killed Robert Gabbert. You've heard Cecilia. She shot and killed him in self-defense of her family. To save her dog, Ferris.

"Now, Mr. Briscoe here says that Ferris, that any dog, is property.

"Did you know that in some parts of the world a woman in the eyes of the law is viewed as property? Did you know even here in the United States, up into the 1800s, women were viewed as property? Under the doctrine of coverture, from English common law, a woman was legally considered a possession of her husband."

Mr. Sewell noted the looks of anger on the women's faces. "I know. Absurd right? A person, a man, a woman is not property. A living, breathing, loving animal is not property.

"But yet, even in those arcane times, if a woman was murdered, the assailant was charged with murder, not criminal damage.

"But I'm not arguing 'basic biology' with you. I'm not saying Ferris is human. I'm saying he's family. And what defines family? Love.

"Did you know that sixty-five percent of American households have a pet? A study found that only one percent of pet owners considered their pets property. *One percent*! Did you know that a study found that over sixty percent of pet owners considered their pets family members? Another survey found ninety percent of owners considered their pets part of the family. Millions of Americans can't be wrong.

"We all know a dog is man's best friend. How can that 'friend' be property?"

He stood and walked to the other side of the jury box.

"You've heard the witnesses. The ones who have a dog or a cat, they buy them a Christmas gift. You also heard them say they didn't buy their car, their television, their oven, their couch, their gun Christmas gifts.

"They buy their children, their wife, their mother a Christmas gift.

"But they don't buy their patrol car, their front door, or their desk a Christmas gift.

"*They buy gifts for their family, but not their property.*"

Mr. Sewell motioned to Michael, who was standing in the back of the courtroom. He opened the door and someone handed him a camouflage leash.

A soft muttering of "ahhs" was heard through the crowd as Ferris slowly walked in. Overwhelmed by the size of the crowd, he kept his head down and his body close to the only one he knew, Michael.

Many reached for Ferris, as he walked by, to pat his golden fur. Those farther away leaned in to get as good a look at him as they could.

Ferris walked obediently at Michael's heel. He looked around at all the people, not stopping for any until he saw Briscoe. He sat in front of him and looked at him. Most thought Briscoe was glaring at Ferris. Many expected him to growl at Ferris. Ferris licked his hand, and all were stunned when a smile slowly appeared on Briscoe's face. One even creeped onto Mr. Derby's face, the jury foreman.

Ferris looked around for a new attraction. Michael lost control when Ferris saw Cecilia. Ferris jumped onto her, placing his paws on her knees and hitting his head against hers. She laughed at his clumsiness while he licked her face. She pulled him close, rubbing his neck the way he liked, and cried. She hoped this wouldn't be the last time she'd be able to be this close to Ferris. When she let him go, he licked her tears away.

Cecilia smiled. Looking into his eyes, she briefly forgot she was in a courtroom, at the end of a trial to determine her future.

A hush had come over the crowd. Despite his whispered tone, Mr. Sewell could be heard telling the jury, "Now that's love. I don't know about you, but my *property* does not *love* me like that."

EPILOGUE

CECILIA SAT IN the backyard on one of the two Adirondack chairs. Dressed in a purple asymmetrical top and a patterned skirt, she stretched her legs out. Ferris sat next to her.

Her phone dinged. A Google Alert for the town of Folley. It was official. Folley's prosecutor had won the state senator race. She wondered if he would have won the campaign if he had won the case. She transferred the article to a folder on her phone.

It joined articles and tidbits on other post-trial events. Michael had sent a picture of himself standing by the F150, which Cecilia sold to him at a very reasonable price. Cecilia had saved Abigail's news conference on her first case on her own. Wyatt sent the link of a video of his acceptance speech at the state's animal association Man of the Year dinner. He included a picture of himself and his companion for the night, Ferris.

The folder even had an article about CB's Diner. The Food Network heard of the diner's popular special and featured the restaurant on an episode. CB's Sloppy Joes would be available across the country for sale in grocery stores in the fall.

Cecilia shut off her phone, returning her attention to the scene before her. She marveled at the beautiful sunset. The oranges, the pinks, the purples. The beauty of it all. She wondered if it was always this beautiful. Or had it changed? But she was probably the one who had changed.

She finally saw what Joey could see in this place. The beauty of life in the country.

Ferris's ears perked up and he ran for the far fence. Seconds later, Holden hopped over the fence and patted his friend on his head. He grabbed a ball from his backpack and threw it. Ferris chased after it.

Cecilia smiled as she watched Holden approach her. "You know you can come to the front door now."

"I know." They watched as Ferris got distracted from the ball and ran after a squirrel. "More fun this way."

"Vinnie get off okay?" Cecilia asked.

"Yep, he's the sheriff's problem now."

She laughed and he loved how it made her whole face glow. "You're going to miss him," she told him.

He didn't disagree. He sat next to her in the other chair. Out of his bag, he pulled out a six pack of Mountain Dew bottles.

"Bottles?" she asked. "How fancy."

He opened one and handed it to her, then opened one for himself. He held his up and considered what to toast to. She held hers up, waiting for him.

"To the future," he chose.

Cecilia heard Ferris before she saw him. He collided into the two of them and their sodas, spilling soda everywhere. Laughing, she wiped the soda from her face, then held her bottle up again to complete the toast.

Cecilia leaned in and kissed Holden. "To our future."

A writer's best friend is word of mouth.
If you enjoyed this book,
please write a review
and tell your friends and family.

Thank you
A R

Acknowledgements

Saving Ferris was born at the Writers' Police Academy. If you are a writer, check out this amazing hands-on writing conference. I cannot thank Lee Lofland enough for inventing and organizing this phenomenal event.

As always, thank you to my wonderful editor, Lourdes Venard, and my brilliant cover artist, Karen Phillips.

Thank you to my fabulous beta reader, Jackie Robins, for her continued support.

And, of course, thank you to *my family*—my mom and my little doggo, h.

We miss you, H. Always.

Made in United States
Orlando, FL
01 April 2023

31629705R00215